"THIS MESSAGE IS URGENT. . . .

"Professor Kreider, I'd like to ask you to drop whatever you are working on and examine a new problem for me. We have discovered a group of objects buried in the Soleco gravity well!

"I repeat, we have identified at least one hundred ellipsoidal objects in the Soleco gravity well. At the radius of the objects' orbits, no material listed in our ship's library is capable of withstanding even a fraction of a percent of the resulting tidal stress.

"Please understand the magnitude of this discovery! Without our most advanced instruments, we couldn't even measure conditions so close to Soleco's event horizon. The physical survival of physical objects under such circumstances . . . Professor, we have no understanding of this phenomenon!"

Wil McCarthy

FLIES FROM THE AMBER

A ROC BOOK ·

ROC
Published by the Penguin Group
Penguin Books USA Inc., 375 Hudson Street,
New York, New York 10014, U.S.A.
Penguin Books Ltd, 27 Wrights Lane,
London W8 5TZ, England
Penguin Books Australia Ltd, Ringwood,
Victoria, Australia
Penguin Books Canada Ltd, 10 Alcorn Avenue,
Toronto, Ontario, Canada M4V 3B2
Penguin Books (N.Z.) Ltd, 182-190 Wairau Road,
Auckland 10, New Zealand

Penguin Books Ltd, Registered Offices:
Harmondsworth, Middlesex, England

First published by Roc, an imprint of Dutton Signet,
a division of Penguin Books USA Inc.

First Printing, April, 1995
10 9 8 7 6 5 4 3 2 1

For Cathy

ACKNOWLEDGMENTS

This novel would not exist in anything like its current form without the patience and assistance of a great many people, including: Steve Bell, Shawna McCarthy, Cathy McCarthy, Gary Snyder, John Stith, Amy Stout, Connie Willis, and the members of the Northern Colorado Writers' Workshop. Thanks, guys!

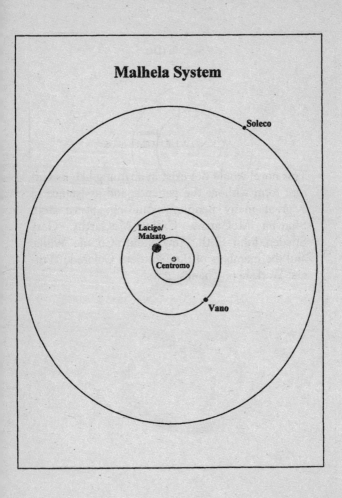

Malhela System

Soleco

Lacigo/
Malsato

Centromo

Vano

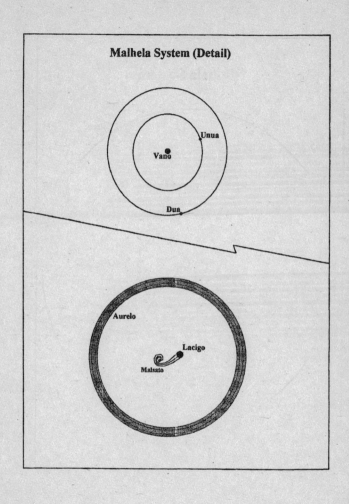

Malhela System (Detail)

Prologue

"Exalted Creature, they flee directly into the nebula."

White frills expanding in anger. "Pursue them."

This place had been a stellar creche, a coming together of gasses, a birthing place of new suns. But as the ages raced by, as Fleet pursued the Enemy at the very edge of lightspeed, things had changed. One of the young stars exploded, touching off neighbors. Now, within the cloud hung stars gone prematurely ancient, withered dwarfs and collapsars among the newly born. The result was not beautiful, nor safe to travel through.

"Particulate matter in the nebula, Exalted Creature. We dare not."

"Also collapsed matter, vermin, and they have the Shield! If they brave the time fields to graze a collapsed body, and they do not emerge for an age of ages? No! We have come too far to give them up."

"We risk the Fleet, Exalted Creature."

"Pursue them!"

Tight, angry silence. And obedience.

Fleet changes course yet again. The nebula looms large, shifting colors as timespace contracts ahead. Soon, Fleet screams through a sleet of tiny particles, and then larger particles, and larger ones still.

"Great danger ahead!" warns a lesser being.

Exalted Creature raises frills again. "We do not curl back when—"

Words uncompleted.

The glittering Shield does not easily lose integrity, but when a flake of matter strikes . . . Exalted Vessel, in its beak-point position ahead of Fleet, becomes a splatter of radiant liquid.

Death strikes with suddenness.

But Death, like all things, must yield in the presence of superior force—Exalted Vessel is destroyed, but its vector has scarcely altered. It roars still toward the heart of the nebula, in timespace-contracted pursuit of its ancient Enemy.

All Fleet's beings are privy to the sight, and they are made brave by it.

PART ONE

ELTROVADO

To the open ear it sings
Sweet the genesis of things
Of tendency through endless ages,
Of star-dust, and star-pilgrimages,
Of rounded worlds, of space and time,
Of the old flood's subsiding slime,
Of chemic matter, force and form,
Of poles and powers, cold, wet, and warm:
The rushing metamorphosis,
Dissolving all that fixture is,
Melts things that be to things that seem,
And solid nature to a dream.

—Ralph Waldo Emerson,
"Woodnotes II," 1837

Chapter One

"Pay dirt," said Troy. He leaned in his harness, brushed his gauntleted hand against the gravel, scraping it aside. Something white and faceted glittered beneath.

Myk Poole leaned closer, cursing silently as his arm caught on one of the harness bungies. He tugged it free, jerked at his harness until it let him move the way he wanted to. Damn the thing anyway, weren't the spacesuits clumsy and clowny enough?

"What is it? Is it diamond?"

"No," Troy said. He scraped again at the gravel, sending handfuls of it spinning away in the light gravity. The fingers of his hand closed on something pea-sized, some kind of crystal, something gray-white and lustrous. "It isn't diamond."

But they had known that anyway. The neutrino detector had gone wild on them, the echoes showing veins inside the planetoid, veins of something dense and strange through which the ghost particles refracted and reflected like light in mazed mirrors. Neutrinos, the antisocial problem children of the subatomic world, could zip through whole planets without touching or interacting, could pierce unstable atoms, pierce the nuclei themselves and keep right on going, forever, unaffected and unaffecting.

"Perfect crystals can trap some tiny fraction of the

neutrinos as they pass through," Dao Vitter had said. "Particularly when the crystals are large. That's how our detectors work. I'd say we're looking at one very large, very perfect crystal."

Myk had snorted at Dao's suggestion. The echoes were of something large, yes, something nearly half-kilometer across. The veins reached through the core of the planetessimal like gigantic, spidery fingers that were caught in the act of curling in, of trying to clench. And yes, diamonds were not unheard of in the Aurelo debris ring or here in the Centromo, where carbonaceous rocks sometimes collided at tens of kilometers per second, heating and fusing and squeezing until the carbon assumed its densest possible structure.

But the diamonds were found in small pockets, near the surfaces of shattered boulders. Their neutrino echoes were localized and shallow and very, very faint. They did not form large, perfect crystals. Nothing did.

"Let me see," Myk said now to Troy Biandi.

"Here," said Troy, handing the crystal over to him. "Don't drop it."

Myk reached out and took the crystal between the glove-caps of his thumb and forefinger.

His fingers cast many shadows in the brown-orange light of Vano, in the blue-white of the Milky Way and the starlike radiance of Lacigo. Not bright even now, with the dwarf no more distant than Vano, no more distant than his home and his wife and his tiny daughter, who had probably already begun to expand her vocabulary beyond "gawawa."

The object in his hand was . . . beautiful.

The color was like brandied milk, like vanilla icing with sprinklings of sugar to make it glitter, hints of oil to make almost-rainbows of its surface. Lustrous gray-white, said the dull and ordered part of his mind. Opaque, crystalline mineral of unknown composition.

Parallelogram facets glinted out at him, flashing in the light of the many suns. The faces interlocked to form little starbursts which interlocked to form tented hexagons. The whole thing, perfectly symmetric and practically spherical, was no larger than Myk's smallest fingernail. Thirty facets, fifty, one hundred, he had no idea how many.

Minerals weren't found this way. He had never heard of mineral that was found this way. Crystalline, yes. Faceted, sometimes spherical. He had once seen octahedral pyrite that looked for all the world like children's dreidels, or gems cut for large and gaudy earrings. But the pyrite's surface had been rough, its edges and corners ragged on close inspection. Not like this, not at all like this.

The corners of this new crystal looked sharp, well-defined, like the edges of well-cut diamond. Myk wondered what would happen if he reached up and drew the thing hard against his helmet visor. Would it leave marks, would it scratch? Would it cut right through the ceramalloy like one of Troy Biandi's digging tools?

"Dao was wrong," Troy said.

"What?"

"Dao was wrong." Troy leaned over the pit he'd made, peering in, reaching in with his hand. His boots were off the planetoid's surface, his low-gravity digger's harness making him look like some failed acrobat tangled up in the equipment. "There are more crystals in here. It isn't all one piece."

Myk huffed cynical breath. "Did you really believe it was?"

"No. No. But the neutrino echoes . . ."

"Dao thinks everything works in the perfect theoretical way. He hasn't spent enough time with his hands dirty."

Troy pulled out another crystal, held it up in the light and looked at it. "This is something new. This is something very important. He was right about that."

Myk pressed the raised square of ceramalloy on the neck of his suit, somewhere near where his Adam's apple would be. "*Grailseeker*, this is team one. Come in."

There was pause. Then: "Jafre here. Go ahead, team one."

"We found it."

"Great! That's great. What does it look like?"

"It's unbelievable. It's nothing we've seen before."

"What does it *look* like?" Jafre repeated.

"It *looks*," Troy cut in, pressing his own SHIPKOM toggle, "like we're all quaking *rich*."

There was another pause.

"Return to the ship right away," Jafre said. "Bring samples back with you."

"Will do," said Troy. "Team one out."

Chapter Two

Jafre hated docking. It reminded him, every time, of how ancillary his function aboard *Grailseeker* truly was, reminded him that he was neither pilot nor navigator to the ship but rather the *administrator* to her crew. He might as well be their astrologer for all the good he was during dock ops.

He sat in his chair quietly and looked out the window.

Unua, the planet where almost everybody in Malhela system actually lived, and to which *Grailseeker* was now returning, was beautiful sight for Jafre's sore and weary eyes. Much more alive in appearance than Dua, Vano's airless outer planet. Much, much better than the vast, empty spaces between the system's stars, or the dark smudges of dust and rock that were the Aurelo and the thrice-damned Centromo. *Grailseeker* had been away too long.

Below, Unua was all red and gray and dusty orange, expanses of desert cut through by spiky mountain ranges and the occasional forests of dark brown.

Unua was the second ugliest planet in all the universe, Jafre was convinced. Only Dua was darker, more empty. In his spare time Jafre watched the holies, he *consumed* the holies, drank in images of Earth and Mbali and Grove and all the other wonderful planets occupied by humans luckier than he was, and he wished he could go and *see* these places with his own two eyes.

But the distant stars were not for Malhelans, not until they got their industrial surplus high enough to make starships plausible luxury. Meanwhile, Jafre the would-be explorer made his living digging up rocks. No, he reminded himself. Not even digging, not even that much.

Jafre had struggled and manipulated his way to captaincy, but no amount of scheming could get him off this tiny canvas on which he was painted. Nothing in all the world. . . .

Chrysanthemum, the starship of his forebears, hung like brightish star above the gloomy limb of his planet. *Chrysanthemum,* which had not moved from its current orbit in one hundred and fifty years. *Chrysanthemum,* the one and only spaceport the Malhelan economy could support.

"This is not ordinary matter," Dao Vitter had said of the crystals they'd found, practically screaming with excitement. He'd said a lot of other things, too, about "strange quarks" and "unusual gravitic and inertial properties" and "a natural origin for this material is *extremely unlikely.*"

With two black holes and two dwarf stars dancing the Malhela for billion years, you'd expect to find some exotic substances kicking around. "But not this exotic," Dao had said. "This find is very important. We mustn't disturb it any further."

"No?" Jafre had replied with naked avarice. And so, over Dao's strenuous objections, they had shoveled the stuff into *Grailseeker*'s hold, several tons of it, and lit out for home once again. Damn the consequences;

they'd had no other luck, and Jafre did have to turn profit on this voyage.

Scientists would be invited from Earth to study these crystals. He would invite them himself if he had to. He would build great antennae and scream at the stars that he had found something worthy of their attention, that he had earned his rightful place among them. The scientists might come, and if they did they might, just maybe, take Jafre with them when they left.

Meanwhile, he was going to get darkly, stinkingly rich selling his crystals to the highest bidder. The thought cheered him up somewhat.

"Ten minutes to contact," said Guelo, his navigator.

"Very good," Jafre said in his best official tone.

Chrysanthemum was swelling visibly now, its rounded shape coming clear in the window. In the wan, brown-dwarf light of Vano, it looked mottled in the same red-gray manner as the world it circled. It looked like planet, really. Probably, Jafre thought, the third ugliest planet in the universe.

"Let me see what you've brought, son," said the white-haired man who had detached himself from the crowd of gawkers who had come up the gangway to block the exit of *Grailseeker*'s crew.

"Get out of our way," Jafre snarled at him.

"I beg your pardon," said the man. "Don't you know who I am? You have to listen to me, you have to humor me; I'm the oldest man in the world!"

"I know who you are," Jafre said.

Jack-Jack Snyder had been, in the dim past, the third president of Unua, and founder of the Library of Trust and the Bank of Forever and handful of other useless institutions. And yeah, he was supposed to be seventeen gazillion years old, like from the twenty-second century or something. What did that actually make him: five hundred?

All the more reason, Jafre thought, to keep him at arm's length. The Originals were still around, most of them, but they were small in numbers, lost in the shuffle of their three million or so descendants. Most times they were easily ignored.

Today, alas, was not one of those times. Jack-Jack not only didn't get out of the way, he strode forward with his arms spread wide, as if he meant to embrace Jafre and the other men like long lost sons. Which, Jafre supposed, they probably were. As the saying went, everybody was related to everybody in colony this small.

"Darkness," he cursed, as Jack-Jack's arms closed around him.

"I'm so proud," Jack-Jack said. "I am *so* proud of you all." His voice was light, as if with barely suppressed laughter.

"Thank you, Captain Shem," Asia Gill said after Jafre had sat back down. Her gaze swept the room, the long table and its twenty inhabitants. "Will there be any *further* rhetoric?"

Uncomfortable silence.

"Okay, then, the matter is settled. Excavation at the discovery site is suspended until further notice."

Jafre's fingernails dug painfully into his palms. Knowing it would come down this way did not mean he was resigned to it. It did not mean he had to like it. He cleared his throat loudly. "Madame Director, I object."

"Of course you do." Asia smiled. She pulled out one of the stones, let it sparkle and roll in the pit of her hand. "But I haven't impounded your cargo or your mineral rights. Not yet."

"Small mercies," he said. And yet, he supposed the

victory was important in its own way. They had given some of the crystals to Asia, to help focus her contemplation before the hearing. They'd also given some to the portmaster and, worse yet, to Jack-Jack. Jafre wondered how many he'd have to hand out before he was done. He had no other leverage, no other means of persuasion.

"Now," said Asia, "we seem to be in agreement about the general interstellar broadcast, but do we have any thoughts on content?"

"At least five gigs multimedia," Dao Vitter said without getting up. "There's too much to talk about in less time than that."

A woman across the table was shaking her head. "Much too expensive. We know almost nothing; how can you fill up that much space? With full data compression, even *one* gig of general broadcast would eat up about ten megawatt hours. That means no lights, anywhere on the planet, for three minutes. You'd never get the populace to agree to that."

"This is important," Dao said. "We're inviting Terran scientists to travel almost forty light-years to see this stuff. What do we tell them? 'Please come soonest, we've found some rocks'?"

"It *is* imperative," Jafre agreed, "that Earth be informed of the full scope of our discovery. Ancient though the samples may be, if Dao's assessment of this material is correct, we're possibly looking at our first evidence of alien intelligence."

And if that *doesn't get the Terrans here,* he added silently, *we'll have to come up with something even* more *dramatic. Notes from God, maybe, or little fucking blue people with umbrellas sticking out of their heads. Something!*

Eighty years, he thought. The time seemed to stretch

before him like dark and featureless desert. *They will be here in eighty years.*

Asia examined her fingernails. "Well, it's really up to the president, but let's push for one full gigabyte. The public is already getting excited, and this may well be worth three minutes of darkness."

"We can't do it in less than five gigs," Dao protested.

"We'll be very succinct," Asia said gruffly, without looking up from her nails.

PART TWO

MALPROKSIME

"You see, wiretelegraph is a kind of a very, very long cat. You pull his tail in New York and his head is meowing in Los Angeles. A radio operates exactly the same way. The only difference is that there is no cat."

—Albert Einstein

"Quantum mechanics, hmm. You put a cat in a box, along with a hammer and some poison and a radioactive isotope . . . I forget exactly how this goes. Anyway, keep some bandages on hand, because I guarantee the cat won't be happy."

—Jack-Jack Snyder

Chapter Three

"I believe that puts you in 'check,'" Yezu said after moving his piece. He frowned down at the projection as if it displeased him in some way. Well, probably it did. Yezu Manaka complained with equal venom about the food, the staff, the accommodations, all of which seemed fine as far as Tom Kreider could tell.

"Yes, I believe it does," Tom agreed. Yezu's horsey, his *Knight*, stood poised to jump on Tom's King, and a pointy-headed Bishop stood by in case Tom's move was to the right. He moved left instead, seeking shelter behind a wall of pawns. He really should have "castled" when he had the chance, to get his rook into play. He seemed to have a problem with rooks.

"You should have castled when you had the chance," Yezu observed dryly. He moved the horsey again, and again it threatened the King. "Check."

"Oh, damn," said Tom.

In their mind-numbing boredom, he and Yezu had gravitated toward one another, and once together had discovered a slight but mutual interest in *Introspectia*'s library of games. They'd perused various simulations, of wars and navigation problems and great, complex biological systems, and simpler games, too, with fake money and bright colors and rules a child could easily grasp. Nothing had appealed, particularly to Yezu, until they had come across the historical cache, and within it, "chess." Its very name smacking of ancientness, of secrets long forgotten, the game had fairly leaped out at them.

Relativity moved them forward in time, true enough, but even so they headed chronologically backward, headed for the primitive conditions and mores of frontier society. How better to prepare themselves?

"You know, we've only a week to go," Tom said, brightening a little from his gaming trance. "I guess we've survived the ordeal, maybe earned the reward. I try not to get too charged up, but really it does excite me. Aliens!"

"Possible aliens," Yezu said with an air of crabby wistfulness. "Ech. Possible, dead, extinct, aliens. And we have nine days, subjective, until we reach the planet. Probably another ten years back home."

Ah, relativity. The starship *Introspectia* traveled within a smidgen of a percent of the speed of light, had done so for thirty days since its departure from high Earth orbit. Time dilated at such speeds. Time shrank and stretched and got away from you. When they got back to Earth, in a year or two, their friends and relatives would be almost a century older.

Yezu had a right to complain. What a hell of a price to pay! And relativity had smacked them in other ways, too. "Extremely slow data transfer," as *Introspectia*'s crew called the phenomenon that prevented their sending and receiving personal messages. And also "dangerously accelerated cosmic radiation," for which they took pills, and "enterochronologic disorientation," for which they did not. And there was nothing to see from the observation ports except streaky blackness, although viewscreens could show you the cluster of blue stars huddling ahead of the ship, the cluster of red stars trailing behind. Static views, or nearly static, changing only a little from day to day, never showing anything new or surprising. Even Malhela system, their not-so-distant destination, was indistinguishable from the general murk.

"Show a little heart," Tom said. "We've come a long way, to see something very strange."

Yezu shook his head, flashed a sad little smile. "I study archaeopaleontological drift patterns. I should be in a quiet nook somewhere. I've left a wife behind, did you know that?"

That stopped Tom. A wife? Tom had left his parents and a pair of brothers and maybe a dozen friends, people whose lives would go on and on without his playing a part in them. Bad enough. But a *wife*? "That, uh, must have been very hard."

"Exceedingly so," Yezu said. He tapped the table here and there, and his knight hopped another few spaces.

Hence all the worry about time, Tom thought. How awful, wondering every minute where she was, what she was doing and with whom! *She* packing in a year's worth of experiences every day while *he* sat here playing games, slowly, almost frozen in time!

Something flashed between Tom and Yezu in that moment, a kind of invisible line that marked them now as friends rather than mere acquaintances. The feeling did not entirely please Tom Kreider, as it meant Yezu's troubles were now, in some way, also his own.

Suddenly uncomfortable, he cleared his throat.

"That's check again," Yezu said quietly.

"Oh, damn." He moved a piece. "There. Do you, uh, need someone to talk to or anything?"

"I need someone to play chess with." Yezu's eyes were serious.

Tom nodded and continued playing.

The activity room did not seem very large, nor as loud and crowded and bustling as you would expect. A single homunculus scuttled about unhurriedly, moving and straightening things, brushing away nonexistent dust. Only three of the five tables were occupied, about ten people in all, including Tom and Yezu. There were over a hundred scientists on this mission, and this left Tom wondering what they all *did*, where they spent their time. Maybe they had all paired off to spend the voyage testing the springiness of their mattresses. Half the passengers, and a good sixty percent of the crew, had double-X chromosomes and the bodies to prove it. *This* made Tom wonder why *he* hadn't paired off, why he'd spent the past few days with Yezu and not with some blond and leggy radiologist of Nordic or Slavic descent.

Ah, well. He watched Yezu move a piece, then leaned over and moved one of his own. Quick, not taking the time to think as this game really seemed to demand. Well, the match seemed equal, at least, Yezu's half-hearted contemplations not apparently more effective than Tom's intuition.

Whoomp!

That was the sound of the door preparing to open. Tom looked up. Presently, the door did open, and a new, eleventh person strode in. Good fortune? But no, the newcomer showed no evidence of femaleness, of tall and leggy Nordicness. In fact, he seemed a perfect likeness of Jhoe Freetz, that mouthy little guy from the soft sciences. Sociology or something. Not good fortune at all, that.

Jhoe spotted them and walked over to the table. "Hi, gentlemen."

"Hello," Yezu said, looking up for a moment.

Tom nodded. "Hi. Out for a stroll?"

"Out looking for something to do, more like," Jhoe Freetz confided. "I've spent about two hundred hours in softlink with the ship's library, and my brain has just *quit*. I tried reverting to multimedia documents and even listening to blank narrations, but it didn't help. I have become a vegetable."

"And you thought you'd share that with us," Yezu said, not looking up this time.

"Precisely." The grin Jhoe exposed held white, straight, perfect teeth. Expensive teeth, if Jhoe had lived anything past about eighty years.

One of Tom's favorite aphorisms stated, "over a hundred you've already blund'red," which he took to mean that you could not and should not trust young scientists with anything difficult, not until they'd had their chance to blunder and fail and learn patience. Other people took that aphorism to mean very different things, but then "other people" demonstrated their bovine stupidity so regularly and so reliably that Tom felt he could set his symbiont clock by them.

"Playing a bit of chess," Jhoe observed, his (vain? youthful?) teeth still glittering whitely. His face, too, reminded Tom of a woodcarving, ruggedly handsome in a way that didn't often occur in nature. His brown hair trailed down past his shoulders in a lazy fan shape that, really, might take hours to sculpt every morning. His skin was a richer, darker shade than people usually wore, and his eyes sparkled improbably. Corneal symbionts, playing games with the light? His nails were painted with clear varnish.

"That's right," Yezu said.

"Great," said Jhoe. "I keep meaning to learn that game, and now I seem to have the time. Do you mind if I watch?"

Tom bristled inwardly. If this guy started saying,

"Ooh, I see a good move for you," and "Oh, you've really messed up with that one," Tom would chuck him out on his rear.

Yezu looked at Tom, his face blank, simply waiting to see what sort of response Jhoe Freetz would get.

And what am I so snappy about today? Tom thought. True, Jhoe wasn't part of the actual mission, had come along not to study Malhelan artifacts but to study the Malhelan colonists themselves. And, yes, he had perfect teeth and a perfect face, and maybe a slight propensity toward ornamentation. But he had counted the same costs, braved the same hardships as anyone else here.

Tom licked his lips and framed up the politest smile he could muster. "Oh, please do."

Jhoe Freetz looked relieved. "Thanks. I, uh, haven't had such an easy time making friends here. That's why all the library time . . ."

Tom felt his cheeks heating a bit. A long time ago, when he'd first arrived at North American University, he'd spent a quiet week poring over multimedia orientation guides and pocket histories, trying to get his bearings. Those hallowed halls had really thrown him, after the cheery hustle and hurry of East Boston. Everything so big and so serious! But he'd met others as the days wore on, young men like himself, and young women on the prowl for young men, and faculty members ready to take young men and women under their wings. . . . He'd celebrated his forty-fifth birthday with a whole circle of new comrades.

"I, uh, don't think any of us have made friends," he said to Jhoe Freetz. "Not really. What sour old nuts we've all become!"

Jhoe cleared his throat, shuffled his foot. "I know what you mean. I know . . . it seems like it was once much easier, but then you wake up one day and realize you haven't made any new friends in a really long time. How does that happen?"

"I wouldn't know," Tom said, with a lot less edge in his voice. "But I *do* welcome you to join us. Bad enough that Yezu and I have only each other for company."

"Well, then. I'll get a chair."

"Please do," said Yezu, his face firming up now that he knew Tom's mind. "You can play against me once I've crushed this gentleman here."

Tom laughed, taking in the activity room with a broad glance. "You've mistaken this for one of your *dreams,* Yezu. Come back to reality and move your piece."

Chapter Four

"Please, ladies and gentlemen," one of the stewards called out, "form neat rows! Make room for your neighbors!"

The observation lounge had filled up rapidly, the good spots on couches and tables gone, and after them the good leaning-against spots on bulkheads and structural supports. Already, people here and there had begun to complain that they couldn't see, that they couldn't get comfortable, that somebody or other had elbowed them or stepped on their feet.

This last complaint seemed particularly petty, in light of the reduced gravity they enjoyed right now. The internal centrifuges had been eased off gradually, the room gimbals swinging nearly ninety degrees, keeping "down" perpendicular to the floors as *Introspectia* flipped tail to its destination and began, gently, to decelerate. But the thrust acceleration held things down with comforting though not troubling authority, and the locked 'fuges meant a clear, undizzying view from the portholes.

Here and there, homunculi wended through the leg-forests of the crowd, looking for things to clean up or carry away. But they seemed ill at ease, their movements sudden, ungraceful, poorly planned. *Too many damn people in here*, their sullen faces seemed to say.

Tom felt a little smug, seeing how he and Jhoe and Yezu had arrived here over five hours earlier. With the deceleration, they'd dropped back out of relativity's grip, and now you could once again see stars through the portholes. Three transparent but thick layers of diamond between you and them, of course, but you were really seeing the real thing, not a recording or simulation or other cheesy second-best.

So they had spent the hours sipping fruit-flavored intoxicants and watching the stars drift slowly by as the ship made its turn. Shoals of gravitation drew near, the dancing, degenerate masses of Malhela system, and now *Introspectia* had to earn its keep, had to do something other than accelerate or coast along a straight-line course. This system was home to people, too, people who didn't like to have starship motors bathing their ships and planets in deadly radiation. *Introspectia* had squirted ahead a cautionary message last week, warning the Malhelans of the danger zones the ship would sweep through.

"The outer mass of the system should come into view in about two minutes," the steward said, dutifully repeating what everyone already knew. Why else had they come here to the observation lounge, come here on the mission at all? But Tom's drink-fuzzled mind couldn't muster up any real sense of annoyance. Let the man do his job.

The steward had brought silence, had caused all heads to turn in his direction. He seemed to bask in the attention. How often, after all, did he have such sights to point out?

"The object, known as Soleco by the inhabitants of this system, is a 'collapsar,' or 'black hole,' or 'hypermass,' consisting of a degenerate star approximately five times the mass of Earth's sun, which has been compressed almost to the diameter of the Earth itself. We're giving the object a wide berth, as it possesses a strong gravity gradient, or 'tidal force,' which could damage or even destroy *Introspectia* if we pass too near. Because the object's escape velocity exceeds the speed of light, Soleco *absorbs* light rather than radiating it, and will therefore not be directly visible. However, the object does possess a faint 'halo,' consisting of gas and dust in close orbit around it. The halo is very faint, and gravitational doppler shift will cause it to appear reddish in color. We should also observe the effects of gravitational 'lensing,' as Soleco's pull will bend the rays of light passing near it."

"How close will we be passing?" somebody asked.

The steward smiled faintly. His blue-and-gold uniform encased him stiffly, and suddenly he seemed a bit small inside of it. "I, uh, don't know. I can find out, if you like."

"What does the name mean?" another voice from the crowd called out.

The steward relaxed. "Although the inhabitants of Malhela speak Lenglish just as you and I do, the original colonists used an extinct language called Esperanto to name objects and other features in the system. Because the outer hypermass orbits so far out from the system's other major bodies, the colonists chose to name it 'Soleco,' or 'loneliness.' Before you ask me *how* far out it is, don't, because I don't know that either.

"The colonists named the other collapsar 'hunger,' because it draws matter off the co-orbital white dwarf, known as 'futility.' The brown dwarf, primary to the only inhabited planet, is called Vano, or 'pride.' These other objects will be visible to us a little later."

"I see it!" Someone shouted.

Fingers began to point.

"I see the hypermass!" "Soleco!" "The collapsar!"

Tom leaned forward in his seat. There, indeed, visible at the edge of one of the portholes! As promised, a dark puckering in the field of stars, a hidden mass greedily drawing all light and matter toward itself. He could see no reddish halo.

"Oh, my," said Yezu Manaka. "Oh, my God. Long life or no, I never thought such a sight . . ."

"I don't see a halo," Jhoe Freetz said. "Do you gentlemen see it, do you see a halo?"

"No," Tom said to him without turning away from the view. "I . . . don't see anything, really." He saw, really, a *non-thing,* an absence, wrapping the starlight around itself like some kind of blanket. *It would wrap this ship around it, too, if it had the chance, stretching and squashing* Introspectia *like a bar of hot taffy.*

"Such beauty," Yezu said, his voice low and breathless.

"I can't see!" A voice shouted.

"I can't!" "Neither!" "The window stands in the wrong place!"

"Ladies and gentlemen," the steward said loudly, "will you *please* be patient? *Introspectia* will continue turning for the next forty minutes. The view will continue to change during that time. If you can't see right now, you *will* see in a minute or two. If you *can* see right now, the view may escape from you shortly. Please wait patiently. Soleco will reappear through another porthole."

Presently the hypermass, the puckering non-thing, slipped behind the edge of the porthole Tom had been viewing it through. Eclipsed, temporarily, from his view. The crowd continued to mutter.

"Such beauty," Yezu said again. "My God. Thank you

for dragging me up here so early. What a view we've had! This was worth all the waiting."

And worth your marriage? Tom thought but did not ask. *Worth a hundred years of your life?* He himself had not been all that impressed with the view.

"I never did see a red halo," said Jhoe.

Bustle and crunch in the throngs behind them, noise around the exits. Already, it seemed, some people had tired of the view, had now other activities calling out more urgently for their attention. Which made Tom wonder yet again what everyone *did* on this blasted voyage.

Here and there, some people still complained that they hadn't seen the black hole, or that their neighbors were elbowing or stepping on them. And from other heres and theres came sighs of awe and grunts of disappointment, as people caught their first view.

The puckering reappeared at the edge of the next porthole. Yezu sighed with awe.

"The next major change will occur in two hours," the steward called out, "when the co-orbiting Lacigo and Malsato become visible. You will probably find that view more dramatic than the present one."

"Let us keep these seats until then," Yezu said quickly.

"I have to relieve myself," Jhoe complained. "All this drink, you know."

"Go, then. We'll keep your seat for you."

"I don't mean *now*, just sometime soon."

"Well, whenever you need to. Once Soleco disappears for good, maybe we can take turns."

"Will you people quiet down?" somebody behind them snapped.

"I think we shall require more drinks," Tom informed his companions, ignoring the voice from the crowd.

"Big, silly pink ones with hats and straws and fog bubbling out of them."

"I find considerable merit in that suggestion," Jhoe said. He handed his empty glass to a passing homunculus and waved for the attention of a steward.

Chief Technical Officer Miguel Barta peered, with eyes insubstantial, at the data his instruments were bringing in from the Soleco hypermass, and he cursed to see it. Something was happening, something he hadn't expected and, no doubt, hadn't been trained to cope with.

"Hey," he said to his tech aid, Lahler. "These readings don't match the projection, not at all. Open more buffer space for the instruments."

"None left," said Beth Lahler, her voice flat.

He turned and looked at her over his shoulder. A young woman, new, first voyage. And taking orders from him! She had a quick mind, and yes, admit it Miguel, a nice set of curves and a very nice face to go with them. Not that he was supposed to notice. But just now her appearance did not seem so nice, with the glazed eyes, the softlink harness sprouting cables from her head like Medusa-hair.

Miguel, also in softlink, shifted his cybernetic "gaze" into the data buffers and saw that she'd spoken truly. No margin in the buffer space.

"Damn," he said. "Cut some loose from the engine monitors."

"Already did that. And from the navigation backups. Really, Miguel, we don't *have* any more."

"Then damn again," he said. Without moving, he signaled the bridge for comlink.

Almost instantly, a face appeared on the holie screen in front of him. "Chelsea," the face said.

Miguel had spoken with the captain, Lin Chelsea, several times before, and to his credit, he did not flinch this time. Like most of *Introspectia*'s bridge crew, Chelsea had wiring that ran *deep*, portions of the link harness hooking in to penetrate her eyes and ears and nostrils. An accident victim, a humanoid robot partially disassembled. No cold, link-eyed stare from her, just the jumble of the sensory interface, less human than the face of a bug. And yet, Miguel had once heard her laugh.

Damn, these were strange times he was heading into.

Miguel's first mission would be called a "paperwalk" by some, just a flick out to Centauri and back on a diplomatic sprinter. Hardly time to get used to the ship and barely a decade gone by in the outside universe. But the second trip, oh . . . He'd spent forever in the belly of a Priority Cargo barge, making the "third circuit" from Sol to Procyon-A to Procyon-B and back again. He'd returned to Earth forty objective years later to find things . . . changed.

And now, on *Introspectia* . . . A good job, responsible and variously rewarding: chief technical officer! But this time around, he paid his price in centuries. Not yet to his hundredth birthday, he would return as a bleeding *fossil*. But a rich one, yes.

A remote scuttled across Miguel's console, its motion a blur of glittering eyes and legs. He stared as it ran by, fighting down the impulse to shriek and swat it with his fist.

"Did you *want* something, Mr. Barta?" demanded the thing-captain.

"Uh, yes. Yes. My instrument readings puzzle me. I need more buffer space to sort things out."

"You agreed to the allocation schedules," Chelsea

said. And yet, Miguel sensed a slight expansion of his buffer space, a token gesture on the captain's part.

"Yes, Captain," he said, "but I read something odd about the Soleco hypermass, a slight asymmetry in the gravity potentials."

"Really?" The thing-captain sounded slightly interested.

Miguel leaned forward. "Captain, in a gravity gradient that steep we should see almost perfect symmetry. We're not dealing with what I'd call a large discrepancy, but the mass imbalance seems to run right up against the event horizon. Either my instruments have gone twidgy or I have to revise my definition of the word 'impossible.' "

"I see," Chelsea said, her mouth curling peculiarly around the words. Miguel felt invisible tendrils probing at the edges of his data. "Can you offer me anything more specific? Are we looking at a science bonus if I cut you more space?"

A shrug. "I really don't know. I can't do much analysis with the observation data chewing up my buffers like this."

"Can you *guess*?" A little more space opened up in his buffers, like a too-tight belt beginning to loosen.

"I, uh, prefer not to," Miguel said carefully. "I mean, with only a few months' experience and all. But it *looks* . . . I don't know. It looks like we've got some mass concentrations down there."

"Down there?" Chelsea repeated, now sounding genuinely interested. "Mass *concentrations*? You mean down deep in the tidal stress?"

"Yes," he said. "Very deep."

"I see."

The captain's thing-face vanished from his holie screen, and in buffer space a door was flung wide, opening a huge portion of the ship's computing resources for Miguel to plunder.

"Good heaven!" he said, then turned to Tech Aid Lahler. "Triple our data rates, would you?"

"Already have, Miguel," she said, and beneath her Medusa-hair she flashed a sickly and lopsided smile.

"Oh, *my*," Yezu gasped. "Will you look at *that*?"

"As if I have something else to do?" Jhoe said.

"Will you three *shut up*?"

The white dwarf, Lacigo, had come into view along with its collapsar partner, Malsato. Futility and Hunger. The dwarf looked small, as its title implied it should. It looked like a bright star, like the inner moon of Mars as seen from the planet's surface. Barely a disc, barely a shape to be seen in the pinpoint glare. The new collapsar did not pucker space as the other one had, or not as much. But something better to see—it sucked a visible plume of dwarf-stuff off Lacigo and drew it in, spiraling! Close in, the plume seethed with tones of orange and red, the primal scream of matter leaving the conventional universe, swirling into the shower drain of dilated space and time surrounding the black hole.

Unfortunately, Jhoe and the physical sciences had never really gotten along. He'd ducked them in school and ignored them in life. . . . But here on *Introspectia* the physical sciences affected him directly, like a punch in the nose. Well, he supposed they affected him back on Earth, too, but in routine ways he'd never noticed or thought about. Anyway, the ship's navigator had offered a Remedial Relativity course in the second week of the voyage, and out of boredom Jhoe had gone, and had really drunk it in. Not so hard, he'd discovered, once you got past the numbers and into the actual facts of the situation. Navigator Jones had told clever stories, with characters like the Relativistic Snake and the Telepathic Twins.

Jhoe had been particularly fond of Black Hole Bahb, who spent eternity swan-diving into the star he was named for. The closer he got, the redder and slower and more squished he became, falling forever as time slowed down and, at the so-called "event horizon," stopped entirely.

Of course, Bahb, with the advantage of being imaginary, could do whatever he wanted, but Jhoe had learned that in the real universe, nothing of substance could survive in the contracted spaces near a black hole's event horizon. Tidal forces, like the ones the Moon induced on the Earth but millions of times stronger, would crush solid things to powder, then crush the powder to atoms, then crush the atoms, and the protons and electrons that comprised them, into something that Jones had called "quantum electromagnetic vortices" or, more simply, "dots."

"I've got to capture this moment," Yezu muttered quietly as he stared out the portholes. "I've got to remember this forever. I could watch a simulation but it could never recapture the . . . the . . ."

Jhoe knew what he meant.

Together, the two stars formed a thing of beauty, like a pair of lovers alone on the dance floor. You could see the gravitational center between them, the point about which they both revolved, bathed in a glow of yellow-white light. No movement visible in the pair, but movement implicit in the sweep of hot gasses, like arcs of dress fabric trailing breezily after the dancers.

Such a false, deceitful beauty! Malsato, with firm hand and unbreakable grip, was slowly crushing its lover to dots, and then devouring the dots. Jhoe had had a lover like that, once, an emotional hypermass about whom all things circled, and into whom all things fell, to be utterly destroyed. Shareen. Ai! A decade gone, almost, and still her name stung across his heart like a lash.

Never again. Jhoe Freetz, like Soleco, had learned to live alone in his cold and distant orbit.

I could really use another drink, he thought suddenly. He'd had many drinks, many more than he normally would. He was, in a word, pissed. So one more couldn't hurt him, right? Just a drop in the bucket. But when he turned from the window and looked around, he saw the steward had gone.

"And here at last, our destination," Yezu said, pointing a finger at the porthole. An object—he hesitated to call it a star—had become visible there, a brown-orange ball that glowed dimly, like a piece of hot iron. Not a bright object, no, not bright at all.

"Vano," Jhoe Freetz said beside him.

"I didn't think it would look *that* dim," Tom Kreider muttered groggily.

Jhoe stared somberly out the porthole, a strange expression on his face. "They live in darkness," he said. "Lacigo gives no more light than a full moon on Earth, and Vano gives off far less than that. The name Malhela means 'poorly illuminated.' "

Like Tom Kreider, Jhoe had drunk too much and had sunk therefore into a moody near-stupor. Yezu clapped a hand on Jhoe's knee. "You know a lot, my friend. Did the steward tell you that?"

"No," Jhoe said, turning, looking surprised. "Yezu, I'm NAU's authority on fourth-wave colonies, particularly Malhela, Algonqia, and Nunuilakai. Didn't you know that? Why did you think I was on this mission?"

"I hadn't wondered," Yezu admitted.

"Well, now you know it. While you gentlemen dig up rocks out in the debris fields, I will live on Unua, learning and studying the ways of the Malhelan people. With that dim little dwarf—" he pointed out the window at Vano "—as the sun in my sky for at least a year. Maybe more, if you all find what you hope to find out here."

"It sounds like a fascinating job. The university must feel very lucky to have you."

Jhoe turned, smiling unhappily at Yezu and at Tom. "Hardly. The place is a snake pit, no hope of advancement. Anyway, they don't have me anymore. We've been gone nearly five decades, right?"

A fist grabbed Yezu's heart and shook it, and he felt it crying tears of blood within his chest. Talina! Fifty years older now, fifty years more distant!

"Oh, yes," Tom said. "So we have."

Yezu closed his eyes, opened them. Stood, brushing away the loose appendages of Tom and Jhoe. "Excuse me," he said.

"What?" said Jhoe.

"I have to go," Yezu told him, stepping away toward the exit. His grief had taken him, as always, from behind, unexpected and brutal as a daylight mugging. Always he would have these long hours of comfort, of ease and forgetfulness, and then . . . Oh!

"I have to go," he said again. "I have to go."

"What did I say?"

"Oh, goodness," Yezu heard Tom Kreider saying. "You haven't heard about this."

And the voice of the tour-guide steward: "We'll see Vano only briefly at this time, so please get a look now if you want one. You may see it here again in approximately eighteen hours, during docking maneuvers as we arrive at Port *Chrysanthemum*."

Tears were forming in Yezu's eyes, again, again. Surely his eyes should have exhausted their tears by now? But Talina! She too had cried, for months before he left and no doubt for months afterward. But she had gotten over it, certainly, and had gone on with her new life which contained no Yezu. Her tears had dried up fifty years ago.

And with that thought, Yezu's tear ducts opened up for real.

"Haven't heard about what?" Jhoe Freetz was asking as Yezu slipped out the lounge's exit. "Really, Tomus, what did I say?"

Chapter Five

Jafre stared out his office window, stared out across the meadow as the park lights brightened, as Lacigo slowly dimmed and dipped below the horizon. Half-night: Vano still hung high against the stars, like heap of coal someone had shoveled up into the sky. Too red to read by, as they said, and too dim to dance.

"Mister President, are you even listening to me?" said the man on the other side of Jafre's desk.

On Earth, the meadow would have been green, dappled here and there with colored flowers. The setting sun would be yellower and much, much brighter than wan Lacigo, and framed in sky of rich blue. Here, all of it was gray and brown. Ugly, but still it was with reluctance that Jafre pulled his gaze away.

"I was hoping you'd left," he said finally. "Would you care to? There's still time."

The young man, one Rodgar Twidd, fumed. "Mister President, I'm quite serious. Unless those demands on your screen are met, *to the letter*, the Youth Coalition will picket the docks at Port *Chrysanthemum*. I'm sure the Earthers will be curious to learn—"

"The Earthers," Jafre cut in with his no-kidding-now voice, "have better things to do than listen to whiny children." He glanced down at the list before him.

"Eliminate the children's curfew? Full suffrage at age twenty-five? Are you actually serious about this?"

Rodgar Twidd leaned forward, his eyes and nostrils flaring, fingers spread on the far edge of the desk. "Yes. We are."

" 'We'?" Jafre leaned back and grinned humorlessly. "The Youth Coalition is, what, about twelve people? I'm not exactly quaking in my shoes." He touched a button on the desk and spoke loudly: "Martin, would you send security in here, please?"

"Yes, sir," said a voice from the desk.

Twidd recoiled, looking both insulted and alarmed as the door opened up and two of Jafre's guards hulked in.

"You can't arrest me," Twidd protested. "I'm just speaking my mind. I've got the *right*—"

Four meaty hands grabbed him and hauled him to his feet.

"We can't arrest him," Jafre told the guards in mocking voice. "He's got the *right*. Help me out, hah? Call this kid's mother."

Now Rodgar Twidd turned bright red and struggled hard against his captors. "Oh, come *on*! Mister President, come *on*, I'm not some fifteen-year-old—"

"The Earthers have child activity laws, too, you know," Jafre told the young man as the guards led him away. "Stricter than ours, I believe. I doubt you'd find sympathetic audience with them. And—" his voice dropped in pitch "—if I were you, I wouldn't try it."

"Darkness," Twidd cursed, "we *won't* be ignored! You can't . . ." But he was out the door by then, and his protests faded quickly into the background.

Twidd and his cohorts would, in fact, be ignored. It seemed the only fitting punishment for their annoying him like this.

Jafre swiveled in his chair, looked out through the

window again. But Lacigo had gone, leaving Vano and the park lights the only sources of illumination. Damn. He'd waited over eight decades for the Terran ship to arrive, counted the setting of Lacigo nearly four thousand times, literally *counting the days* of his Malhelan exile. And here he'd missed the last one.

Well *damn* the Youth Coalition.

A bell chimed. "Jafre?" said the voice from his desk.

"Yes, Martin?"

"Your wife is on the line."

Jafre put a hand to his brow. "Tell her I'm dead," he said, and then sighed, because he knew Martin would do no such thing.

Indeed, on Jafre's telkom screen, the eighteen demands of the Youth Coalition vanished, and the image of Asia Gill replaced them.

"Why aren't you here?" she demanded without preamble.

"Because I haven't left yet," Jafre said reasonably. The matching reasonable expression had found its way onto his face, and he made the extra effort to keep his hands relaxed in his lap. It would not do to let Asia know she'd annoyed him, to let her know she had affected him at all. Such knowledge was never of positive benefit to their relationship, or to Jafre's end of it, at least. "Just some small affairs to attend to. Did you get my suit fluffed?"

"Have you tried on your new boots?" she countered, unwilling to answer his question directly.

"My new boots?" Jafre said, not questioning her but musing privately, as if he couldn't quite remember the answer but would in a moment or two. In fact, he had tried the boots on several times and was quite satisfied with their fit. But Asia's eyes had that shifty look that said she was in the middle of something, that she was hurrying through this call as part of grander schedules, and Jafre simply couldn't resist dragging things out a bit for her. Never mind that he should be hurrying himself.

But Asia knew this game as well as he did, and she was ahead of him this time; she just rolled her eyes and clucked. "Get your ass up on the next shuttle, my dearest. I expect you on *Chrysanthemum* in four hours."

"Yes, dear," Jafre said, and smiled thinly, acknowledging both his defeat and his grudging admiration. It never ceased to amaze him that for all her power, for all her burdens and responsibilities, the Director of Port *Chrysanthemum* and the Fleets of Malhela still had the time to call him up to nag like any other wife.

Before she vanished from his screen, light played momentarily across her necklace as she reached for the cutoff switch. The necklace sparkled with a dozen examples of that most beautiful of stones: centrokrist.

We'll have some trouble on account of that, he realized, and at that his smile split into a wide, unselfconscious grin. The thought displeased him not at all.

Chapter Six

The gangway had an actual red carpet on it, some soft, bright fabric that it seemed a crime to walk upon. And yet, ahead of Tom and Yezu a few dozen people had already done that, and some of their shoe prints were clearly visible in the pile of the carpet. Tom stepped out onto it.

"You *did* lose it in the endgame, sir," Yezu said for the third time that morning as he matched pace and they strode on down the gangway. A man and a woman waited near the bottom.

"Yezu, will you leave it alone? I failed to establish control of the center. I failed to develop my pieces effectively."

"Nonsense. Your queen bored through my ranks like a rock drill, and I couldn't dig her out until you fed me that bishop. That destroyed your entire defensive structure."

He slowed a bit, nudged Tom in the ribs and nodded toward the couple at the base of the ramp. "And who have we here?" he asked in a much lower voice. "The red king and queen?"

The man wore a jacket of bright crimson, with puffy white lace bursting out at the cuffs and neck. Lights in the corridor were white and harsh, and the buttons of the man's jacket seemed to catch the glow and sparkle peculiarly with it. Shiny orange boots laced up toward his knees.

The woman's face peered out between the hugely billowed shoulders of an elaborate, floor-length dress of shocking scarlet. She wore a necklace of gold woven around bright, faceted stones. Blond highlights streaked the woman's hair, which piled high above her in a sculpture of curls and pins. Both she and the man displayed broad, professional smiles, and they touched and spoke with the men and women debarking from *Introspectia*, each in turn.

And presently, it was Tom's turn.

"Jafre Shem," said the man, commanding Tom's attention back to him, holding crossed fists out in front of him, flat. His smile seemed entirely too broad. "President of Unua."

"Uh . . ." Tom gripped the man's hands and shook them briefly, not quite sure what was expected. "Tomus Kreider, Doctor of Planetology. I'm, uh, pleased to meet you."

"Asia Gill," said the woman beside Jafre Shem. She offered Tom the same crossed hands, but with the backs turned down toward the floor. "Director of Port *Chrysanthemum* and the Fleets of Malhela."

Tom gripped her hands as well, shaking them in what seemed an appropriate manner. "Tomus Kreider, utterly charmed."

"What goes on here?" Yezu said behind him, his voice at once polite and impatient. "Where are those people going?"

Ahead, the line of debarked passengers, moving rapidly once past the constriction of the Red King and Queen, snaked around a corner and vanished.

"Why, to the reception of course," said Jafre Shem. "If you'll just, ah, follow them . . ."

Yezu cleared his throat in the way Tom had learned meant he was displeased. "We have come a long way, sir, and sacrificed much. Have you some sort of briefing for us? Can we see a sample of the material you've discovered?"

Jafre Shem's smile stretched to an improbable width. "You already have, Earthman."

"I don't understa—" Tom watched Yezu's eyes lock on the buttons, the elaborate, sparkling buttons on Jafre Shem's jacket. "Oh, no. Oh, you *haven't* . . ."

Tom shot a look at Asia Gill, at the jeweled necklace dangling down into the upper reaches of her bosom, draping upward between her shoulder-puffs. Pea-sized polyhedrons, the stones reminded him vaguely of opals, of cut and polished pearls, of peizoluminescent quartz under megabar pressure. But really, they resembled nothing Tom had seen. And Tom had seen much.

Above the necklace, the woman's smile faltered, and her eyes flashed a signal of . . . guilt?

"You *haven't* . . ." Yezu repeated dully.

"Please move along," Jafre Shem said in a low voice. "We'll talk at the reception, ah?"

"Tomus, they have—"

Tom grabbed Yezu's arm and pulled him away from the two, down the corridor where the other passengers all had gone. Toward the reception. "Yes, my friend, apparently they have."

"But . . . But we've come so *far*. Do they mock us? Do they regard this as some kind of joke? Very poor taste, I should say. Would you wear a piece of the pyramids around your neck? Or a piece of the first lunar lander?"

Ahead, the corridor curved up and away in classic spin-gee architectural style, but Tom followed the crowd, turning left onto a corridor that ran long and

straight, parallel to the station's spin axis. Faint music
carried on the air, flutes or bagpipes or violins, with an
eerie voice crooning in the background.

"Will you relax?" Tom said quietly. "I think you *need*
a good party right now."

"Precious stones." Yezu's voice was distant. "Back
when *Earth* was the frontier, rare minerals were the
only form of hard currency."

"Yes? Yezu, what are you getting at?"

"I don't know. I don't know. Let's wait for those damn
painted bureaucrats at the party."

The music seemed much louder now.

More cocktails, of peculiar color and flavor. Slender
women, wrapped in pink and bright green fabrics and
with little stones sparkling on their fingers and wrists
and earlobes, held out little silver trays with little bits
of food on them. Conversation rumbled low and loud
as Terran visitors tried to coax or bully information from
the servants of their absent hosts.

Tom and Yezu tried to pounce on the Red King and
Queen as soon as they entered, but many others tried
as well, and Malhelan security officers, clad in garish
yellow costumes, had to push the crowd back so that
the two could pass. And pass they did, up toward the
dais at the head of the chamber. Tom heard a few
shouted questions he couldn't quite make out, and
then Jafre Shem was up and facing the crowd, hands
raised, his gemstones sparkling in the harsh light.

"Welcome to all!" he shouted, projecting his voice
without amplification. "We are pleased to welcome
these honored guests to our system, humble though it
be. For four centuries now, we have labored alone to
build world for ourselves in the darkness, with only the

distant voices of our friends to keep us company. And now, our friends have arrived in person!"

There came a smattering of applause from, Tom thought, the smattering of Malhelans in the crowd. But Jafre held his palms out just as if he were silencing a throng of millions. "Malhela is no longer alone; our friends have come, across the great emptiness of space, to study the substance we call 'centrokrist,' the substance which we believe to have originated with an ancient, nonhuman intelligence in this system. Such profound discovery! *Humanity* is no longer alone! *Humanity* now has friends from the great emptiness, even if those friends are absent. It is in joy that we share this knowledge with you, the scientists from our mother world."

A little more applause this time. Again, Jafre held his hands up to silence the invisible millions.

"Let's move up next to the dais," Tom murmured to Yezu. "I want to be right in front of him when he comes down from there."

Together, they pushed through the crowd—three hundred people, maybe more, in this small chamber that might serve as a dining hall for fifty or sixty. Room to move, yes, room for the elbows and the trays of food and drink. But not a *lot* of room. Already the air had grown warm and humid and did not promise to improve over the course of the reception.

Pale gems glittered here and there in the crowd.

"There will be time later for lectures and meetings and laboratory sessions," Jafre boomed. "In fact, large block of space has been cleared out here in Port *Chrysanthemum* for your use. Just let our people know your power and datastream needs and we will accommodate you as best we can. Right now, though, we encourage you to relax, to get to know us as people. Certainly we are very eager to know you! For—"

The applause came again, still sparse but much more vigorous this time, and evidently unexpected. Jafre seemed a little flustered and a tiny bit irritated. He paused for a moment, then bulled through. "For your enjoyment, we have beer, and yogurt, and delicious chokeberry wine fermented—very carefully!—from the fruit of the toxic choker tree. If you're hungry, please try the sausages and the butter wheat crackers. There's plenty here, and it will all go bad if you don't eat it, and that would hurt our feelings."

He laughed. "Now, Asia Gill and I will step down from here and mingle. We're happy to answer your questions, but please, do try not to smother us. There are others in this room now, and more arriving soon, who may be better able to help you. Thank you all for your patience!"

He leaned over slightly, waving his hands as if brushing dust away. Tom, who had just stepped up level with the podium, stepped back again, and Jafre Shem hopped down into the space he had occupied.

"Ah, Mister President?" Tom said as carefully and as formally as he could. "Could we have a word with you?"

"When can we visit the discovery site?" Yezu blurted out, leaning over Tom's shoulder. "Once we've enjoyed your hospitality I'd like to get right to work, and I must see the material, the 'centrokrist,' in its original matrix to properly—"

"I'm afraid I can't help you," Jafre said, his voice quietly slicing through the crowd noise. "Fleet scheduling is Asia Gill's sphere, not mine. And, ah," he nodded sideways, to the place, five meters and a score of people distant, where the Red Queen smilingly attempted to push through a knot of anxious, question-sniping scientists. "She seems to be rather occupied. Anyway, there's not much to see anymore—I mean at the excavation site. The veins, really, are mostly played out."

Yezu Manaka leaned forward, his hand gripping Tom's shoulder tightly. "I knew it! Those buttons, those necklaces! You've plundered it all, haven't you? The very thing we've come here to study!"

Looking nonplused, Jafre Shem leaned backward a little and came up against the dais. "I can assure you, we have set aside significant amount of the centrokrist for your study. More than enough, I should think. If you will excuse me?"

Yezu shook his head. "Don't brush me aside, sir. I've come here to study the *lay* of the centrokrist as much as the substance itself."

Jafre tried on a half smile, then dropped it and scowled. "It's been long time since I was out there. I really can't help you. If you ask around, I'm sure you'll find somebody who remembers those things. Now if you don't mind, I really do need to circulate."

With that, the Red King puffed himself up and strode past Tom and Yezu and into the crowd, into the teeth of other people's anxious questions.

The music started up again, raining down from a set of primitive, ceiling-mounted sound generators. Guitar music this time, the sound of a glass rod picking and sliding at the strings while a drum rapped slowly in accompaniment. Light sounds, perhaps friendly ones. But the tune rolled out with slow turgidity, like a funeral dirge.

"*There* you fellows are!" a voice called out, and behind it Jhoe Freetz elbowed his way through the masses. And behind him, a tall, white-haired man.

Jhoe stopped, half turned. "If you please, allow me to present—"

The white-haired man, still moving forward, spread his arms. *Like a kind of trap,* Tom had time to think, and then Jhoe, grunting in surprise, was shoved against him, and he against Yezu. The long arms came together, encircling and squeezing.

"Hey!"

The man chuckled in deep, gravelly tones. "Ho, what beautiful children. And from Earth!"

"Sir," said Yezu, his voice rising in alarm. His face was squished up very close to Tom's. "What do you intend here?"

"Oof," Jhoe Freetz added, his breath warm against Tom's cheek.

The arm-trap loosened a little, and the white-haired man chuckled again. "What *beautiful* children. I was once a child from Earth, did you know that?"

Yezu grimaced politely. "Perhaps you've mistaken us—"

"Uh . . . Tomus, Yezu," Jhoe said, "allow me to present Jack-Jack Snyder."

"I'm the oldest man in the world!" the man said brightly. He let go with his arms and stepped back. Tom, suddenly leaning too far forward, fought to unhook his thumbs from his belt so he could flail properly for balance.

Jhoe looked earnest, excited. "I'd read so much about Jack-Jack Snyder in the early histories, just imagine my surprise at finding him still alive. Well, actually *he* found *me*, when I was practically still on the boarding ramp. At any rate, I'm very pleased."

"A social scientist to study my planet." Jack-Jack beamed. "Of course I came to fetch you. Who better to share the vaulted troves of my memory?" He laughed again.

Tom believed instantly this man's claim to great age,

to an Earthly origin that must, by definition, predate the colony on Unua. The man's hair, not gray but *white*, tied back in a heavy bun that nestled behind a palm-sized bald spot. His skin looked deeply lined and saggy, pale even against the cream color of his suit. No puffs or ruffles or lace there, either, just a smooth and conservative cut of minimalist elegance. A single, thumbnail-sized jewel dangled sparklingly from one of his earlobes. Centrokrist? Yes, surely.

Behind his smile, the man's teeth gleamed white and perfect, like new laces on a raggy old pair of slippers.

"Um . . ." Tom said.

Yezu came sharply erect as someone bumped him from behind. He cast a look of annoyance over his shoulder, then turned and pointed it at the old man. "Quite a grand entrance. What have you got there, hanging from your ear?"

"What do you think it is?" Jack-Jack asked with mock innocence. "A piece of history? An object, perhaps, slightly older than myself?"

Yezu reddened. "What have you people done?"

"You are a very angry young man."

"Don't insult me. I was born a hundred and eighty-four years ago, and that does *not* include relativity."

"Really? How wonderful. The stone, as you've guessed, is a centrokrist, the wearing of which marks me as a man of refinement. Something you aspire to, I trust, and I wish you well in the endeavor."

Yezu looked a little puzzled at that, not sure if he was being placated or insulted.

"Oh, come on," said Jack-Jack. "Should we have frozen ourselves until your arrival? Should we have held our collective breath and nailed our collective feet to the floor? Please understand, we were as interested as you. But eventually the novelty wears off. Let an old man tell you something, hey? The novelty *always* wears off."

"You seem like a very peculiar person," Yezu grumbled unhappily.

Jack-Jack's smile was warm. "My boy, you see to the heart of things. It makes me proud."

"Uh," Jhoe Freetz cut in, uneasily, "Mr. Snyder has kindly arranged for my transport down to the surface. I have to go and pack my things."

"Right now?" said Tom. "Why not stay for the party, and pack later?"

"Well, I'd like to, but—"

"These people are mostly idiots," said Jack-Jack, waving his arms to indicate the crowd around them. "They won't tell you anything you really need to hear. I, on the other hand, am the oldest man in the world, and my flight leaves in two hours. Come now, I won't take no for an answer." He laughed. "Really, I actually won't!"

"I've already agreed," Jhoe said, a little tersely.

Tom shook his head, letting his disapproval show. "If you really feel you must hurry, then I won't try to dissuade you. I've never been to an interstellar reception before, though, and I intend to enjoy myself. Should we say good-bye now? I guess we won't be seeing you."

"Not for awhile, no. As I said, I'm going back to the ship to get my things together, and then . . ." He shuffled a little. "I'll try to contact you when I'm settled. Um, best of luck to you both. In your research, I mean."

"What research?" Yezu muttered, still glowering at Jack-Jack.

Jhoe shook his head. "Have I missed something here? Has Mr. Snyder offended you in some way?"

"Please, boy, call me Jack-Jack." The white-haired

man did not quite have a smile on, but his eyes twinkled.

"I'm sorry."

"Oh, nonsense. Now, your little friends here"—he looked at Tom and Yezu—"are very amusing, but I think we really ought to go." He stuck a hand out, in the normal, Terran way. "Boys, it's been a pleasure."

Silently, bewilderedly, Tom shook the man's hand. Yezu stared at it, declining. Unruffled, Jack-Jack withdrew the hand, and then faded back suddenly into the crowd.

"Uh," Jhoe said, looking after Jack-Jack and then back to Tom and Yezu again. "He seems sort of . . . Damn. I don't particularly know why, but I keep doing what he tells me."

"He does seem a bit overwhelming," Tom said, still staring after Jack-Jack.

Jhoe nodded, digging at his shirt clasps. "Yes, exactly so. I have to go, okay? Good luck?"

"Certainly."

"Enjoy your stay with them," Yezu said, unhappily, his eyes also on the old man's retreating form.

"Well," Jhoe said, and then he was gone as well.

An elbow or two emerged from the crowd to jostle Tom, but he didn't turn. Crowd sounds competed with the mournful guitars while he stood there, blinking. Impatience and overbearing were generally traits of the young. Never had he encountered a person like Jack-Jack, or even guessed that one might exist.

"People can get very strange, I think, living in isolation," Yezu said after a while.

Absently, Tom nodded. His grandparents had all died before two hundred years of age, but from time to time he *had* met a few very old people. Retired NAU faculty, the relatives of his friends . . . They'd always seemed quiet, slow, a little confused. And sheltered! Why, the idea of T.T. Feng bulling around in a crowded room like this was ... ridiculous.

"I haven't been called 'boy' in a very long time," Yezu said. "This place will take some getting used to."

"Yeah." Tom sniffed. "Welcome to the frontier. You want to try that chokeberry wine?"

"Actually, no. What I'd really like to do is wring that fellow's neck."

Tom followed Yezu's gaze across the room, looking not at Jack-Jack now but at Jafre Shem.

The president of Unua stood hunched against the wall, beside one of the exits. He spoke, hurriedly, with ... Who was that? The woman wore an *Introspectia* uniform, but one colored light gray rather than blue beneath the gold trim. Her hair, also gray, hugged her scalp in a tight crew cut. Tom felt certain he had never seen her before.

Jafre Shem seemed very, very interested in speaking with her.

"I'd call it bad form," Tom said to Yezu, "to threaten the life of a public figure. Bad diplomacy, too—you could create an incident! Spill a drink on him instead. Who there speaks with him, by the way? I don't recognize her."

"Lin Chelsea, I would think," Yezu said.

"The captain?"

For the most part, *Introspectia*'s crew had made themselves available and approachable, if not entirely warm. Chelsea, though, had been a voice on the intercom and nothing more. Tom had heard that she lay strapped to a couch somewhere, fed by tubes and linkwires, literally and permanently mated to her ship.

But it seemed she had a human face after all, at least when the occasion demanded it. He pictured her, with faceless grin, fishing a mask of skin from a jar of reddish liquid. . . . Oh, what an ugly thought!

"Yes," said Yezu, "I think so."

"Well. Fancy meeting her here. I wonder what the conversation is about."

Jafre looked decidedly more animated than he had previously. Indeed, he looked ready to kick off his orange knee-boots and dance a little jig for the captain. But Tom thought he looked a little furtive, as well, like a man with a secret and not much time to tell it. Mouth very close to the captain's ear, with a hand hovering nearby, as if to deflect his voice away from unwanted listeners.

Chelsea, for her part, looked politely and patiently attentive.

Yezu grunted. "I hope she's reading him the Articles of Doom."

"She looks more like she's listening to a pitch. What could he be trying to sell?"

Presently, a young man, black haired and blue/gold clad in standard *Introspectia* style, materialized at Lin Chelsea's elbow. He leaned toward her, much as Jafre had done, and spoke hurriedly.

Jafre puffed up visibly. "Can't you see I'm *speaking*?" he snapped at the crewmate, his voice inaudible but his mouth quite clearly forming the words.

Lin Chelsea held up a hand to silence him, and nodded at the crewmate to continue. Jafre turned nearly as red as his shiny jacket, and stuffed his hands in his pockets and *glared* at the captain and the crewmate. He did not seem at all accustomed to being ignored.

Tom watched the young crewmate speak. There seemed an urgency about him, an impatience or frustration. ". . . *gravity well* . . ." Tom watched him say. "Something something in the *gravity well*."

The crewmate must have been speaking very quietly, because the Red King leaned forward, as if straining to hear. Chelsea waved him away again. Whatever the crewmate said, it had certainly gotten the captain's attention.

"That looks like something important," Tom said.

"Huh," Yezu said, looking away. "If it is, I suppose we'll know soon enough."

"I suppose so," Tom said, and found that he wanted a glass of chokeberry wine after all.

Beth was still in the tech blister when Miguel got back. She smiled as the door whoomped shut behind him.

"That didn't take long. How's the party?"

"Crowded and bright," he said. Indeed, it seemed surprisingly dark and gray in here after the harsh lights and screaming colors of the station. His eyes fairly throbbed, even now.

"Was there dancing?" Beth's eyes sparkled. She tucked a lock of hair behind one ear.

"I didn't notice. Listen, it seems we won't debark after all. Captain wants to light out for the hypermass again in twenty minutes."

Beth's smile drooped. "Twenty minutes? Why the hurry? Good heaven, what did you say to her?"

"I just told her our theory." Miguel shrugged. He and Beth Lahler had hypothesized that a large rock fragment had fallen down the Malsato gravity well, and was somehow breaking up much more slowly than it should do. No other scenario seemed to fit the instrument readings, and the fact that *Introspectia* was here looking for unusually tough rocks lent more than a little credence to the idea.

"I guess she bought it," Beth said, a little sarcastically. "What, did she worry about losing a science bonus or something?"

"Well, I did mention that we might be missing the final breakup. That got her attention. I didn't see credit lights in her eyes, though; I think she's just honestly curious. Anyway, we'll be back here in a couple of days. Maybe they'll throw another party."

Beth smiled again. "If they do, will you dance with me?"

He shook his head, ruefully. "Ms. Lahler, I'm an officer. Best I can do is *watch* you dance, and even that might get us in trouble."

Chapter Seven

Air screamed past the window, which still radiated an intense, prickly-dry heat. Jhoe's stomach churned again as the lander banked, cut through a layer of cloud. Ten other people on board, and none of them seemed to have any trouble so far. And how could that be?

After popping from a launch tube somewhere on Port *Chrysanthemum*'s hull, the lander had fired a long series of pulses with its fusion motor, slowing the vehicle down in its orbit. Slowing it down *all the way*! The damn thing had *fallen* three hundred kilometers before it started asserting aerodynamic control, and that had been ungentle when it came.

The sky had faded quickly from black to dark brown, and from dark brown to a color which, Jhoe thought, would have to be called *deep* dark brown, in the sense of actual three-dimensionality, of tremendous distance showing through the murk. Like looking down into deep, deep water. Unua's atmosphere was twice as dense as Earth's, and towered nearly three times higher above the lowland plains.

". . . we'd brought what we perceived as all the best of Earth," Jack-Jack's voice droned beside him. "Art, science, philosophy, music. All the cream, skimmed off the top of Earth's enormous vats. And we came here prepared to *work*, to batter and beat this planet until it yielded us comfort. To batter it gently, I mean; we went to great lengths to avoid ecological disturbances and such. Why do you think the cities are so far from the mountains, and the seas? My point is that we *brought* the best, we *were* the best, we *did* our best.

"You see what I'm talking about? *This* was the context against which the first generation rebelled! Little brats, all of them, but by the second decade they outnumbered us three to one."

"And you've been waiting ever since for someone to complain to," Jhoe quipped, perhaps a little irritably.

But Jack-Jack simply chuckled. "That's right, more or less. Touché. You make me proud."

"You know, I've heard most of this before. I've combed through every broadcast this system has ever sent."

"For a long time," Jack-Jack said, not seeming to notice Jhoe's remark, "the children still came running to us when things blew up on them. Mommy, Daddy, what do we *do?* They were cheeky enough to take on the world, they just didn't know a damn thing. But eventually, that stopped bothering them. Now, *their* children grew up very confused. Frightened of everything, and with pure foolishness foisted off on them as parental wisdom. They barely even knew their grandparents existed, we who had built the walls they were cowering behind!

"The third and fourth generations, well, they sort of found their own way. Space program, industrial program, arts and sciences . . . They'd learned to ignore their parents, you see, to sort of amputate the stupidity they'd been brought up with. They're not so bad, really."

"But not your own," Jhoe observed, putting a hand on his stomach to settle it.

For the first time since he'd accosted Jhoe, Jack-Jack Snyder looked tired. But still, he smiled. "No, son, they're nothing of mine. I, *we*, are sort of the inflamed appendix of their society. They've never cut us out, per se, but we've been drugged and palpated and chilled with ice packs, and I think they'll all breathe a little easier when we're gone."

I should be recording this, Jhoe thought, suddenly regretful. Jack-Jack's metaphors had exactly the sort of colorful charm Jhoe had expected to find here. Surgery! People born with vermiform intestinal appendices! Had Malhelan society really been so brutish? Or . . . was it still? The thought chilled him slightly. Interstellar broadcasts didn't show everything about a culture, didn't show much at all that was bad.

"Gooh!" he said as the lander heaved through another pocket of atmospheric turbulence.

"The thing that really makes it all . . ." Jack-Jack started up again, but Jhoe filtered him out, and reached for his sickness hose.

Sweat popped out on his brow as the little craft groaned and vibrated around him. The suction of the hose pulled cool air against his face, but not enough, not enough for comfort. Well, damn Malhelan technology anyway. There was a hard and unpleasant texture to this place that he somehow had never anticipated.

His gorge rose, and his breakfast came right along behind it, and he discovered that the mask end of the sickness hose had a top side and a bottom side, so that it could fit comfortably over the nose and chin. But he was holding the thing upside down!

No, indeed, he thought, as noxious fluid, only partially caught by the mask, squirted out along his cheeks. *The broadcasts didn't show everything.*

* * *

Jhoe walked, on unsteady legs, out onto the paved surface of the landing field. He felt sweat evaporating off him, sucked away by the dense, dry atmosphere, and his bag hung heavy on his shoulder. The gravity here felt much stronger than 1.16 gee. Beside him, Jack-Jack babbled on unheard.

Darkness above, a muddy brown sky. The field itself was illuminated with bright yellow lights that cast long and unpleasant shadows.

In the gloom a hundred meters ahead, there waited a building. One which, Jhoe fervently hoped, had a sink for him to clean up in, a couch for him to sprawl out on until his head and stomach stopped spinning.

". . . and we didn't even have communication!" Jack-Jack proclaimed, cuffing Jhoe's shoulder with a loose fist. "Ah, those days will never come again."

"I'd certainly hope not," Jhoe muttered.

The building looked peculiar in the darkness ahead. Its sides were shiny and rippled-looking, with curved supports bulging visibly beneath them like the bones of a giant beast, stretching out against its skin. A slight breeze whooshed by, and moments later the sides of the building began to sway noticeably.

With a shock, Jhoe realized the thing was little more than a glorified tent, a sheet of thick fabric stretched over a more-than-slightly flexible truss. It had doors and windows that looked normal enough, and a roof of different stuff than the walls, or at least differently colored. Some attempt, then, to have it at least *look* like an actual building. But Jhoe could not be comforted so easily. The whole structure seemed ready to collapse at any moment.

"You call that thing a building?"

"Why wouldn't I?" Jack-Jack said, without breaking his long stride.

"It's soft." Jhoe said. "Why in God's name is it soft?"

Jack-Jack chuckled. "Oh, you'll find out soon, I imagine. Have I told you yet about our first expedition to the Other Ocean?"

"I'm really very tired," Jhoe groaned. "I'd just like to lie down for a while."

"I'm sure we'll find you a comfortable nook," Jack-Jack said.

Jhoe noticed a young man standing on the pavement ahead, holding up a white placard with red lettering on it: UNUA UNFAIR TO ITS YOUTH. The young man, a boy really, probably not yet out of his twenties, looked nervous, his eyes darting back and forth as if he expected to be arrested at any moment. Which he probably would, Jhoe reflected; if this society bore even a passing resemblance to Earth's, as he believed it did, there would be little tolerance for the tantrums of youth activists. Indeed, this bold child attempted to embarass his elders in front of *visitors*.

The young man suddenly fixed his attention on Jhoe, as if noting his difference from the others around him. "Are you from Earth?" he called out.

Jhoe politely but firmly ignored this question, and was gratified to see Jack-Jack doing the same. Children, when they misbehaved but were not under your direct supervision, were perhaps best ignored in any society.

Jhoe became aware of a feeling of unease. Not about the boy, but about . . . something else. He heard a low rumbling noise, like thunder rolling off the distant hills.

The building ahead began to shudder, though there was no breeze just now. Then Jhoe's knees began to feel even wobblier than they had, and the ground beneath his feet began to shake.

"Ah," said Jack-Jack, "just on time!"

The pavement felt fluid, suddenly, a wave-tossed lake of black, slow-motion water. Jhoe lost his footing and fell, grunting loudly, atop his bag.

"Oh my God!" he cried, rolling over onto his back, looking up at Jack-Jack, who remained standing, his arms held out sideways, moving and bending as his balance shifted. "Oh! Oh my God!"

Quite suddenly, the ground stopped shaking.

"Oh my God," Jhoe said again, more quietly.

"Just a quake," Jack-Jack said, smiling slightly. "We get them all the time."

Jhoe nodded. "Right. Yeah. I knew about that."

Jack-Jack extended a hand to Jhoe. "That's why the buildings are soft. That way, they don't fall down so much, and don't cause much havoc when they do."

"Right," Jhoe said. "Okay."

"Never been in a quake?" Jack-Jack asked, hauling Jhoe to his feet. The old man did not possess any particular strength, but his grip was steady enough, and Jhoe did not weigh a lot. Even at 1.16 gee. "Not even on Earth?"

Jhoe brushed himself off with shaking hands. "Once, I think, as a very young child. Rare. We destress the faultlines, you know."

"Is that accusation in your tone, young man? You wound me. We haven't got much in the way of geologic engineering, it's true, but there also aren't any faultlines for us to relieve. It's all driven by tidal stress, what with Vano so close. . . . Shakes the crust up, even though it's very thick."

"Oh," Jhoe said, nodding. "Yeah. I guess I knew that. I guess I read that somewhere."

So much for his expert status. He *had* known about the ground quakes, and yet, in another way, he hadn't. Certainly, the thought hadn't troubled him until now.

Other people were brushing past them, now, Malhelans unconcerned by the shuddering instability of their planet. Only one other man had fallen. Jhoe shot him an unsteady, embarrassed salute.

"Are you from Earth?" the Unuan boy called out again. "Hey! Hey! Are you from Earth?"

Once again, he was ignored.

The man who had fallen waved a hand at Jhoe and walked over to him with small, cautious steps. "Hi. You're Jhoe Freetz? The social scientist?"

"Yes."

"Don Kowalski," the man said, shaking the hand Jhoe held out for him. "Synergicologist."

"Nice to meet you," Jhoe said, tiredly.

"And you. Listen, I heard you two talking just now, something about a trip to the ocean? I wonder if I might tag along with you. That's, ah, that's where I'm heading. Hopefully."

"A synergicologist!" Jack-Jack said, with evident delight. "Come to study the interaction between Terrestrial and Unuan ecosystems?"

"Yes, that's right."

"Wonderful! I've been saying for centuries, we need to study that whole thing more carefully. How splendid that you're here."

"Are you really going to the ocean?" Don Kowalski asked.

"Er," said Jack-Jack, "actually, no. I was talking about a trip we made four hundred years ago. But I could arrange it for you, if you like."

"Really?" The man's face split into a grin. "That would be great."

The Unuan boy came up to them again, moving forward with uncertain steps. "Excuse me. Are you folks from Earth? Would you speak with me for a moment?"

He had dropped the placard somewhere, and now, since he had framed his question with at least a modicum of politeness, Jhoe felt compelled to answer. But Jack-Jack beat him to it, saying quietly, "Not now, *vireto*. Save yourself some trouble and go home."

His voice was gentle, reasonable, even a little indulgent. But it seemed edged with threat, as well, a paternal warning that left no room for argument. The young man, looking quite crestfallen, seemed to realize the remark had been the end of any hope of conversation. Glumly and without another word, he turned and walked off into the gloom.

"Youth activists?" Don Kowalski asked.

Jack-Jack watched the boy's retreat with sympathetic eyes. "Unfortunately, yes. We've started to have trouble, these past fifty years. The world's getting too slow and comfortable, I guess. Very sad, really. It's one of the reasons we left Earth in the first place. Of course, when we left I was about a hundred and was not considered young. I'm the oldest man in the world, by the way. Have I mentioned that?"

"I believe so," Jhoe said with tired diplomacy.

Jack-Jack flashed his teeth and cuffed Jhoe on the shoulder again. "Just teasing. Every day is a history lesson with me, eh? But even history ends. You can manage from here, I hope. There's someone waiting for you inside."

Jhoe blinked, momentarily confused. Was he being abandoned?

"Oh, come on!" Jack-Jack said, putting an arm around Don Kowalski's shoulders and grinning broadly. "Share me! There's lots to go around! I wanted to see you safely down, and to have a little chat, and I've done that. But I'm much too old to play tour guide. They've

got somebody from the Power Board to do that for
you."

"The Power Board?"

"Oh, yes. Very important, the Power Board. Keep the
lights on, keep the citizens from getting frightened. It's
quite an honor, really. You should be flattered."

"Um," Don Kowalski said, extricating himself from
Jack-Jack's embrace. "Maybe I could find my own way.
Maybe the electricity guy could help me?"

"Nonsense! I wouldn't hear of it!"

Already, Jack-Jack was leading the other man away.

"There are some things you should know about the
Other Ocean. Saline? It'll take your skin right off. . . ."

Jhoe faced the flimsy terminal building once again.
The voices began to fade, leaving him. Leaving him
alone in this place, so far from all he had known. He
felt very small, suddenly, on the spaceport field. And
dry-mouthed, and uncomfortably warm in this strange
air, beneath this strange sky. Even the pavement
seemed strange, a sand-colored, vaguely bumpy surface
that *gave* with curious softness beneath his feet. Not
pavement at all, then, but some kind of thick rubber
sheet? Deep cracks ran along it in places.

". . . and you move slowly, so the andlius won't
bite . . ." Jack-Jack's voice carried on the breeze.

"Didn't anyone assign a liaison or something?" he
heard Don Kowalski ask. But Jack-Jack talked on, unconcerned. Voices fading now, bodies lost in gloomy
shadow between the field lights.

Dubiously, Jhoe started toward the building. The
other people, the Malhelans, had already dispersed, but
several of them had gone in here. The heavy fabric of
the walls shone yellow-white in the lights and cast
weird shadows on the ground. Paler, brighter light was

visible behind the windows, but they looked milky, translucent. Perhaps hung behind with gauze curtains?

The wide double door had been painted a bright green that burned into his eyes even through the night-time gloom. The door had a pair of brass handles, things apparently meant to be grasped and turned and pulled to disengage the latching mechanism, and a low concrete ramp leading up to it. It seemed the sort of building which, in a children's story book, might house a wicked witch or a family of trolls.

Three more strides carried him to the top of the ramp, where he paused, grasped the handles, turned them, pulled. The doors swung wide. Cool air and brightness greeted him.

Rows of chairs inside, bolted to the floor. Rows of holie screens hanging down from the ceiling (which, unlike the walls, looked straight and flat and solid). Dozens of people in here, men and women in bright clothing. A voice, improbably high and lilting in its delivery, spoke quietly from a sound generator somewhere.

". . . departure in twenty minutes. *Brava Navedo*, now boarding for departure in twenty minutes. *Fiera Navedo* will begin boarding in one hour, for departure at . . ."

A man, standing nearby, turned toward Jhoe. "You're letting the heat in." He wore a formal suit, cut broadly of glossy yellow fabric.

"What?" said Jhoe.

"You're letting the heat in," the man repeated. "Close the doors."

"Oh. Right." Jhoe had already stepped through the doorway, but the doors had not shut themselves behind him. Of course, that would be too easy. He turned and, with some hesitation, grabbed the inside handles and pulled them toward him. Turning them and pulling in on them at the same time seemed a little awkward, but as the doors swung to he found he really only needed to pull. The latch, fortunately, engaged by itself.

The yellow-suited man looked at him oddly as he turned around again.

"Has something disturbed you?" Jhoe asked. He felt acutely aware of the traces of bile on his face, on his shirt. The flight crew had given him a moistened, scented cloth to freshen up with, but still he did not feel quite clean. His hair, he suspected, had also seen better times.

"You're from Earth," the man said, making a simple statement of it but falling short of actual rudeness. "You people are down here already?"

"Oh, yeah, just a couple of us. Others will follow soon, I think." Relaxing, Jhoe stuck out his hand. "Doctor Jhoe Freetz."

The man stared uncertainly at the hand.

"Oh, my apologies," Jhoe said quickly. His first faux pas on Unua: he *knew* they did not shake hands in the Terran way. He crossed his arms, palms down, and offered those to the man instead.

Relaxing visibly, the man reached out, crossing his own arms, and grasped Jhoe's hands. Gently, he shook them. "Salutes, Doctor Jhoe Freetz. My name is Lano."

Jhoe gave a smile and the hint of a formal bow. "It pleases me to meet you. I only wish I could be more presentable."

"My name is Sheyla Awk," said a voice at Jhoe's side. He turned to see a small-framed woman standing there, and another woman behind her. A man, clad in a white shirt and light blue overalls, was moving up, and in moments Jhoe found himself surrounded by Unuans holding crossed hands out at him.

Momentarily, he fought down a sense of fear. Earth

people did not behave this way toward strangers. Nor did Lunans, nor Martians. Violating en masse his space-of-reach! And yet, there seemed no menace in this, but friendliness only. Their faces were all smiles and curiosity.

He thought of the long, lonely weeks on *Introspectia*, of the difficulty of approaching Tomus and Yezu. That effort had intimidated him greatly. He had made no other friends.

And he thought, then, of Jack-Jack, who had accosted him almost without introduction. Who had assumed control of Jhoe's movement and activities for hours, and then abandoned him, with equal brevity, in an unknown place.

The waltz of social graces ran differently here. Perhaps here they did not waltz at all.

"It pleases me to meet you, Sheyla Awk," he said, reaching out to shake the small woman's hands, offering her a smile.

He shook hands almost continuously for the next several minutes. "It pleases me to meet you, Vickie. It pleases me to meet you, Potter Chino. It pleases . . ."

"Are you through yet?" a woman asked him over the heads of the crowd.

He grinned widely at her, pleased now by all the attention. He felt like a Source Link personality, connected to disparate admirers he had never met. "Your turn will come soon!"

"I'm Uriel Zeng!" the woman called out, evidently annoyed. "Will you please hurry up?"

Jhoe, shaking another set of hands, looked squarely at her. "When your turn comes, yes, I will."

The woman made a face, her eyes rolling upward, lips curling back momentarily to reveal the teeth below.

"That's it," she said. "I came here as favor. You can find your own quaking ride."

She started to turn away, and Jhoe saw that her clothing did not resemble that of the other Malhelans he'd met. She wore a jumpsuit, colored a fairly mild shade of green, like uncut grass, and bearing patches and insignia of various sorts on the front and back and shoulders.

Technicians look the same, he thought wryly, *on any planet.*

"Wait a minute," he called out to her.

She paused.

"Did you come from the Power Board? Did Jack-Jack send you?"

Jhoe's Malhelan friends, sensing their time had passed, began to melt away.

"I came from the Power Board," the woman said coolly. "I don't know anyone named Jack-Jack."

"Jack-Jack Snyder? One of the Originals?"

"I don't know him. Are you coming with me or not?"

Earthly society considered Jhoe a fairly young man, and in general, for the sake of propriety, he tried to behave as one. But he did, after all, have almost thirteen decades' experience in dealing with difficult people. Finding, suddenly, that thirteen decades were quite enough, he dropped the last bits of his grin.

"Miss, I get very tired of being shuffled around like a box of freight. I've had a very long and difficult journey, and I'll thank you to behave more civilly toward me."

The last of Jhoe's admirers slipped away, finding they had business elsewhere in the terminal.

The woman's expression did not change. The distance between the two of them did not shrink. "You're staying, then?"

Jhoe sighed, the weariness rushing back into him. "I feel tempted to decline your offer, miss, but I suppose, politically speaking, it would be unwise. It would also leave me stranded."

"Fine," she said. Then, in a voice of false courtliness: "I would be delighted if you would accompany me to the chopter pad. I take it you'd like to rest before seeing the city?"

"Yes, I would," he said, opting to ignore her sarcasm. Things were off to a bad enough start already.

"Shall we go then?"

Hefting his bag once again, he nodded as politely as he could. Which, he thought, wasn't very. She started moving, and he followed her.

Just then the walls around them began to quiver, the floor to ripple beneath their feet. A floor of palm-sized hexagonal tiles, he saw, hinged with some flexible caulk so that the quake could roll right through without cracking the tiles. And roll it did, in low, solid waves that moved with visible speed, that snapped at Jhoe's feet like rugs being pulled out from under him, one after the other.

"Damn it!" he shouted as he wobbled off balance. This planet seemed *determined* to make things difficult for him.

"Steady," the woman said, calmly grabbing Jhoe's elbow.

"Let go of me!" he snapped, then immediately regretted it. Fortunately, the woman did not let go.

They were silent for a few seconds, the woman outwardly calm, Jhoe inwardly, gloweringly angry at everyone and everything.

The quake tapered away, its little shockwaves fading. The floor became flat and solid once again.

"I'm sorry," the woman said, politely. "I thought you might fall."

Jhoe found his anger cooling. He licked his lips, shook his head. "No, miss. *I'm* sorry. That was very thoughtful of you."

"Stop calling me 'miss,'" she said. "My name is Uriel Zeng."

Jhoe hefted his bag up higher on his shoulder, and offered her his crossed fists. "It pleases me to meet you, Uriel Zeng." His voice was serious.

She looked at him for a moment, and then snorted. "Yeah, okay. Are you coming?" She did not shake his hands.

They left the terminal building through a different exit than the one Jhoe had come in by, and walked out onto a differently colored, differently paved surface. The darkness and the thick, dry heat swirled around them like a strange fog. Politely, Jhoe turned and closed the doors behind them.

"It's hazy out today," Uriel Zeng said, ahead of him. "I guess you won't see much of the sky."

"I suppose not," Jhoe said. "Do you think it'll burn off when the sun comes up?"

Uriel snorted again and flicked him a contemptuous look. "They are up, Doctor. Both of them."

"Really," Jhoe said, his voice calm while his eyes darted, taking in the murky blackness around him.

But for the peculiar, double-clicky sound of their shoes on the rubbery pavement, the walk continued in silence. He didn't think Uriel would ever guess how horrified he'd really been at this moment.

Jhoe opened his eyes, and came fully awake when he saw the gray-white plastic ceiling above him. In the dim light it looked glossy, with the sort of cheap ugliness you almost never saw on Earth. And here and there, it had *cracked* in little spiderweb patterns. That cut right through his sleepy confusion, let him know right away that he had not awoken in his NAU dormitory, nor his parents' mountain home, nor in his cabin aboard *Introspectia*. That he had awoken, rather, on a gigantic bed in the penthouse of the Verva Hotelo, city of Verva, planet Unua of Malhela system. Thirty-eight light-years too far from home, he rather suspected.

Uriel had brought him here, after a harrowing flight through dark, hazy skies and an even more harrowing landing on the hotel's roof. She'd strutted around a little, spoken briefly to the staff. And then, like Jack-Jack, she'd abandoned him to his fate, which, not surprisingly, turned out to consist of many hours of deep and unbroken sleep.

He kicked off the light sheets now and sat up, looking around at the apartment. Uriel had called it "splendid" or "fabulous" or something, and tired as he felt he hadn't really questioned her assessment. But now . . . He saw that someone had stenciled monochromatic images directly onto the plastic walls, plants and animals and craggy ridges in black silhouette, without even frames to surround them. Here and there he saw clear plastic tables, and atop them plastic vases full of dead flowers that seemed, against reason, to have been arranged with some pretense of artfulness. Round, meter-wide windows circled the room at shoulder height, and through them he could see a distorted image of city and sky. Daytime sky? A ruddy glow bathed the room, like firelight.

Jhoe wondered whether Uriel Zeng knew the word "shabby," and if so, what dire conditions might cause her to speak it aloud.

"Lights up," he said, then sighed when he remembered that the room had no computer. Rolling over, he hunted for the manual switch on the wall behind him, found it, turned it. The lights came up, white and harsh and entirely too bright.

The sheets, vaguely slick, very thin and very soft, tickled against his skin as he slid out of the bed. His feet found the floor, and were not uncomfortable there. Textured plastic, neither hot nor cold. He walked to one of the windows.

I can't believe I'm here, he thought. *I never expected this, never in all my life.* The Malhela expedition, grand adventure of a lifetime, had never seemed particularly real to him, not even in the cramped months aboard *Introspectia.* He hadn't felt the magnitude of it all, deep down in his heart, but then it had been his reason, not his heart, that had led him here.

Suddenly his heart, thumping heavily inside his chest, seemed to catch up with events. He felt a wash of joy, and terror, and excitement of a sort he hadn't experienced for more decades than he could count on his hands. Sprawled before him in lens-distorted glory, the city of Verva lay waiting for his attentions.

Low buildings lined up in crisp regiments all around, and lamps hung from their corners and sides, illuminating the streets below. People moved about down there, looking like chessmen on a strange, oversized board, and ground vehicles big and small zipped between them. Above, the sky simmered with a twilight glow that looked at first like haze backlit by a rising sun. But when Jhoe craned his head a little, he saw that the "haze" had a definite edge, a definite circular shape. It was the brown dwarf, Vano!

Vano looked like a ball of iron in a dark, hot fire, except that—staggeringly—the thing filled a good quarter of the sky, dwarfing all that lay beneath it. Like a thunderhead made of sputtering flame, like God's burning fist about to smash this planet to flinders. Jhoe's mind could not quite take it in.

It had looked so different through the windows of *Introspectia's* observation lounge! Space was so large around him there, a full 360-degrees in every direction he could look. But with *ground* beneath him for reference, he could appreciate better the enormity, the *proximity,* of the star. And people *lived* here, on the hot and shaky ground directly beneath it. That seemed, suddenly, like a kind of miracle.

His pessimism had fallen away like a shed skin. He knew, now, that the ground tremors occurred mainly when Vano loomed at its zenith, and eight hours later when it lurked at nadir behind the planet. Four hours until they started today? Something like that.

Uriel didn't seem to joke about the tremors, but neither did she seem concerned by them; they came every day with little variation in intensity. One simply planned around them and gave them no further thought.

And the tent-buildings, soft and ridiculous as they were, held no special place in Unuan architecture. In yesterday's terror flight he'd seen quite a variety of construction styles, and now he could see more, and more clearly. Nothing soaring, towering, skyward-reaching like you saw in Terran cities, but here below was a little puebloish thing that seemed cast of red cement, and there a graceful dome of burnished metal.

There, an ugly tent, and next to it a beautiful, sweeping one that looked like some kind of three-dimensional math function graph. And over there, a low and narrow building that looked like somebody's caricature of a brick shit-house.

The Verva Hotelo looked much like an Earthly resort, though not a large one. According to the safety card he'd read before going to sleep, the hotel was so solidly constructed that it would more likely fall *over* than *apart*, in the case of an unusually powerful quake. And remembering the squat shape of the place, Jhoe thought its falling over an extremely unlikely thing.

Unua. Malhela. A century-long expedition.

He drew in a deep breath, let it expand him and strengthen him. The time had come for him to stop acting helpless, to stop acting like a child away from his mother for the first time. The city, the whole *world*, lay waiting for him.

A shower? No, Unuans did that only weekly. A sponge bath, then, and a dab of cologne in his hair. Yes, that would do nicely. But first, some business!

Pushing away from the window, he flopped once more onto the bed, reached across it for the bucket-shaped device, labeled TELKOMILO, that lay on the night table. Like the floor, a thing of textured plastic. It weighed less than he expected.

He fussed with controls for a few moments before he got the thing to produce a hum, and then a holie image of one of the hotel staff. The image focused on him, smiled. "Salutes, Doctor Freetz. What can I help you with today?"

"I'd like to order some breakfast."

"Certainly! Would you like to eat in your room?"

"No, I think I'll come downstairs. I'll find the restaurant on the ground floor?"

"Indeed you will," the clerk agreed with the same unfaltering cheerfulness. "Would you like us to prepare something . . . familiar to you?"

"No," Jhoe said. "Quite the opposite. I'd like you to surprise me with something uniquely Malhelan. Can you do that?"

"Of course. Will you be requiring anything else?"

"Yes, actually. Could you link me through to Port *Chrysanthemum*? I've got to check with some friends."

The clerk looked at something down below screen level. "Uh, yes. Can you pause for couple of minutes?"

"Yes."

The smiling face vanished, and the word PAUSE appeared in the screen, cast in shiny brass letters. Faint music started to flow from somewhere behind the screen.

Well, the world could wait a few minutes for him.

He sat patiently, fidgeting very little. One hundred and twenty-six standard years had taught him the art of waiting. Other arts, too, like rationalization, shifting blame, farting silently in a crowded room. So many skills to be mastered, thank heaven he had the time. He wondered what wisdom his next century might bring.

PAUSE vanished then, and a new face appeared in the telkomilo. Not a scrubbed and cheery face like that of the clerk, but a tired one, with mussed hair and a comlink hanging askance from one ear.

"Port *Chrysanthemum*," the tired face said.

"Hello," Jhoe said to it. "I would like to speak with one of the Terran scientists, a Doctor Tomus Kreider."

Wordlessly, the tired face vanished, and PAUSE returned to the screen. In silver letters, this time.

Again, Jhoe waited, and after a time, the face of Tom Kreider appeared behind the screen. *Large as life and twice as ugly,* as NAU staffers often said. Like the comtech, he appeared very tired.

"Yes?" Tom said. Then he looked at Jhoe and his face brightened a bit. "Oh, hello."

Jhoe grinned at the older man. "You seem surprised, Tom. Did you expect some other person to call?"

Tom smoothed his hair back, straightened. Behind him was some sort of equipment rack, and the noise of several people speaking at once. "Yes," he said, "as a matter of fact, I did. I hadn't expected to hear from you so soon, and things have really gone to hell up here."

"Really? What's happened?"

Tom blinked. "You haven't heard? *Introspectia* lit out of here about nine hours ago, headed for Soleco. Some kind of scientific emergency, it seemed like. The captain kept denying any problem, but she was hustling everyone around and really didn't seem inclined to discuss it. The Red King is screaming at us all about breaches of protocol, and—"

"The who?"

"The . . . oh, sorry. The, uh, the president. Jafre Shem. Yezu and I have shared a sort of joke about him."

Jhoe's smile had gone. "And how fares Yezu?"

"Asleep right now, I believe," Tom said, smoothing his hair back again. "As if we didn't have enough going on, he got a half-hour personality fax from his wife. It really upset him, I guess; he wouldn't talk about it, but afterward he played a really savage game of chess."

"I . . ." Jhoe waved his arms, trying to express a thought. "I don't completely understand your circumstances. What kind of situation have you got right now? Are you working yet?"

"No," Tom said. "And there lies part of the problem—most of us up here never got the chance to unload our equipment. We're setting up temporary laboratories with all sorts of makeshift gear, but there isn't enough to go around, and . . . Well, a Malhelan ship departs for the Centromo tomorrow, and Yezu and I plan to be on it. We just hope our equipment will catch up with us before too long."

"*Introspectia* really left in that much of a hurry?" Jhoe asked. "Why? What could drive them with such urgency?"

"I've just *told* you I don't *know!*" Tom snapped. Then, "Forgive me. I haven't had any sleep since you left. About ten hours ago?"

"About that much, yes."

Tom nodded. "Okay, well, listen: I'm glad you've got off to a better start than we have. I'd love to chat, but I really do have to go."

"I understand," Jhoe said, though he didn't, completely. He hadn't expected turmoil from above, and certainly not from *Introspectia*'s calmly efficient crew. Abandoning him, as Jack-Jack had, as Uriel had. Stranding him here on the planet! What in heaven could have happened up there? Headed for Soleco, Tom had said. Why? What secret emergencies could a dead star hold?

"Well, good-bye then," Tom said, and then the telkomilo went blank in Jhoe's hands.

"There you are!"

Jhoe looked up from his breakfast to see Uriel Zeng stomping into the restaurant, an impatient expression on her face.

"Good morning," he said.

"I've been looking all over for you."

"I've been right here."

"Well, hurry up! We're due at the power station in forty minutes!"

"Power station?"

Uriel nodded impatiently. "Yes, you were supposed to have the tour today."

"That's odd," Jhoe said, "I don't recall asking for one."

"Well," Uriel said, "I arranged it for you." She held

up a hand. "I know, I know, I said I'd tell you before I scheduled anything. I forgot! I'm sorry! But we really do have to go if you want to see the facilities today."

The Unuan government had assigned Uriel as Jhoe's guide and liaison, which he supposed was thoughtful of them. She seemed to interpret the role rather broadly, though, as if she were somehow in charge of him, as if she somehow had the right to command his obedience. Jhoe could think of no reason why she might actually be so entitled.

He took a last bite of his "pitch cakes," dabbed the corners of his mouth with a napkin, and offered Uriel a patient, an *old man's* smile. "And what, precisely, would I see if I went?"

"The power station," Uriel said, blinking. "You know, one of our geothermal turbine emplacements. They're very important for the functioning of our society."

"Oh, I believe you. Still, it doesn't sound like something that would interest me very much. If you want to introduce me to your society, why not let me follow you on a normal day's work? I think I'd get a much better feel for—"

"You're impossible, you know that?" Uriel said, with what seemed like genuine anger. She flicked a thin plastic card onto the table. "Here's your itinerary for the week. I spent a long time on it."

"Well, I'll have a look," Jhoe said, picking up the card. "It's very kind of you to work so hard, but I wish you hadn't gone to the trouble. I expect I'll have a few ideas of my own."

Uriel did not appear to take that remark very well.

Today's flight seemed only slightly rougher, only slightly more frightening than yesterday's. Given Uriel's bitter mood, this seemed to Jhoe like a sort of blessing.

She could be flying much worse than this! Still, it might help her mood, and his stomach, if he improved relations a little.

"Let me thank you again for your efforts," he tried saying. "You were very thoughtful to draw up that itinerary for me, and I could have been a little more appreciative. But you were angry at me before that, and yesterday, too. I wish I knew why."

She cast a brief, hooded look in his direction, then jerked her eyes forward again and pulled hard on the controls. The chopter dove, swooped, and turned, cutting near the top of a relatively high building. She jerked again, and the vehicle leveled out.

Manual controls! Not a link harness, not even a manual link interface. Jhoe had noticed this yesterday, as well: Uriel did not *guide* the vehicle, suggesting a course for its control system to follow. Uriel actually *was* the control system! The levers she pulled and twisted at seemed integrated with the actual mechanisms of the vehicle, so that the roughness or smoothness of the ride was fully a function of her own dexterity.

Incredible! Together they hung, suspended in the air by a bubble of metal and plastic, which was in turn suspended by whirling blades turned by motors inside the metal-and-plastic bubble. And the whole, improbable contraption under direct human control. He wondered what would happen if she made a mistake.

"Uh," he said as the chopter swooped again, "this seems like quite a complicated vehicle. It must be very difficult to operate."

"My license is up on the panel," she replied without turning.

Jhoe looked. Atop the panel sat a row of primitive indicators, brightly marked discs and spheres floating in clear fluid inside clear plastic bubbles of their own. And behind this, yes, a hologramatic card of some sort. He pinched the card between his fingers, pulled up on it against resistance, a clip or bracket of some sort. The card came free in his hand.

"Good heaven," he exclaimed after examining her holograph and biograph and chopter licensing information. "Have I read this wrong? Have I misunderstood your calendar?"

She looked at him, less angry now. "What?"

"This says you were born only thirty-four standard years ago."

"Yeah? So?"

"Thirty-four years? Really? I would have guessed you were much older. You don't carry yourself like a little girl."

"I'm not little girl!" Uriel snapped, her mood turned sour again. "Darkness, everyone thinks you have to be hundred years old to know what you're doing! I'm assistant deputy administrator at the Power Board. I fly chopters, fix high-voltage lines and generators. I've been doing it for five years."

"Forgive me," Jhoe said quickly. Faux pas number two—people grow up fast on the frontier. "I meant no offense. It's just that achievements like yours happen rarely on Earth, even among very exceptional people. Our young people mainly sit around and complain."

"It's rare here, too," Uriel admitted, her eyes focused on the rushing scenery ahead and below.

Aha, thought Jhoe, *low standards of modesty.* A usual thing, here, or restricted to young achievers? Or to Uriel herself?

"Then you'll accept my apology?" he asked sincerely. She sniffed. "Yeah. Whatever."

* * *

". . . and this is—Doctor, you have to step out of there before the door closes. Right. And this is the deputy administrator's floor."

It looks just like the other three, Jhoe wanted to say, but did not. Low against the cityscape, the Power Board building did not present an imposing edifice. But considering that quakes would come again in an hour or so, Jhoe liked it low and plain, free of the heavy and possibly fragile ornamentation that an equivalent building on Earth might wear.

"And over there is the deputy administrator herself." Uriel pointed between a pair of columns, toward a corner office. Jhoe craned his head, saw a red-haired woman in there leaning over a telkomilo, growling something.

"Come on, I'll introduce you," Uriel said.

Jhoe followed her into the office. The red-haired woman looked up as they entered. "Uriel, I'm glad you're here. We've got lines down near the southwest transformer station, and Powell is threatening to shut it down, to keep it from shorting."

Uriel staggered, grabbed at her heart melodramatically. "Shut it down? Shut it down? Oh, darkness."

The red-haired woman did not smile at this. "Darkness is right, *virineto*. Remember, the backup transformer is offline? Powell pulls that switch, the southwest goes brown, we're out a week's pay at least, so I want you to get a chopter out there *now*, and kick his rear end really hard. Oh, and get those lines up while you're at it."

"Luna!" Uriel said, her voice rising almost to a whine. "I've got full queue today! Send the zeta team out on it."

"Kiss me. The zeta team *is* out on it, but last time I checked zeta was under *your* little wing. Let's not fight about this, okay? The call is pretty urgent."

Uriel huffed out a loud, long-suffering sigh and jerked a thumb at Jhoe beside her. "Can I bring him with me?"

The red-haired woman seemed to notice Jhoe for the first time. "Oh, you're that Terran sociologist." She mimed slapping herself on the forehead. "I signed the auth two weeks ago, you'd think I'd remember." She winked at Jhoe. Then, to Uriel she said, "Of course you can't take him with you. Has he got a license? Has he even got a *suit*? Go on, I'll take charge of him for now."

Uriel Zeng seemed very displeased by that. She glared at the red-haired woman, then at Jhoe, then back at the red-haired woman again. "You promised I could do this," she said, then turned and vanished.

It occurred to Jhoe, with no small degree of surprise, that Uriel had perhaps *volunteered* to be his guide. How odd! Why did she then act as though she hated him?

"I'm sorry about that," the red-haired woman said, smiling vaguely. "I hope we haven't caused you any distress. Now that I think about it I did promise her, but hey, the electricity comes first."

I hope, Jhoe thought, *this woman doesn't expect me to spend the day cooped up in her office.* A whole planet awaited his exploration!

"Uh," he said, holding crossed fists out before him, "Doctor Jhoe Freetz. It pleases me to meet you."

"What?" said the woman. Then, "Oh. Right. Power Board Deputy Administrator, Luna Shiloh."

She grabbed Jhoe's fists and shook them lightly. She had said her title in a lilting, hyperbolic way that suggested self-deprecation, as if she found her name and her job title somewhat foolish. She had put on a crooked grin, and as she looked at Jhoe she tried, without much success, to straighten it.

He liked that, liked the easy unaffectedness of it. He returned the smile.

"Hey," she said, her expression shifting suddenly, "what the hell is going on with your ship up there? Our allocation tables were favoring the spaceport pretty heavily, because there were supposed to be all these landings, and they needed the radar and the lidar and the lights. . . . But hardly anyone's come down, and I heard rumor that the *Introspectia*'s left dock already! Quakes, what are you people up to?"

"Uh," Jhoe said, "I really don't know that much about it."

"Did the ship really leave?"

He grinned slightly. "Everyone seems determined to abandon me in inconvenient places. Yes, the ship left port last night. Something about that black hole, Soleco. I don't know, I guess the crew was really excited about something and they wanted to go back and check it out. I didn't catch any of the technical details."

"Huh." Luna Shiloh raised her arm, checked a readout of some sort that she had strapped there with a band of metal. A watch? A wrist watch? "It's late enough I could break away for lunch, I guess. Should we find someplace with a news holie? Catch up on the latest?"

"I just ate about half an hour ago," Jhoe said. *And I've come here to study* you, *not to watch you watching holies about us.*

She frowned. "Well, I can't leave you here alone, can I? Come on, I'll buy you a drink."

"It's a little early for that, isn't it? By my clock, anyway. I've only been up for a couple of hours."

Luna rolled her eyes at him. "Okay. Come with me

now, and I'll buy you a drink later on to make it up to you. Okay? How would that be?"

"Oh!" Jhoe said, understanding at last. "You're asking me *out,* for a *drink.*"

Ordinarily, he considered the reading of people and circumstances one of his stronger talents, but Malhela seemed to have jammed his gears. Now, though . . . he felt red warning diodes light up in his brain. He had not been *out,* for a *drink,* since the days of Shareen Brugiere. Shareen, the emotional hypermass who had gracefully, waltzingly crushed him to dots. Again, the thought of her stung him, stung his heart. Oh, damn romance! Damn women and their games.

"Doctor Freetz," Luna said, looking perplexedly at him, "is everything this difficult on Earth? Would you like me to leave you here with somebody else?"

"No," he said distantly, with resignation. Love at first sight was an exceedingly rare phenomenon, but so-called "contextual infatuation" happened frequently. Especially to those who found themselves alone and far from home. And knowing this wouldn't help him; Luna Shiloh had a kind of beauty, a kind of charm that, if turned in his direction, he doubted he could resist. Would she seize him? Would he become locked, redshiftedly, in a swan-dive through her distorted spacetime? "Falling forever," he mumbled, "like Black Hole Bahb."

Then he realized, with some alarm, that he had spoken out loud without intending to. Just like a complete, blithering idiot, and good heaven, that was one of the warning signs of contextual infatuation! He was suddenly acutely aware of how he must look to Luna Shiloh, and then he felt another tingle of alarm, because acute self-consciousness was another symptom!

"What?" Luna said.

He felt his face warming. "Nothing. Nothing! It would please me to drink with you, Luna Shiloh. Shall we go?"

"Uh, yes," she said, frowning at him peculiarly.

PART THREE

EN TEMPO SENMOVIGA

*Pretty! in amber to observe the forms
of hairs, or straws, or dirt, or grubs, or worms!*

> —Alexander Pope,
> *Epistle to Dr. Arbuthnot,*
> 1734 A.D.

*The bee is enclosed, and shines preserved in amber,
so that it seems enshrined . . .*

> —Marcus Valerius Martialis,
> *Epigrams,* c. 100 A.D.

Chapter Eight

Where before he'd had only a trickle of data, Miguel had lately dealt with a smothering flood. He fairly drowned in it, and still somehow he seemed to know nothing at all! Day after day, he sorted and collated, compressed and regressed and, with more than a hint of regret, deleted. Even so, the buffers had begun to fill up again. All *Introspectia*'s data storage capacity lay in his hands, its allocation subject to his whim rather than the captain's. Not enough? Ridiculous!

The problem, then, must lie with him. He had failed, in some way, to make full use of the resources he controlled. Could Tech Aid Lahler help? At his suggestion, she had confined herself mainly to the routine task of filtering and tagging the incoming data, staying away from the subtler and orders-of-magnitude more complex task of analysis. A bad idea on Miguel's part? She did seem much more comfortable, much more at home with the link technology than Miguel. She'd grown up with it, he supposed, or at least with the idea of it. How ironic, that he should be charged with telling her how to use it!

"Lahler," he said.

She turned, smiled, waited. Ever the eager and pleasant assistant.

Nice curves, Miguel thought for the thousandth time,

and mentally slapped himself for the thousand-and-first. Another bad idea, one that just *waited* to get him in serious, serious trouble!

He scratched his forehead, at the itchy spot where link harness met skin. "I, ah, need some help with this. Conceptual help, I think. All this data surrounds me, and somehow I just can't seem to integrate it. This equipment . . . We didn't used to have this equipment."

Lahler, *Beth* Lahler, gave him a pleasant, patient look. "You've done fine with it, Miguel. I think you just . . . hold yourself back a little? Just push it. Just push your mind right into it. After that, you can't *not* know what to do."

"So simple," he said skeptically. "I just 'push my mind into it.' "

Lahler shrugged, made an I-guess-so face.

Well, the time had certainly come for Miguel to earn his keep. Skeptically, almost jokingly, he poked and squeezed at his mind until it felt like a physical object overlapping his brain, and then he pushed it up toward the top of his head, toward the tangle of link cables harnessed there.

Amazingly, it took no more than that.

For a moment he knew thrashing panic, the shock of sensations wholly unfamiliar. Like falling into an icy stream! Of information! Of frozen frozen frozen—

"Steady," said Tech Aid Lahler from the chair beside him. "I'll monitor, I'll guide you. Good heaven, what are you doing?"

"I can't—" he gasped. "I—"

And then, like a pond suddenly freezing over, his mind seized into a state of glittery, crystalline calm.

"That's it," said Lahler. "See? Nothing to it. You should have told me before that you needed help."

Miguel Barta did not reply, did not feel the *need*, just

now, to reply. All at once, identity had shifted, expanded, changed. Miguel Barta had become thing-Barta, a piece of the seething group mind that controlled, nay, that *was* Introspectia. And thing-Barta felt a sense of freedom, of power, for it knew in its heart that it could do, astonishingly well, the task that had been layed out for it. With link-borne senses it sniffed and caressed and tasted the data and, with greater effort, visualized it.

No more difficult than walking, this. No more difficult than sitting in a chair. Slowly, almost leisurely, thing-Barta turned its full attention to the instruments, and through the instruments to the Soleco hypermass beyond.

And . . . And . . . And then thing-Barta knew, with crashing, crashlike suddenness, an amplified and clarified and back-filtered sense of awe so achingly powerful it bordered on the religious. So close to the event horizon . . . Matter could not exist in that environment! Gravitational stresses would tear atoms apart, tear *everything* apart, leaving only the quantum electromagnetic vortices that theorists knew as "dots." And yet . . .

"Tech Aid Lahler," he said, in a loose and wavering thing-voice. "Have you continued to guide me? Do you *see* that?"

"Yes," Lahler replied flatly.

Miguel shuddered a little. "Good. Good. I thought perhaps I had . . ."

"I see it," she assured him, and even through the link harness she looked stunned.

At the event horizon of the black hole, the data revealed a group of ellipsoidal objects, tens of meters across and quite clearly solid. Against all sense, against all *possibility*, several hundred of the objects huddled right up against the edge of the darkness, frozen, unmoving.

Lahler's eyes locked onto Miguel, demanding answers, demanding leadership. "What do we do?" she said.

Miguel pulled away from the images, pulled his mind clear of the link, back into the slow and narrow and softly focused environment of the real world. Impossible. Impossible. Good Lord, what would he tell the captain? "I don't know," was all he could think to say. "I really . . . don't know."

Run a full instrument diagnostic? Disengage from the link system and proceed with manual analysis? Have themselves declared insane? Damn, and damn again.

It was shaping up to be one of those mornings.

"You see?" said Dade Soames as Tom and Yezu got the airlock shut and started fumbling out of their bulky spacesuits. "Not so bad, really. Not so bad at all."

Dade, first officer of this narrow, tube-shaped flying prison known as *Wedge,* had made it his project to mollify the two of them, to convince them that things were not really so bad. But now they had seen the centrokrist mine for themselves, and Dade's expression looked more hopeful than reassuring.

Tom unscrewed a glove, tossed it into a locker. Cursed when it bounced right back out and fluttered past him. He'd thought the gravity on this tiny planetoid a blessing when they'd first touched down, but in fact it did not do much for him at all. A twelfth, a twentieth of a gee? Not enough to hold anything down, not really.

"Your miners have not destroyed the deposits quite as thoroughly as we had originally feared," he said, acknowledging Dade's point without concession or agreement.

Yezu simply pulled his helmet off and glared.

The Malhelan "fast" cruiser *Wedge* had taken three weeks to get them out here, nearly half as long as their trip from Earth had taken. A journey of mere light-hours, and yet so arduous! The ship's interior did not offer much space or comfort; Tom and Yezu had been crammed into tiny bunks, less spacious than coffins, less airy than the spaces under their beds in the vast (and private!) *Introspectia* cabins.

And the weightlessness! Gravity had varied considerably over the course of *Introspectia*'s journey, but thanks to centrifuge management and careful trajectory design, it never got below about a quarter gee. The Malhelans, with their tiny fusion engines, could make no such accommodation. Captain Biandi had encouraged them (actually, *ordered* them) to exercise their muscles. But he had no equipment for it, and so Dade Soames, quite the helpful first-mate, had shown them the *memlukto* ("self-wrestlement") exercises used by the Malhelans themselves.

Much of it looked, Tom thought, like a kind of masturbation, though of course *that* activity was nearly impossible in these close and privacy-free quarters.

But the ship did not offer many other activities to those without duties to perform. Had they not found a chessboard, stenciled on the bulkhead in a shadowy corner and staffed by magnetic pieces that had to be moved by hand, Tom would have gone quite thoroughly insane.

Yezu, he thought, might already *be* insane.

"The tunnels," Dade Soames said now, with a hopeful half-grin, "have been expanded only very slightly beyond their original dimensions. They really are very good indicators of the shape of the original deposit."

"The *empty* tunnels," Yezu snapped, heaving a boot

into his locker. Like Tom's glove, it bounced right out again and skittered across the floor, out of sight. "The looted, raided tunnels we have come so far to examine."

Dade sighed unhappily. "Did you see the remains of the core deposit, at least?"

"Yes," Tom said, "we saw them. Yezu took a lot of readings, else we'd have been back an hour ago."

"Readings," Yezu said witheringly. "Yes. I see exactly how a sliver of a corner of an edge of the deposit lies within its matrix. How exciting. Yes, well worth a century's journey."

Dade looked truly unhappy now, as he had so many times on their cramped journey out here. "Look," he said, "I'm sorry. How many times do you expect me to say it? Captain Biandi was one of the first people to see the centrokrist and, yes, to plunder it. *I* was one of the first to make jewelry of it. It was wrong of us, yes! It was difficult to resist, but it was wrong, and we're sorry."

"It doesn't help," Yezu muttered bitterly.

Dade clenched his teeth for a moment. "Well, Doctor, I'm sorry for that, too."

He turned and skated away, his feet sliding easily across the floor in the low gravity.

Tom shook his head. Dade Soames was aware of Yezu's problems. Damn, the whole *crew* was aware of Yezu's problems, and no one more than Tom. Yezu's wife, after remaining faithful to him for the better part of a decade, had divorced him and remarried. So her personality fax had informed Yezu, with simulated tearful eyes. She still loved him, yes, and dreamed of him often! But the decades must change her, wear away the personality Yezu had known and grind out a new one in its place. Too much time, far too much. They would meet, she said, when Yezu returned. Perhaps she would find herself once more unmarried, perhaps they would fall in love all over again. Or, she had said, perhaps not. Good-bye Yezu, hello Tom's Unceasing Headache.

"We have sympathy for you, my friend," he said now to Yezu, "but everything has its limits. Dade has done a great deal for us, and shown a lot of patience with your naggling. It's past time for you to stop this."

Yezu looked away, saying nothing.

Suddenly, a man in light gray fatigues appeared, skating up to them, stopping short with an expert skid. Techman Boyce.

"Doctor Kreider," he said, pulling up onto his forehead the goggles that served as primitive cousin to a link harness.

"Yes?" said Tom.

"I'm getting wideband transmission with your name coded as recipient. It's the *Introspectia*, I think."

"*Introspectia*? Are they still out at the Soleco hypermass?"

Techman Boyce shrugged. "I can't decode a point of origin. Most of the signal is wideband analog with modulations way outside audio range, and the digital part of it just looks like random bits. I'm wondering, is this some kind of encryption?"

Yezu looked up at the young man. "Probably they've sent a personality fax. You don't have those here?"

"We don't have those here," Boyce agreed, nodding his head. "I have no idea what you're talking about. Can you show me how to read one?"

"Not easily," Yezu said. The rage had gone out of his voice, leaving only a resigned, defeated sort of tone.

Tom once again felt a spasm of sympathy for his friend. Such an awkward fate he wrestled with, such a lose-lose scenario! Lose his wife on the one hand, or lose the opportunity of a lifetime, of *ten* lifetimes, on the other. It showed real caprice on the part of the gods, that the universe should contain such mischief.

"They probably have not left Soleco," Tom said, "or we'd have heard about it before now. Just beam a signal back there on the same frequency range, telling them not to fax. What . . . you just want banded multimedia?"

"How about a regular old holie transmission?"

Tom nodded. "Okay, just tell them that. I don't doubt they can arrange it."

Nodding, Boyce raised his arm and checked a wrist chronometer. "Yeah, okay. Round-trip light time from here to Soleco is over four hours, though. Can you wait?"

"Of course I can wait," Tom said, somewhat annoyed. He was no bouncing thirty-year-old, after all, and anyway no other option had presented itself.

"Right. Sorry." Boyce ducked his head. Then, after popping the goggles back down over his eyes, he turned and skated off, down the long axis of the ship toward his station near the bridge.

And so, they fed Yezu's new data from the tunnel, and a little that Tom had managed to put together, into *Wedge*'s poor excuse for a computer system, where it merged and melded with the data already there, information downloaded from the labs at Port *Chrysanthemum*. Then, they beamed the resulting mess *back* to *Chrysanthemum*, along with a request for updates as the data was processed.

That done, they dug in and began a little processing of their own.

Tom saw, for the first time, the brilliance and eagerness with which Yezu Manaka operated in this, his native element. Hypotheses spun from his fingers and lips, flying into the computer to be collated, assessed, accepted or rejected. And each time a new puzzle piece clicked into place, it seemed to kick Yezu into still higher energy levels.

"Look how these Penrose grains shear off at the tunnel boundary!" he exclaimed at one point. "Back up just a few microns and the structure seems unaffected. Flaws at interface less than one in seventy thousand, and the tesselation displays a fractality of well over two point six. Probability of natural occurrence?"

"Insufficient data to complete calculation," the computer grumbled back at him.

"What has the fractality got to do with it?" Tom asked, feeling that his thinking, already five minutes or so behind Yezu's, had begun to lag even farther.

"It can't come together like this," Yezu told him shortly. "The quark complexes should interfere. Left to themselves, they should *interfere!*"

It went on like that for quite some time.

Back at Port *Chrysanthemum,* the scientists had already gone over and over the quark complexes that made up the "atoms" from which the Penrose grains were "crystallized." But the crystallization itself, the methods or conditions by which such a ludicrously complex three-dimensional structure might come together, continued to escape them. But now, Yezu seemed right on top of the problem.

Heavily "charmed" matter comprised most of the octahedral and tetrahedral grains, accounting in part for both the unusual gravitic properties and the echoes of pedial, triclinic internal symmetry. This much they had already known. Now it seemed another dispute had ended, as matter doped with "strange" quarks made up the other grains, the hex-needles and the irregular, polyfaceted "pluggers." These pieces interlocked, almost perfectly, in a nonterminating and nonrepeating fashion that gave the centrokrist its incredible hardness and toughness.

Individually, centrokrist deposits lacked cohesion, falling apart into small crystals (this word seemed inescapable despite its incorrectness), a few no larger than a poppy seed, some about the width of Tom Kreider's thumbnail. The bulk of them were more or less pea-sized. At the edge of each crystal, the myriad grains came together to form a flat plane. *Truly* flat, the "burr" between grains never more than a single atom high. That this should happen at all seemed remarkable to the scientists, Terran and Malhelan alike. That it should happen in such a way that each crystal formed a regular polyhedron . . . Tom had not really believed this when he'd examined the Malhelans' original call for help. Now, seeing it with his own eyes, thinking it through with his own brain, he still didn't believe it.

It was just bad luck, Tom thought, that the crystals came out of the mine so perfectly sized and shaped for jewelry. A little larger or lumpier and the deposits might have been safe from depredation; in eighty years, no Malhelan scientist had yet been able to crack or crush or melt even a tiny sample. The Terrans, of course, had done so on their first day aboard *Chrysanthemum*. But not easily, no.

The edges of the actual deposit, inspected so meticulously by Yezu, proved now to hold charm and strangeness in equal proportion, along with more heavy "bottom" quarks than Tom would ever have guessed. And, too, more voids and irregularities, more and larger burrs on the crystal surfaces. So then, the "pink centrokrist," or "heavy centrokrist," must find its origins here. Nice to have a theory, finally; in their plundering days, the Malhelans had never paid much attention to what came from where.

"It almost looks like a shock front," Yezu mused as he stared at the holie display. "Like the 'bottom' matter once resided within the body of the deposit, and then something forced it through to this edge."

"Yeah," Tom said, pointing with a finger. "Maybe they used to fill up these tiny voids here."

Yezu sat up straighter. "Yes, I think . . . Yes! Tomus, you've got it! A high-energy burst of some kind could initiate quantum tunneling . . ."

It struck Tom, quite suddenly, how strange and beautiful the crystals really were. On the macroscopic scale, something like pearls, like diamonds, like opals. And yet, completely unlike these things. When examined personally, without the mediation of scientific instruments, they possessed a . . . an almost supernatural quality. Ghost stones.

Stranger still on the microscopic level, like a clever fractal display a computer might cast up in a fit of boredom. And, again, entirely unlike this.

And on the atomic level, more strange than anything anyone had ever examined. Holding it up against conventional matter, he could perceive little in the way of family resemblance.

"Damn it," Yezu said, startling Tom from his thoughts.

"What?"

"I can't . . . We need that mix data from Port *Chrysanthemum*. We won't get much further on this track without it."

"Oh." Tom had no idea what they might need the mix data for, but this hardly surprised him. He felt awed by Yezu's progress. And, yes, a little annoyed as well; in a properly functioning universe, Tom's colleagues labored in *his* shadow, never the reverse. Still, they'd gotten a week's work done in only a few hours and the results . . . Well, they were fascinating, to say the least.

"Maybe we needed a break anyway," he said. Port *Chrysanthemum's* reply would not reach them for at least another hour. "Maybe we can go talk to Dade."

Yezu eyed him narrowly. "You think I owe him an apology."

"Yes, well," Tom said.

"I don't think so. I . . . well, I could stop acting so unfriendly, I suppose."

"Shall we, then?"

"Oh, all right. Lead the way."

They unstrapped and rose from their stations, feet sliding unsteadily on the deck until they got their balance adjusted. Then, a quick skate down the length of the ship. In *Wedge's* narrow, linear spaces they soon came upon Dade Soames, curled up in his coffin-bunk, playing with a handheld data unit of some sort.

"Hello," Tom offered, tentatively.

Dade looked up. "Oh, salutes to you. How is the analysis going?"

"Very well," Tom said. "Very well indeed. But we've come to an impediment of sorts. Until some data arrives, we've put ourselves off duty."

"Well, that's nice." Dade put his data unit away in the tiny locker behind his head, and removed from it another object: a plastic bottle, long-necked and with a pointed straw-spout sticking out the top of it. The sort of thing one used to carry and dispense beverages in microgravity. He sat up as much as space allowed, and kicked his blanket down toward his feet. "Yezu, I have a peace offering."

Frowning, Yezu reached out to touch the bottle. "Yes? A bribe to clear your conscience?"

"It's fire wheat whiskey," Dade said, pressing the bottle into Yezu's hand. "Not exactly a bribe, though—it's not the best stuff. Besides, I won't let you drink it without me."

"Really," Yezu said, neutrally. He sniffed the end of the straw. Took a small sip from it. Frowned again.

"A bigger hit will kill the taste a little," Dade suggested.

Yezu squeezed, leaned back a little, took down a good swallow. Yellow-brown liquor sloshed gently, slowly inside the bottle as he lowered it. His frown had deepened. "I've tasted furniture polish better than this."

Dade smiled a little. "I used to keep better, but the guys kept stealing it. This is the nastiest stuff I could find."

"I believe it," Yezu said, handing the bottle back.

"Does sort of warm you up, though, doesn't it?"

"Yes, but . . . not in a good way."

Dade raised the bottle, took a healthy tug at the straw. Grimaced. "Bleah. I always *forget* just how awful this *is*. Darkness."

Still grimacing, he offered the bottle to Tom.

"Uh, no." Tom said, recoiling a bit. "Thank you anyway."

But Dade held the bottle out still, shaking it, waving it in Tom's face, and with a sigh, Tom took it and, reluctantly, sipped from it. Fire burned across his tongue, continued to burn there as it spread down his throat and into his stomach. He fought not to make a face, and lost the fight.

"Oh, my word," he said around his grimace. "I've never tasted worse."

He passed the bottle back to Dade, who drank from

it and passed it to Yezu. Who drank from it and passed it back to Tom again. Who, against his better judgment, drank from it once more.

"Now I'll have two reasons to be angry at you," Yezu said to Dade, after choking down his third sip.

A crewmate leaned out from another bunk. Shipman Lake. "Hey, you drinking Dade's whiskey? Darkness, you're brave."

To shut the man up, Dade passed him the bottle, and after drinking, Shipman Lake did in fact retreat, wincing and shuddering, back into his shadows. "Quaking hell," he muttered, or something very like that.

"You know," Dade said to Yezu, "it doesn't take relativity to shake your life apart."

Yezu looked at him with a sort of cautious curiosity, and gave a little sideways nod to show he was listening.

"You went to sea," Dade continued. He looked weary, perhaps a little sad. "You put career travel above your marriage, and your marriage broke under the strain. The story is as old as civilization."

"Dade used to be married to that Power Board lady from Verva," said Shipman Lake from his bunk.

"Really?" said Tom.

Dade nodded, taking another pull at the fire wheat whiskey.

Yezu took the bottle, took another drink of his own. "Do you miss her? Do you sometimes wonder if you can . . . you know, if she'll . . ."

"It was a long time ago," Dade said, holding up a hand to slow Yezu's obvious dip toward despair. "We were married thirty-eight years, but . . ." He shook his head, definitely looking unhappy now. "Decades ago. Yes, I still miss her sometimes."

"Thirty-eight *standard* years?" Tom asked.

"Yeah," Dade said quietly. And that put things nicely

in perspective; Unua completed each orbit around Vano in just over seventy days. An eyeblink, a moment. Tom didn't think they even called it an "Unuan year," called it anything at all. But even at Tom's age, thirty-eight standard Terran years seemed an awfully long time.

"There's a lot of misfortune to be rationed out," Dade said. "We all choke down our share."

And then, thoughtful silence took the place of conversation for a while as the bottle made its rounds.

Eventually, Techman Boyce skated up, goggles riding up once more on his forehead. Tom stuck the bottle out at him.

Boyce didn't take the bottle, and pressed it off to one side when Tom held it up closer to his face. "Doctor Kreider," he said, "I've got your transmission from the *Introspectia*. I think you'd better come look at it."

"Oh," Tom said, feeling disappointed somehow. Since the very dawn of civilization, human males had honored the Ritual of Bad Liquor, and Tom had just begun to feel a sense of connection to all those departed pioneers. Firelight and earthen mugs, sincere but empty fisticuff threats . . . By refusing the bottle, by raising the specter of real work, Boyce had effectively broken the spell.

"What's so important?" Dade asked irritably.

"Just . . ." Techman Boyce looked unsettled. "Just come look at the message, okay?"

"Darkness," Dade said, struggling out of the bunk and unfolding himself, working out kinks in his elbows and knees.

So Tom and Yezu and Dade followed Techman Boyce to the comm station.

The face of an *Introspectia* crewmate was frozen there on a holie screen, little jagged lines frozen across the image like razor wire. Something familiar about that face . . . Yes! He was the young man who'd burst in on Captain Chelsea at the reception, leading her out from under the Red King's nose. Why would he be calling Tom aboard the *Wedge*?

Boyce worked a couple of controls, and the razor wire vanished, and the man's face unfroze and began to speak: "This is Miguel Barta, Chief Technical Officer aboard the Solar Commercial Starship *Introspectia*. I am trying to reach Professor Tomus Kreider. This message is urgent.

"Professor Kreider, I'd like to ask you to drop whatever you are working on and examine a new problem for me. I recognize my presumption in this, but I trust you'll agree with my reasoning. We have discovered a group of objects buried deep in the Soleco gravity well. I count between one and two hundred objects, ellipsoidal in shape, approximately eighty meters in diameter.

"I repeat, we have identified at least one hundred ellipsoidal objects buried in the Soleco gravity well!

"At the radius of the objects' orbits, gravity gradient covers a range between ten million and one hundred million per second squared. No material listed in *Introspectia*'s library is capable of withstanding even a fraction of a percent of the resulting tidal stress. We've collected and re-collected our data, analyzed and re-analyzed it. We waited this long to ensure the validity of our conclusions, and by now we have a very high level of confidence.

"Please understand the magnitude of this discovery! Without our most advanced instruments, we couldn't even *measure* conditions so close to Soleco's event horizon. The physical survival of physical objects under such circumstances . . . Professor, we have *no understanding* of this phenomenon.

"I don't have anything more to say. Please . . . respond to this message as soon as you possibly can."

Miguel Barta's face froze again, and the jagged razor wire sprang up once more in front of it.

"Darkness," Dade said with a low breath.

Yezu cleared his throat. "It seems . . . perhaps we've come for something important after all."

Chapter Nine

Miguel cursed at the equipment, wishing he could *pound* on it until it did what he wanted. Such slow communication—if only he could send and receive some goddamn personality faxes! Passive radio transmissions across the breadth of Malhela system . . .

He stayed awake through four straight shifts, sending and receiving and collating and relaying and banging his forehead against the panel in frustration. Still, conversation of a sort did emerge over time, and the summary in his log file looked like this:

BARTA: What holds these objects together? Could the centrokrist material survive these stresses?

DIETRE: I don't think so. Checking . . . No, it has nowhere near the required tensile strength. Centrokrist only beats our best materials by a factor of a hundred or so.

QUINT: I don't think *any* atomic bond could hold so strongly.

KREIDER: Wait a minute. We know the mass of unbroken centrokrist increases logarithmically with volume. Probably, the gravitic interaction between exotic quarks is responsible for this. We've never seen a really large sample, but I can tell you it would have a low mass, in comparison to its size.

DIETRE: What's that got to do with anything?

KREIDER: Less mass in the same gravity means less tensile stress. Let's think about this. Could someone have designed this material specifically to survive in high-gravity gradients?

MANAKA: What purpose do these objects serve?

BARTA: None that I can imagine. Nothing *exists* down there, just a kind of very, very diffuse haze.

KREIDER: We *have* got a timescale for alien activity in this system, from the dated centrokrist deposits here in the Centromo. The depositions and impact histories come in around nine hundred and eighty million years. At that time a nebula covered this whole area, right? An awful lot has changed since then.

DIETRE: Alien activity? Let's not jump to conclusions.

QUINT: Oh, come on, Dietre! Can you seriously suggest a natural origin for all this? If so, I'd like to hear it.

MANAKA: Won't the objects just spiral into the hypermass? No? Tomus says no. Very well, then, colleagues, let's congratulate ourselves; we've discovered an entirely new sort of fossil.

BARTA: Come again, Doctor?

MANAKA: The gravity gradient you were talking about; you measured it in seconds squared.

KREIDER: One *over* seconds squared.

MANAKA: Yes, fine, but do you see? It has to do with time.

DIETRE: <Sigh> Only indirectly. We measure the spacetime slope in gravities per meter. Meters per second squared, per meter. All the units cancel, right? Except the seconds.

BARTA: Doctor Manaka has a point, one I've studied rather closely. With gravitic spacetime distortion, plus the velocity necessary for a circular orbit, the ellipsoids remain in a highly dilated time frame. Even the least affected of them ages at only a thousandth of our rate.

MANAKA: Yes! Fossils, buried in a kind of strata! Like flies in a drop of amber.

BARTA: *Black* amber, Doctor. Gravitational redshift stretches everything out to thermal noise, barely distinguishable from cosmic background. I've taken most of my data from gravity imbalances, but I can barely distinguish those, either. Some neutrino tracings, shadows in the Hawking radiation . . .

DIETRE: I have a lot of trouble with all this, with the *extremes* of it. How closely do these objects orbit the hypermass?

BARTA: From what I've observed, none of them are more than a hundred meters above the event horizon.

QUINT: Good heaven!

DIETRE: Oh.

KREIDER: Good heaven!

MANAKA: Time machines. Well, time capsules, anyway. Fossils by design, you see? I speculate, of course, but it does make sense. Can we possibly retrieve them?

QUINT: Impossible.

DIETRE: Impossible.

BARTA: I don't think so, Doctor Manaka. If you like, I can walk you through the math.

MANAKA: Tomus has offered to do that. Damn. What luck we have, finding things we cannot hold on to!

BARTA: Yes.

KREIDER: The crewmates here on *Wedge* want to know if you have talked to Unua yet.

QUINT: Port *Chrysanthemum* has become a rumor hive.

BARTA: Captain Chelsea will talk to the president very soon, I think. Ladies, gentlemen? Forgive me, please, but I haven't slept in a long time. I'll leave you to your work.

<Replies not logged.>

And so, Miguel brushed a handful of remotes off his panel, watched them scatter, then promptly yielded his station to Tech Aid Lahler. He went then to his cabin and, with minimal tossing and turning, slept.

"Checkmate," Yezu said, for the third time that shift.

Tom sighed. Since *Introspectia*'s last transmission, Yezu had scurried from task to task, wanting all at once to suit up and go outside, to stay in and run some simulations, to continue the conversation with the scientists at Port *Chrysanthemum*, to sleep. Tom had finally convinced him to calm down and play a bit of chess, but Yezu's nervous energy had carried over to this, as well.

"Good game," Tom said.

Silently, they moved the magnetized pieces back to their starting positions. Tom, cross-legged on a box on the floor, had to stretch his arm halfway up the bulkhead to reach the hand-painted board. Yezu hung upside down from a pipe on the corridor's "ceiling," leaning and turning at the waist to reach his own pieces. Even with the low gravity, the pose looked uncomfortable in the extreme. But Yezu had offered no complaint.

"Can I play the winner?" Dade asked. He had watched them for hours, occasionally asking questions of them, occasionally smiling smugly to himself.

"Perhaps you'd rather play the loser," Tom suggested.

Dade sniffed, rubbed his nose. "Tomus, I've been playing this game since I was eight. Who do you think painted the board here?"

"You did that?"

"Good guess. Are you up for another round, Yezu?"

Yezu blinked, seemed to think for a few fidgety moments. "I feel as if we have a lot to do, but really I suppose we don't. How frustrating! We must wait, always wait and wait and wait, and we don't even know what for."

"Shall I take that as a 'yes'?"

"I suppose so. Yes, damn it, I'll keep playing. I must say, you seem awfully calm about this. Your crewmates, too, seem not very excited at all. Alien artifacts!"

Tomus vacated his position and, shrugging, Dade assumed it. "Try to remember, Yezu, we've been living with centrokrist for eighty years. We were never sure it was an artifact, but . . . well, maybe we were sure. Anyway, you get used to it."

Yezu pursed his mouth sourly. "This discovery won't change your life, eh?"

"No," said Dade. "With all that time compression and tidal force and whatnot, no. If I can't touch it and it can't touch me, then it's just a curiosity. And I guess I'm not all that curious. You understand?"

"No," Yezu said, shaking his head. "Not at all. Not at all."

"Well, just my opinion. Maybe it doesn't make any sense. It's your move, by the way."

* * *

"Darkness," Jafre snarled as he switched off the telkom, blanking the white-haired visage of Lin Chelsea. "Quaking *whore*."

The Terrans were finally, really, actually here, on the cutting edge of nowhere. Ready to take Jafre away, yes? Nothing here but earrings and coat buttons, as easily studied on Earth as on Port *Chrysanthemum*. *More* easily. And yet somehow, despite his best efforts, the Terrans had gone and found something big, something that would hold them here longer, maybe *much* longer, than they had really expected. Damnation and darkness!

He would have to think about this. Chelsea would expect him to reply, his eyes and voice dripping with wonderment and gratitude. *How fortunate we are for your presence!* Something like that. Darkness, how much shit was he going to have to eat to pull something like that off?

He considered getting some coffee to nurse while he thought about it, but no. The caffeine would chew on his nerves, chew on his stomach and bladder. Herbal tea, perhaps? No, no. Why, at times like this, did he feel such need to hold hot drink in his hands? What useless instinct had he tapped into? Forget it, forget it—something was happening here that had never happened before, and he was going to need all his wits to work the curves.

Working curves was something Jafre knew how to do. He felt the old, bitter strength beginning to stir inside him. He *would* make something of this situation. When Ralfh Chang faced him down in the senate, back in '39, Jafre had spoken names, had pulled favors and leveled threats. Calling up the magic, feeling it flow through his hands. The shriveled, desiccated husk of Chang had been carried from the field, soulless and without future. Five decades ago. And Jafre had sharpened his claws on many bodies since then!

Captain Chelsea, he dictated in his head, trying out a friendly but businesslike tone. *Your discovery sounds very interesting. Please return at once to Port* Chrysanthemum *for consultation. Please also refrain from telling anyone else about this until the Unuan government has had time to assess potential impacts. I do hope you and I will have opportunity to talk.*

Hmm. Too weak? *Get back here, you bitch. Nobody roots around in my system without asking first.*

Feeling something land on his shoulder, he jumped, grunted, turned.

Asia stood behind him, frowning, her hair in disarray and lit from behind by the bedroom lights. She looked as if she'd been asleep.

"Jafre, what is it?"

"Don't do that!" he snapped at her.

"What's going on, what are you doing?" Asia's yellow robe was falling open at the collar, the dark edge of an aureola peeking out on one side. Her feet were bare.

"Just got a transmission from *Introspectia*. It seems they'll be staying a while longer than I'd anticipated."

"What's going on?" Asia repeated.

Jafre put his fingers against his forehead and rubbed. He should get Asia to massage his back for him, that would help him think. He should be nice, warm her up for that. "I'm sorry," he said. "I'm not thinking straight. The Terrans have discovered artifacts buried in the Soleco gravity well, where *artifacts* have no right to be. Alien. Artifacts. I think . . . that's something important. *They* will think so, at any rate."

Asia seemed to be waking up quickly. "Are you serious? What kind of artifacts?"

"Eggs, I guess." He shrugged. "Giant centrokrist eggs."

"You're kidding! Darkness, are they hollow? Is there something inside them?"

"I don't know. Maybe." His voice, he realized, didn't sound quite right. He'd let a sliver of his anger leak through again. Damn!

Asia picked up on it right away. Her eyes narrowed. "You're up to something. Is this all true, what you're telling me?" She pulled the robe tighter around her, covering her cleavage with folded arms.

Jafre sent her one of his disarming, confused-but-covering-it smiles and reached out to touch her arms where they crossed. "I have never lied to you, my dear."

"Hmm," was Asia's only reply. Her face was slack, neutral in a way that suggested she wanted to look like she wasn't thinking. Which meant, of course, that she was.

Jafre moved his hand, dug for the soft breast hidden behind her arm. Leaning closer, breathing harder. He loved it when she fought him, resisted the forces pulling her into his orbit, because he knew she couldn't hold out for long.

"Heard from Ralfh Chang lately?" he said, easing her arms away, undoing the sash and pulling aside the bright yellow satin of her robe.

"What?" she said, off balance, confused by the question.

Jafre chuckled in private pleasure. His hand slid up across warm flesh, toward her face. His thumb, hooking up over the jawline, began to probe at her lips, demanding they open to admit it. Frowning, she resisted, turned her face away. But he had hold of her jaw, and turned her face back toward him. He rose from the chair.

What does she get out of this? he wondered, in a moment of peculiar almost-empathy, as the director of Port *Chrysanthemum* and the Fleets of Malhela acquiesced and quietly took his thumb into her mouth. Even after all these years, he felt that same little thrill in his belly, in his guts. The most powerful woman in all Malhela, and self-made, her supremacy dating back longer and farther than his own. And yet, in the end she would do almost anything he wanted her to. Almost ... *anything.*

He wondered at the natural force that could do this to her, and thought, for a moment, that it must be something very much like gravity.

Chapter Ten

"I've been hearing rumors," Luna said as she toyed with her eating utensils.

"Really," Jhoe said, and gave her an encouraging look.

"About *Introspectia*. I hear they found something out at Soleco. Some stuff made out of centrokrist."

"Really? That must have excited them."

"Oh, I think it did. I heard the spaceports were clogged this morning with Terran scientists returning to Port *Chrysanthemum*. I'm not sure what they plan to *do* up there. . . ."

"What kind of stuff did they find, exactly?"

"I don't know. Artifacts of some sort. Maybe treasure chests." She chuckled a little.

Jhoe put his elbows down on the table. Artifacts? So Malhela had aliens after all? He felt hairs prickling up and down his arms. "Recent artifacts? Recent *aliens*?"

Luna waved a hand, put on a derisive scowl. "No, of course not. It's all very old, like millions and millions of years." She seemed to study him for a moment. "Why? Were you worried?"

"Well, yes," Jhoe said. "I thought maybe . . . Well, if something changed because of *Introspectia*'s arrival . . . I'd hate to think we'd brought some kind of trouble to you people."

Luna put a hand on Jhoe's own. "Worried for *us*. That's sweet of you, Doctor."

He almost pulled his hand away, but resisted the urge. Day after day, Luna touched him and thumped him and brushed against him, and seemed slightly offended when he flinched away. And here, Jhoe felt very much at a loss; what exactly was her interest, her intent? Mere indifference, in a society with little concept of tactile privacy? A strange, frontier-style overture of friendship? A blatant romantic play, which he had rudely failed to acknowledge?

It seemed all these things, by turn, and others, and none. And why had Jhoe's brain dedicated so much of its time to unraveling the mystery? It hardly seemed relevant to his work.

And yet, Luna had brought him here each evening to the SudVerva Restoracio (one branch, he had found, of a monapellate poligarchy of restaurants which, despite the name, existed mainly outside the SudVerva district). She paid, also, for his dinner and refreshments, and he had no idea whether anyone would reimburse her for the expenses. Should he read something into that?

And he faced still another enigma, one named Uriel Zeng. She took him around the city nearly every day, showing him things, telling him things, discussing things with him. As he understood it, she had made considerable sacrifices to have this task assigned to her. And yet, he had never seen a smile from her, never heard a kindly word, never felt even the slightest, most fleeting touch.

She glared at him, even now, from across the room. As she did nearly every night.

The SudVerva Restoracio sat across the street from the Power Board building, and was therefore frequented by many of Luna's employees and colleagues. But not all of them made a habit of staring at Jhoe. He did not understand, and this bothered him greatly. Had decades of social science taught him so little?

"Hello?" Luna said, waving a hand in front of his face.

Jhoe blinked. "What?"

"I *said*, don't you think we can take care of ourselves? We've been doing it for four hundred years."

Jhoe picked up a spoon, put it down again. "I, uh. I'm sure you can. I mean, as long as nothing really serious happens."

"Oh really?" Her voice sounded sharper now, and a little bit angry. Jhoe chalked up another faux pas. Number sixty?

"You do quite well here," he said lamely. Then, to change the subject as abruptly and completely as he could, "Listen, I wonder if we should invite Uriel over here. I mean, she works so hard with me during the days, and in the evening I . . ."

Luna shook her head a little, forming a vague smile while she did it. "Uriel has been shirking her real duties to do that, and she's gotten everybody angry at everybody else in the process. And she's concocted some sort of personal gripe against *me*, which . . . Let's leave her be, okay?"

"It's *you* she's glaring at? Not me?"

Luna sighed. "Maybe not, I don't know. I really don't care."

"You don't like her much?"

Luna sighed again, more heavily. "She's like a daughter to me. Really. She's a very hard worker, very diligent, but she has no patience at all. Like a spoiled little girl. She's only thirty-four, did you know that?"

"Yes, I did."

"She's come far, done really well for herself. But it's just never enough. Poor, persecuted little Uriel."

Jhoe fidgeted again with the spoon, caught sight of his distorted reflection within it. Wide neck, wide shoulders, a tiny, tapered head sitting atop them. Did Black Hole Bahb's face look like that, as gravity and relativity had their way?

"I didn't know you two were fighting," he said.

"We're always fighting. I said she was like a daughter."

"Hmm."

An uncomfortable silence descended between them. Jhoe tried for a few moments to listen to the conversations going on among nearby patrons, but saw Luna frowning that opaque, incomprehensible frown at him again. *What?* he wanted to ask. *What do you want from me? What do you expect?*

Maybe he should come straight out with that, get the confusion over with once and for all. Yeah. Right. And maybe he should reprogram his symbionts to churn out elephant pheromones. *Me Jhoe, you Luna! Ungh!*

"Um," he said, "would you excuse me for a minute? I need to visit the bathroom. Excuse me, the *sanito*."

"All right," Luna said, still giving him the look.

Jhoe eased his chair back, stood, waded through the noise and confusion of the restaurant. Uriel Zeng's glare followed him as he moved. "Hello," he said as he passed her.

"Salutes," she said back to him, in a distinctly unfriendly tone.

Bother. Had he really traveled forty light-years for this?

He kept walking, found and opened the *sanito* door. What a planet. Quakes and darkness, weird hostilities and demands. . . . Fortunately, *one* thing about Unua really pleased him—the sanitary facilities could hardly be distinguished from those of Earth.

When he returned, Uriel had vacated her chair, and a young man now sat there, sipping something from a low, wide glass that looked to Jhoe's eyes almost like a bowl. Where had Uriel gone? Ah, there she sat, in Jhoe's seat. Arguing heatedly with Luna.

" . . . and you *stole* him!" he heard Uriel say.

"Kiss me, *virineto*," he heard Luna snarl back. "I haven't done a thing except eat dinner with him, and anyway I didn't know you liked him. Darkness, you sure don't act like it."

"I'm sneaking up on it. Being *patient*, like you're always telling me."

"Oh, for darkness' sake, you can't act like you hate somebody and then expect . . . Wait, this is ridiculous. He's hundred years older than you are."

Uriel pounded the table with both fists, making the utensils jump and clatter. "Look around you, Luna! *Everyone*'s hundred years older than me! *Everything* is off limits! No matter what I do or how hard I work, there's nothing *anywhere* that I'm supposed to be able to have."

Luna shook her head, as if in sadness. "This conversation is pointless, *virineto*. Can I have my dinner in peace?"

"Absolutely," Uriel said, pushing off the table, coming fully erect and turning toward the door in a single furious motion. She saw Jhoe standing there before her, then, and froze.

Jhoe felt a keen embarrassment, and found he could not meet her eyes. "Hello again," he said quietly.

"Salutes, Doctor," Uriel said in a voice that was softer than before, but ringing with the same sense of outrage and betrayal. *No fair, no fair!* "I was just leaving."

She brushed past him and, without another word, slipped out of the building.

Jhoe looked around him, saw all the restaurant patrons looking back silently, curiously. His face burned, surely hot enough to melt candle wax, hot enough to *ignite* candle wax. Quietly, he took his seat.

"Um," Luna said, "our dinner is here."

He looked at the platters, shuddered inwardly. Like most of Luna's meal choices, this one consisted mainly of shiny, black, fist-sized bugs. Properly spiced they went down okay, especially with the heavy beers the SudVerva Restoracio served. But he would have to eat, yet again, with his eyes on the ceiling.

"You know," he said to her, "this night doesn't seem to favor me."

She picked up a bug and the curved "flick" utensil meant for scooping the meat out of it. With quick and terrible sounds, she split the carapace in two. She was giving him that look again.

Later, they strolled together down a hot and darkened avenue, with streetlight shadows dancing all around them, tent buildings and low, crumbly plastered-brick edifices lurking on either side. Luna curled an arm around Jhoe's and squeezed it a little.

"Kids," she said.

"Oh, don't bring that up," Jhoe said, mockingly half-pleading. "Good heaven, I've never felt so embarrassed."

"Well, she *is* over twenty-five. I mean, *legally* you could . . ."

"Please," Jhoe said more seriously. "Stop it."

Luna laughed at this. "I'm sorry. She's quite a hand-

ful, though, isn't she? In another fifty years, she'll be a
real force around here, but right now she's—"

"Precocious?" Jhoe suggested.

"Yes, exactly. In a way, I'm proud of her, though." She
chuckled again. "At least she knows what she wants,
and tries for it."

"Well, I could have done without it."

They came to a dark corner, draped in shadows.
Above, the stars burned yellow through the haze. Luna
stopped, pulling him to a halt beside her. She turned,
turning him with her, and fine grit crunched between
their shoe soles and the cracked, rubberized pavement
beneath.

"Kiss me, Doctor Jhoe Freetz."

Kiss me. That phrase seemed popular as an invective, and Luna had used it often in speaking to Uriel.
He wondered what he had done or said to earn it. Faux
pas number sixty-umph?

"Kiss me!" she said again, grabbing his face with both
hands and pulling it toward her. No one handled him
this way, came inside his space-of-reach and intruded
upon his tactile privacy in this way. No one since
Shareen Brugiere. Then Luna's lips brushed against his
own and, finding them in the darkness, crushed against
them with moist firmness.

It occurred to Jhoe that she had meant the phrase,
for once, quite literally. Her kiss shot bolts of electricity
through his body, through his brain. Through his loins,
most particularly. He stiffened, twitched, then melted
in her arms.

Chapter Eleven

SHEM: Captain Chelsea, I'm told you are not, in fact, returning to Port *Chrysanthemum* at this time. Perhaps I was not clear enough: please return at once. Also, everyone seems to know our little secret. Can you offer me some insight into how this came about?

CHELSEA: Mr. President, I apologize for the rumors. We've conferred with our people at Port *Chrysanthemum,* and evidently no one told them not to discuss it. Presently, we plan to take some measurements of the Malsato hypermass. We may head back toward Unua in as little as a week or two. Certainly, our scientists would appreciate the return of their lab equipment.

SHEM: Chelsea, we are obviously working to different protocols. This is understandable, but of course you are in Malhela system now, and under the jurisdiction of the Malhelan government. Being duly authorized by the director of Fleets, I am *ordering* you to return to Port *Chrysanthemum* without delay.

CHELSEA: According to my charter, Mr. President, I don't take orders from anyone but Solar Commercial. Since the corporation currently has no offices in Malhela system, you may consider me an ambassador of sorts. If you have a specific complaint, I'll happily pass it on to my superiors. It will arrive in Sol system well before I do.

SHEM: Darkness and damnation, Chelsea, why are you making this difficult? I have the welfare of millions to look after.

CHELSEA: I understand your complaint, I think. In the interests of diplomacy, we'll coordinate all further releases of information through your offices. And we *will* come to Port *Chrysanthemum*, just as soon as we've finished here. I hope you'll find this acceptable.

SHEM: <Sigh> Very well. Let's please try to do these things a little more smoothly, okay?

<Reply not logged.>

"There you have it," Miguel said to Tech Aid Lahler.

"Yup," she agreed.

"Fascinating? Incredible?"

"Yup."

"Strangest damn thing you ever saw?"

"Um . . . sure."

Down in the Malsato hypermass, another group of objects lurked against the event horizon. Right there in the muddy particle storm at the equator, where Lacigo bled and screamed and fed the nothingness. Down close, the white dwarf's lifeblood redshifted away to dull, seething black that only special instruments could see through. And down farther still, the objects! A stunning discovery.

Or one that *should* stun, Miguel thought. In truth, the thrill had begun to wear off for him. Unlike the Soleco objects, these had come as no real surprise. But like them, these new ones didn't do anything, *couldn't* do anything. Passing through time like bubbles in honey, in amber, in stone.

Miguel had visited the Grand Canyon once, and the top of Everest Mons, and the floor of Trench Marianis in the deeps of the Pacific Ocean. Staggering views, all, but day trips nonetheless. When presented with fixed imagery, the mind did not remain staggered for long.

"I wonder what Unua is like," Lahler said.

Miguel turned and looked sharply at her. "Your work here displeases you, Tech Aid?"

Beneath her Medusa harness she blinked, straightened. "No, Chief, it doesn't. Um, did my question upset you?"

Upset me? Upset me? Miguel slumped. "No. My apologies, Beth, I didn't mean to snap. You struck a nerve, I guess."

"A nerve?" she said, politely prompting him to continue.

"Do you realize I've never visited the surface of an alien planet? Not even Mars. Not even Luna. Here I've burned all these decades, logged over seventy light-years, and I get nothing more than a view from the window and a peek at the instruments for my trouble. Plus the money, of course."

"I *have* upset you," Lahler said.

"No." He shook his head. "Not you. Shall we continue the sweep?"

She leaned forward, put a hand on his knee. "Miguel, *will* we see the planet?"

"I don't know. I have more pull now, as an officer, and even before all this hypermass stuff the schedule had us in system for almost a standard year. But the way things have gone . . . I guess I kind of doubt it."

"Well, if we go," she said, "I hope we can go together. I *have* seen Mars, and Luna, but never . . . with a friend."

Miguel returned her smile tiredly. "Shore leave with

the bossman, eh? It sounds nice. I hope we get the chance."

She nodded, taking her hand back, putting her smile away. "I know, I know. Back to the instrument sweep, right?"

"Yes."

And they turned back to it, Miguel more dispirited than ever. His interest in Beth Lahler had grown, even as his awe for the mystic ellipsoids had begun to wane. His leg still tingled where she had touched it. Useless! Self-destructive! Lord, weren't there enough mysteries dangling out of his reach already?

Sullenly, he pushed his awareness up into the link harness and let the more orderly mind of thing-Barta take over the analysis for him. Once this shift was over, he'd head for his quarters and shower up three days' water ration, on the coldest possible setting!

"So," Tom said, "you have everything?"

Yezu rolled his eyes. "I possess almost nothing, and most of that is still aboard *Introspectia*. What can I possibly have forgotten?"

A new ship, the *Rockhammer*, had arrived at the centrokrist mines with the equipment Tom and Dade had agreed on, laughable instruments of Unuan manufacture which would somehow have to suffice. With all the work and turmoil going on in the face of all these grand discoveries, he supposed he should feel lucky that anyone was worrying about his research at all. And yet, he did not.

And now, even Yezu would abandon him! *Rockhammer* would proceed next to the Aurelo, the debris ring surrounding the Lacigo/Malsato pair, to drop off more pathetic equipment for the researchers at the small centrokrist deposits there. And Yezu would go with it.

"I've basically finished here," Yezu had said. "And no-body at the Aurelo deposits has my background in . . ."

Bah. Yezu had abandoned an entire life back on Earth, and by comparison *Wedge* certainly offered little to hold him. Tom didn't even know why he'd tried to argue about it.

"You've forgotten to say good-bye," he said now to his friend.

"No, I haven't." Yezu skated forward and, shockingly, opened his arms to embrace Tom. "I shall miss your company."

Tom stiffened, acutely uncomfortable with this display. Right out in front of everybody!

Yezu released him, withdrew once more to a respectable distance. "We always have the radio, although I suppose we'll soon have troubles with time lag. Several light-hours to the Aurelo, yes?"

Tom resisted, successfully, the urge to brush himself off. He did not wish to offend Yezu, this man who had somehow become his best and closest friend. "I guess we will," he said. "I think we can cope, though. I've heard people used to play chess by mail. Actual, physical, hand-carried mail. It must have taken a long time."

"Chess? Ech, I've grown to hate that game."

"Yeah," Tom agreed. "Me too. Take care of yourself, all right?"

Yezu gave the helmet a final twist, locking it down against its seals. "Always."

He tipped a salute, and the airlock door whoomped shut.

"Remember, Doc, that's dinner tomorrow at my house."

"I'll remember," Jhoe said, and let the ferry door close itself with soft, pneumatic sounds.

Lars waved at him, then lowered his hands to the controls. The ferry pulled away from the curb and rolled off down the road on its four rubber wheels, electric motors humming faintly as it rounded the curve and vanished.

Leaving him, in a sense, stranded. After that blistering row with Luna, Uriel had ceased to guide and shuttle him in his wanderings. Ceased, in fact, to speak to him at all. Fortunately, the Verva Hotelo had made arrangements for him with a ground ferry company. More fortunately still, driver Lars had offered Jhoe a friendly hand and, aside from brief show-and-tell sessions with his family, seemed to want nothing in exchange. Getting around had not been a problem of late.

Anyway, Jhoe had begun to grasp the flows and rhythms of the city. No longer the lost little boy, he moved about as he pleased, saw what he needed or wanted to see on his own loosely defined schedule. And his peculiar status, guest of the city and planetary governments, celebrity ambassador and visiting researcher, had not hurt matters either. It seemed nearly every door would open for a man of distant suns.

Tonight, he would bring Luna to the kickball games, and dancing afterward. He had set the whole thing up himself, though of course she would have to do the driving. He stepped away from the curb and turned toward her house.

The tent fabric, muddy orange in the dying light, glowed from within. The building, arched and domed and sprawling at the edges, looked to Jhoe like a great dragon that had curled up and gone to sleep. Luna's friends seemed to think it quite a nice little home, so he tried to think of it that way.

A path of flat stones led him up to the door, where a yellow light burned in welcome for him. He took a breath and then released it, and reached out to knock on the door. *Rap! Rap!* It felt thin and oddly flexible beneath his knuckles. From within the house there came rustling and thumping noises, and then Luna's voice: "Just one minute!"

He smiled. On Earth, at least in North America, the door would have studied him and, finding him on the roster of invited guests, opened automatically to admit him. Spouting platitudes as likely as not, in a smooth and annoyingly polite tone of voice. Really, he liked it better this way, this much more personal, much more *intimate* Unuan way.

His pulse quickened. Images and textures flashed though his mind like silent fireworks. Luna's hair, shining in the full-moon light of Lacigo. Her feet on the top of a desk, knocking the telkom over. Her lips, soft against his own, her hands on his back.

Smitten, he thought, with a sense of embarrassment and, comically, of loss. So much for objectivity! Every note, every memory and observation came back with the taint of his personal involvement. And to hell with it anyway! Every time she kissed him it felt like his shoes would pop off, like his feet would leave the ground and never return to it. Her lips burned against his, leaving him painfully conscious of her body heat, and his own, and of the thin layers of clothing that kept them apart.

A clattering, a squeaking, a wash of yellow-white light—the door swung open and there she stood, a slim silhouette against the brightness. A gauzy skirt hung down past her knees, but the light shone right through it, revealing long and supple legs, set slightly apart. His eye followed them upward into shadow, then traced higher still, past the curves of her waist to the curves of her upper body, also plainly outlined through the backlit translucence of her blouse.

"Salutes," she said brightly. He couldn't see her face, but a kind of top hat crowned her head, her longish hair spilling out beneath it. She paused. "Is something wrong?"

"What?" he said. "No! No, of course not. How do you do this evening?"

"Fine," she said, still brightly. "You certainly look nice."

"Oh, thanks." He looked down at himself, at the hideous clash of colors the Verva Hotelo's resident tailor had dressed him up in. Yellow slacks, bright blue tunic, a strip of shiny, shocking red dangling from his neck, two more wrapped in bows around his shoulders. "I decided to go native for the occasion. Do you like it?"

"Yeah." She stepped back from the doorway, her body language inviting him in. As he turned, the light caught her face from the front and he could really see her.

Good heaven. The top hat shone a bright and sparkly green, and the band encircling its base actually *glowed* a luminous blue. Her blouse looked brighter and yellower than Jhoe's slacks, and her skirt, blue and white in alternating diagonal slashes, topped high boots of blinding, sequined white. Her hand clutched something, a vest, he supposed, whose color matched the sparkly green of the top hat.

"And how am I?" she asked, spreading her arms wide, baring her off-duty plumage for his inspection. Unfortunately, the gesture drew Jhoe's eyes toward her breasts, which bobbed, light and unencumbered, beneath the fabric. With effort, he looked back up at her face again, but something dragged his gaze right back down again. He felt a blush coming on. How uncouth and uncontrolled his behavior! But when he finally turned his eye back up to her face, she simply looked amused.

"Uh, very nice," he said.

She winked. "Thanks. Can I show you around?"

Her arms still spread wide. Her breasts still bobbed. Her legs, still slightly apart, seemed to beckon him.

"Don't toy with me, Luna," he said, ogling her once again, but exaggeratedly this time. "I think I remember how to find everything."

Had he actually just said that? Had he actually let his gonads run his mouth that way, actually spouted that rude nugget of juvenalia?

But Luna Shiloh tipped her head back, covered her mouth and laughed with surprise. "Oh! I'm sorry! I was asking for that one, wasn't I?"

Jhoe's face had grown hot, his stomach cold and quivery. "Luna, I apologize. Such a comment—"

"I accept," she said, and planted a kiss firmly on his mouth. "I'll show you the house later. Let's get good seats at the game!"

With that, she threw on her sparkly green vest and bounded out the door like a twenty-year-old preparing to break curfew for the first time. Jhoe's feelings, none too clear to begin with, jumbled up inside him in a big, messy ball. His shoes had not, after all, popped off.

He closed the door behind him and followed her down the stone path toward her personal ferry. *Car,* he reminded himself. *They call it a car.* The term struck him as typically, almost annoyingly, quaint.

Getting into the car proved a little uncomfortable, too. His new slacks seemed to have grown awfully tight.

The kickball hit the bell atop its yellow-and-red striped post, ringing it soundly, and the crowd went mad. With three thousand other people, Luna rocketed to her feet and let out a low, ululating yell, slapping her hands together several times above her head. Lagging behind a little, Jhoe imitated the gesture.

"What happened?" he asked over the roar of the mob.

Luna leaned close to his ear. "Teller and Koto just shared the point."

"Shared? Why?"

"Because Koto got it off the ground, and Teller hit the goal."

"Koto has the darker hair? And the red jersey?"

"Yeah!"

Below in the arena, fifteen men leaped and capered, vaulting over cube-shaped obstacles, chasing and kicking the hollow and surprisingly springy rubber ball. Above, a triple row of lights cast whiteness down upon the field, banishing shadows. The field, green with simulated grass and marked up by orange lines and the white obstacles, seemed the brightest place on the entire planet. The players, decked out in fifteen different schemes of fluorescent color, actually hurt Jhoe's eyes at times.

Considering the temperature and the lights and the stillness of the air within the arena walls, Jhoe wondered how hot they got down there. Pretty *damn* hot, he would bet. And yet they played on, tirelessly.

The bell rang again, and the crowd, still standing, continued its enthusiastic display. Jhoe leaped in the air and clapped his hands.

"Did you see that?" Luna cried. "Two goals in thirty seconds. Did you *see* that?"

"I sure did!"

What a show, what an experience! Earthly sport offered nothing so dynamic, so quick and savage and unpredictable. Never mind that Jhoe had no idea what was going on.

The players sometimes cooperated, sometimes competed, sometimes actively tripped and mauled one another. No teams, at least not in the usual sense, but not a free-for-all either. Alliances seemed to form and dissolve and form again with the ball still airborne, and to shatter completely on the rare occasions when it rolled flat across the ground. And watching the ball proved no easy trick as it careened from the walls and field and obstacle cubes, quick as a frightened bird.

Two of the players smashed together while closing on the ball. Knee and shoulder pads flew, and the men fell sprawling, one of them tumbling backward over a cube. But the ball popped high in the chaos, and the other players pursued it, heedless of their fallen colleagues.

"Are they hurt?" He shouted at Luna.

"I doubt it, but—well, here comes the clown."

A man in spotted clothing and white face-paint trotted out onto the field, ducking and dodging around a knot of players struggling for the ball, and made for one of the fallen men. But the man had gotten up already, grabbing up his pads and shoving them back into place as he ran after the ball. Which had bounced free and changed direction again!

The other man did not rise so quickly, and the clown, without pausing, angled low and scooped him off the ground. Luna cheered wildly as the injured party was hurried clear of a rushing wall of players.

"Rescue! Rescue!" the crowd chanted.

Running hard, the clown came up against the wall. Then, incredibly, he climbed it with his feet, transferring and transforming his speed so that he sort of floated up into the air and then settled back down again. He set his burden down gently. The man sat up right away, looking alert and uninjured. Within moments he was up again and rushing after his comrades. Such verve, such grit! For sure, they grew them tough here on the frontier.

Luna threw her arms around Jhoe and hugged him crushingly for a moment. "Oh, this is so great!" She said. "I haven't been to kickball for*ever*! Thank you so much."

Jhoe kissed her lightly on the forehead. "It pleases me, Luna, to—look! He has—"

The bell rang again, marking still another goal.

"Oh *wow*!" Luna screamed. "Go, Haggen! Go, Haggen!"

Jhoe's neighbor in the stands, a burly gentleman in shiny blue robes, whooped and thumped Jhoe firmly on the back. Merrily, Jhoe returned with an elbow to the man's shoulder.

"Go, Haggen!" the man shouted.

Jhoe thought he might just burst. All those years at NAU, all those decades of work and study and quiet aspiration. When had he ever had a night like this? Even the Olympics paled, *shriveled* in comparison.

"Look!" Luna shouted. "Koto's got the ball again!"

"All right!" Jhoe shouted back, happy just to bask in her enthusiasm. He hoped, at this rate, that he would have energy left for the dancing.

Whirling, whirling through the night air, watching the carnival lights sparkle in her eyes. The music, soft in his ears. The dance floor soft and springy beneath his feet.

"There's a kind of magic," a recorded voice sang, over and over again. "A kind of magic, a kiiiind of magic."

Sweet smell of the rose that Luna had put in her

hair, mingling with dust and . . . just a hint of perfume? And perspiration, human and pleasantly real on her skin.

A kind of magic, a kiiiind of magic. . . .

Wordlessly, he held her close. And whirled.

He pressed her against the car, kissing. Kissing her throat, her hair.

She led him up the path, and somehow they kept their feet even though they never stopped kissing. Never, at least, until the door rose up to baffle her. She opened it with a spike of blue metal. Light spilled out onto them.

She pulled away for a moment, leaned slightly to one side, flipping her hair and running fingers through it. It fell across the lower part of her face as she straightened in his arms.

"I'm ready to show you around," she said, her voice low and breathy, mouth curling into a sort of smile. Her eyes seemed large, seemed to catch all the light and make things of it.

A sudden coldness shivered through Jhoe's middle. Shareen. Shareen had looked at him that way. All at once, the night seemed not quite so warm.

Luna did not miss the shift. "What?" she asked softly.

Jhoe went back half a step, and stopped. "I can't."

Luna slumped, stiffened, cooled. Eyes narrowing, a shark about to bite. "Can't? You *can't?* What's that supposed to mean?"

"I . . ." Jhoe struggled for the words. "I've had . . . bad experiences. I mean, in the past."

She sighed. "Jhoe, you're hundred and twenty-eight years old. *Obviously* you've had bad experiences."

"I mean . . . I . . ."

"You've gone all cold inside? Lost your fire?"

He said nothing. Failure. Failure. What, really, had he hoped to accomplish?

"Jhoe." Luna removed her vest, tossed it inside the open house. Then she spread her arms wide, as she had done earlier that evening. "It's nice and warm over here."

From somewhere nearby came the musical tinkling of wind chimes, a soft breeze rustling the bells.

Luna's eyes were wide, her lips moist and inviting. Her breasts still danced beneath the thin fabric of her blouse. Jhoe felt dizzy just looking at her.

"Oh, to hell with it," he said, and moved in to grab her around the waist. "I'm the kickball clown!"

She looked momentarily alarmed. *"What?"*

"Rescue! Rescue!" Jhoe called out as he lifted her up and carried her through the doorway.

"No!" She shrieked. "No! Put me down!" Her voice rang with laughter, then screamed with it.

Once inside, Jhoe put his heel against the door and kicked it back toward the frame. It swung closed, and latched with a satisfyingly solid click.

"Put me down," Luna said again, more softly.

"Rescue," Jhoe said, and kissed her on the hollow of her throat, just above the upper clasp on her blouse. He lowered her to the floor, then kissed her more firmly on the lips. "Rescue."

She kissed him back. Her hands gripped him, slid over him like warm, soft talons. She moaned quietly.

He found the place where her skirt tucked in back, and he pulled it free. The skirt began to unwrap itself from her body.

We must never underestimate the importance, Jhoe thought, with sudden and peculiar clarity, *of a really close look at the native undergarments.*

Then, as she bent, leaned, eased back and pulled him slowly down with her: *Good heaven, I'm going to take her right here on the floor!*

Though surprised, he felt no displeasure or discomfort at this, his last coherent thought for quite some time.

Chapter Twelve

Miguel$_{(1)}$: "Scanning object 29."
Miguel$_{(2)}$: "Lock."
Miguel$_{(1)}$: "Scanning object 29."
Miguel$_{(2)}$: "Lock."
Miguel$_{(3)}$: "Position comparator. Blink. Blink."
Miguel$_{(2)}$: "Lock. Angular motion stored."
Miguel$_{(*)}$: "How*wee*! Look at me go!"

His mind flew, leaped, meshed with itself like a clock-work mechanism! A practiced orchestra had replaced the banjo-plucking of everyday thought. Yes! Yes! The link had become easier and easier for him to use . . .

Miguel$_{(1)}$: Standardized learning score of 0.962 likely a major factor in promotion to chief technical officer. Solar Commercial has always paid attention to that kind of detail.
Miguel$_{(3)}$: They couldn't have anticipated the difficulty of this assignment. Peering into collapsars!

. . . since Lahler had begun helping him. He found he could set problems for himself and then spin them off as separate subprocesses, autonomous mindlets that merged back into him after completing their work. As if he could cast away fingers and toes, then wait for them to return laden with treasure!

Miguel(*): Lahler, can *anyone* do this? Lordy, I feel I could move mountains!

Lahler: You have a gift for it, I think.

Miguel(*): If every human were hooked up to one of these, just think what we could do!

Lahler shuddered and spoke with her physical mouth. "Don't say things like that, Miguel. A lot of time has passed back home. Sometimes I'm . . . afraid I won't recognize it when we get back."

Won't recognize it. Hmm. A remote, black and chrome and sparkly-diamond, scuttled across the back of Miguel's hand. He flicked it away.

"A sobering thought," he said.

"Silly, I know."

"No," he said, looking up at the link wires sprouting from her head. "Quite sensible. Times do change, sometimes quickly. If we want to really go home again, we'll have to put our faith in the . . . constancy of human nature."

Lahler looked uncomfortable with that thought. "Don't you think human nature could change? How human are we right now?"

Miguel(1): *Touché.*

"I don't know," he admitted. "Even if you took the link away right now, forever, it's definitely made a permanent change in me. So yeah, if you define human nature that way, it changes. I wouldn't worry, though; so many hide-headed old windbags on Earth, talking about how great it was in days gone by, banging the rocks together . . . It would take a long time to change that."

"Longevity works in our favor, hmm?" Lahler said, looking a little less gloomy.

"I've found that it does. But anyway, if you want even a *chance*"—he held up two fingers, close together as if pinching something small—"of visiting the planet, we'd better get back to work."

"Right. The work." She shifted back into professional posture.

The work: plotting trajectories. The ellipsoidal objects did move, if you looked at them long enough. And so, Miguel Barta and Beth Lahler looked, and recorded and analyzed what they saw. Tedious, for the most part, although some of the higher objects moved almost fast enough to measure in real time. And the games with the link equipment made it . . . more interesting.

Miguel sent his little servants out again. A bit more cautiously this time, though—Lahler did have a point.

Miguel$_{(1)}$: Scanning object 30.
Miguel$_{(2)}$: Lock.
Miguel$_{(1)}$: Scanning object 30.
Miguel$_{(2)}$: Lock.
Miguel$_{(3)}$: Position comparator. Blink. Blink.
Miguel$_{(2)}$: Lock. Angular motion stored.

Object 30 moved more quickly than the others he'd logged so far. Interesting. He went back to the Coordinates database . . .

Miguel$_{(1)}$: Scanning object 31.
Miguel$_{(2)}$: Lock.
Miguel$_{(1)}$: Scanning object 31.
Miguel$_{(2)}$: Lock.

Miguel$_{(3)}$: Position comparator. Blink. Blink.
Miguel$_{(2)}$: Lock. Angular motion stored.

... and examined its records on 30. Higher up than most, almost a hundred meters above the event horizon. Gravity gradient ...

Miguel$_{(*)}$: $\delta g_R/\delta R \approx$ -1.04E+07 g_e/m

... steep at that distance, but the effects of time dilation ...

Miguel$_{(*)}$: $\gamma_1 = (1-(V/C)^2)^{0.5}$
$\gamma_2 = 1-2\mu/(RC^2)$
$\gamma = \gamma_1 \gamma_2 \approx (1.06E+03)^{-1}$ (nondimensional)

... began to taper off sharply. Only a thousand times slow, object 30, where some of its cousins ran a thousand-thousand times slower than that! A half-trapped thing, it seemed, drifting along the beaches of time, well clear of the deeps and yet not wholly ashore.

Miguel$_{(1)}$: Scanning object 32.
Miguel$_{(2)}$: Lock.
Miguel$_{(1)}$: Scanning object 32.
Miguel$_{(2)}$: Lock.
Miguel$_{(3)}$: Position comparator. Blink. Blink.
Miguel$_{(2)}$: Lock. Angular motion stored.

Wait a minute. Wait a minute. Something about number 30 bothered Miguel. Something didn't seem right.

Miguel$_{(*)}$: Go back to number 30.
Miguel$_{(1)}$: Acknowledged. Scanning object 30.

Miguel$_{(2)}$: Acknowledged. Lock.
Miguel$_{(1)}$: Scanning object 30.
Miguel$_{(2)}$: Lock.
Miguel$_{(3)}$: Acknowledged. Position comparator. Blink. Blink.
Miguel$_{(2)}$: Lock. Angular motion stored.

Okay. Now in order to let the object move, he had to wait a few seconds. Lordy, what a long time that had become! Waiting . . . Waiting . . .

Miguel$_{(*)}$: Repeat.
Miguel$_{(1)}$: Scanning object 30.
Miguel$_{(2)}$: Lock.
Miguel$_{(1)}$: Scanning object 30.
Miguel$_{(2)}$: Lock.
Miguel$_{(3)}$: Position comparator. Blink. Blink.
Miguel$_{(2)}$: Lock. Angular motion stored.
Miguel$_{(*)}$: Feed all angular positions for object 30 back through Coordinates. Cut an ellipse through five points and compare to the sixth point. Run all possible combinations.
Miguel$_{(1)}$: Transforming angular coordinates. Triangulating. Performing regressions.
Miguel$_{(2)}$: Performing regressions.
Miguel$_{(3)}$: Performing regressions.
Miguel$_{(1)}$: Max residual 3.01E-04 meters.
Miguel$_{(*)}$: So large!

What did this mean? Miguel pulled his "fingers" back, pulled a bit more of his mind from the link, back down into his own squidgy gray matter. The ellipses he'd used to map object 30's trajectory did not fit the measurements with expected accuracy. Nearly a millimeter off, a huge distance considering the precision and special Malsato-tuning of his instruments.

That could only mean . . . that the trajectory was not an ellipse?

Miguel$_{(*)}$: Cut a hyperbola through five points and compare to the sixth point. Run all possible combinations.
Miguel$_{(1)}$: Performing regressions.
Miguel$_{(2)}$: Performing regressions.
Miguel$_{(3)}$: Performing regressions.
Miguel$_{(1)}$: Max residual 7.94E-08 meters.

His stomach lurched. The clarity of the link began to blur a little as, beneath the harness, his forehead went cold and sweaty.

Miguel$_{(*)}$: Compute V_∞ of object 30. Compute departure asymptote and integrate trajectory. At what time will the object emerge into ($\gamma < 1.2^{-1}$ (nondimensional)) spacetime?
Miguel$_{(1)}$: $V_\infty \approx 1.56$ m/s $\approx 0.52C$
Miguel$_{(2)}$: Integrating.
Miguel$_{(3)}$: $T_{(\gamma = 0.83)} \approx T_{NOW} + 5.78E+06$ s
Miguel$_{(*)}$: Oh, shit.

He opened his mouth to scream at Beth Lahler. "Did you follow that? *Did you follow that?* Thanks to Doctor Manaka's 'time capsule' theory, we assumed an approximately circular orbit, but how would it get *down* there? How would it get *down* there?"

"Chief?" Lahler sounded entirely nonplused.

He waved his hands, impatiently sketching figures in the air. "A *hyperbola*, that's how! Oh, just think of it: you fire an object across the edge of the collapsar. You see? You understand? Gravity deflects your straight line into a hyperbolic trajectory, but the periapsis lies *just above the event horizon,* eyeball deep in relativistic effects. Assuming your object has a way to survive the tidal stress, as the ellipsoids *clearly have,* it gets caught in the time dilation and it *hangs* there. For as long as you want it to! For a billion years, if you want it to!"

Lahler sat straight and motionless in her chair. "Chief Barta, you are frightening me."

"This *should* frighten you! It very well *should*! Tech Aid, we don't know what object thirty is, or what it does, or what it's for. But in sixty-seven days, it will be clear of the hypermass and moving toward us at half the speed of light!"

Miguel$_{(1)}$: As will object 34.
Miguel$_{(2)}$: As will object 35.
Miguel$_{(3)}$: As will object 39.
Miguel$_{(*)}$: Enough. Time for this later.

He unbuckled his link harness and, gripping its medusa wires, pulled it slowly off his head. He looked at Lahler the whole while. "Do you understand what I've told you? Would you like to check the work?"

"Yes," she said. "I would." Her face went blank for several seconds. Then: "Checked. I agree with your assessment."

Her face remained neutral for a moment, but then fear began to creep back into it. All at once, their cute little mystery had lost its hypotheticality. As if they had plucked up a strange flower, only to find it squirming and buzzing in their hands!

"Yes," Miguel said to her. "Think about it. Think about it a lot." He rose from his chair. "But call the captain right away. Before you do anything else. All right?"

"Where are *you* going?" she demanded, her eyes large, her mouth pursed small with anxiety.

"To the bathroom, Tech Aid. I've got an emergency of my own."

Chapter Thirteen

Jafre Shem felt like something was gnawing at him down in his guts. A word kept flashing visually in his mind, like a restaurant sign: Emergence! Emergence! But the last letter was flickery and vague, looking sometimes less like an "e" than a "y."

Never, in three decades of presidency, had he faced such clear and immediate threat to public safety. Alien invasion!

Chelsea had tried to calm him, tried to tell him the objects were probably harmless, probably solid and inert. "No living creature could survive the gravitational stress," she had said.

"You told me *nothing* could survive it!" he'd shouted back at her. "But something has! You can talk all you want about your time capsules and your flies in amber, but where's the motivation behind that? Mark my words, Captain, those objects are far from harmless. *Far* from harmless."

He had waited long, long for her reply. And argued with it when it came! Had the woman no sense at all?

Now is the time, his little voices whispered in his head. *Villain or hero, leader or fool. Some have greatness thrust upon them.*

"Shut up," he told the voices. He keyed his desk and picked up a stylus, spinning it thoughtfully in his fingers. Public address was called for here, obviously. Planetary address, systemwide address! No situation had ever needed it more.

No more shall you be painted small on this tiny canvas, the voices tried.

"Shut up!" he repeated. Personal considerations be damned, this was truly something larger than Jafre's ego. For the first time he could recall, his primary concern really was the safety of the Unuan public.

What should he do? What *could* he do?

Order the Fleets of Malhela to alert status. Well, have Asia do it, of course. But yes, that was good for starts.

Build shelters in the cities? Shockproof, fireproof, radiation-proof? Yes, absolutely! As many as they could cast before the emergence! Sensible precaution was something nobody could argue with, in the face of such uncertainty.

He should find jobs for the Youth Coalition, as well. This was exactly the sort of time they'd been waiting for, the chance to make mischief while their elders were distracted, making him look bad, undermining the public confidence. . . Damn them, he shouldn't even have to *think* about such trivia right now. But by striking preemptively, with appeals to their vanity and demands on their time, he could neutralize them as source of dissent. Quakes, they'd be eating out of his hand.

What else was he forgetting?

Of course: water. He would have to increase H_2O mining activities at the poles, open up the ocean pipeline. Damn, would that still work after so long? Anyway, fill the city tanks up and build new tanks if there was time. And cut domestic water rations, and increase the penalties for speculation and profiteering. Ruinous penalties—let nobody dare even to try it.

And fire up the old antennae, contact Earth again: Send help! Alien invasion! Never mind the 37.6 standard years it would take the message to arrive, the fifty or more it would take to ship the cavalry back here. If something really terrible really did happen, if alien monsters swept down to smash the cities of Unua . . . Better the scream of futility than no scream at all.

Damn Lin Chelsea and her smug Solar Commercial attitude! *Introspectia* should be his greatest asset right now, his source of advanced technologies, of devastating energies and micron-precise instrument readings. But Chelsea had, she said, reference handbooks to be used in case of alien contact, and she would be doing what *they* told her to. Handbooks! Some weasel-faced office bureaucrats somewhere, cooking up hypothetical protocol for the event they never *dreamed* would really happen. . . . And Jafre Shem, here in the thick of it and charged with the safety of an entire planet, was expected to stand impotently aside!

He would find some way to make her listen. Failing that, he would doodle-run right past her like a kicker after the ball, dodging the other players and aiming to score.

Even if she jumped correctly, then, he would never, never let her share the point.

Uriel Zeng burst into the office, her face ashen. "I've just heard the most terrible rumor!"

Luna cupped her hand over the telkom receiver. "Uriel, I'm on the telkom here."

"The egg thingies are emerging from Malsato!" Uriel said, breathlessly, ignoring Luna's words. "They're hostile alien spaceships, made of centrokrist and *armed*, and they're *coming out!*"

Inwardly, Luna sighed. Uriel was young, and never had learned much in the way of politeness. And she hadn't learned the ways of rumor.

"I've just heard that same one," she said, trying to project a sense of calm onto her young protegé. "I've also heard that the aliens *are* the egg thingies. And that they eat babies, or they eat black hole matter, or they don't eat anything at all because they're creatures of pure and radiant light, or that they're planning to kick us out of this star system because they were here first . . . Where have you been all morning?"

"Out on the Zulamie cables."

"Well, walk around for a few minutes and you'll get caught up on the rumors. Right now I'm talking to Jhoe, who's a little closer to the source than the rest of us." She took her thumb off the microphone. "Jhoe, Uriel just came in. She seems to be panic-stricken."

"Hi, Uriel," said Jhoe's little face on the telkom.

Uriel, who could see only the telkom's plastic back, paused for a moment to flash a look of displeasure. "Salutes, Doctor," she said coolly. "What can you tell us?"

Luna slapped the top of her desk. "Uriel! I'm talking to the man, here. Do you mind?"

Uriel snorted angrily, then turned to leave. She slammed the door heavily behind her.

"Has something happened?" Jhoe's image asked.

"Oh, Uriel is just being her usual charming self. Anyway, you were saying?"

"Uh, yes. I'd been wondering how the objects could get out of the black hole once they'd fallen into it, but when I asked Tomus, he said they were never really *in* it at all. Just grazing past it or something, somehow taking advantage of the time dilation."

"Right," Luna said, "I got that part."

Jhoe's image nodded. "Okay. He said *Introspectia* had observed two separate groups of objects, emerging on slightly different paths. Fourteen large objects, I think, followed by eight smaller ones. Or something like that—anyway, I know we're not looking at a large fraction of the total population. Three hundred of them? Something close to that. He said all the objects will come out eventually, but the times range from centuries to, well, to millions of years."

"Huh," Luna said. "Not much of invasion."

"Enough of one for my taste," Jhoe admitted, looking uncomfortable. "Doesn't this . . . worry you?"

"Of course it worries me. But I can't really fall apart over it, right? Whatever ends up happening, it will eat up lots of electricity. Crises always do."

"Well, then, I suppose you're lucky to have the job you do." Jhoe ran a hand through his hair. Long strands in disarray, it looked like it hadn't been combed since he'd slept on it last. "I . . . don't feel so good about this. People keep looking to me as the Earthman, the Star Traveler, the Social Scientist, as if that somehow means I know what to do. But I don't. I wish they'd stop asking."

"Oh. I'm sorry, I didn't know this would bother you. Would you like me to ring off?"

His face changed. "Oh, no! I . . . didn't mean you. Anyway, I know what I'll do about this. I'll pray to the God that made me. But nobody wants that advice."

Luna grunted in agreement. The Originals were militant atheists, and the society they established on Unua had reflected this fact. Despite some flirtation with the occult by the first and second generations, religion had never quite got foothold in Malhela system. Like fairy tales, it was something you told to children.

It was nice idea, actually. The cold universe personified as someone to talk to, someone who looked in on you and worried about your problems. Did Jhoe believe in that? Really? His face was earnest behind the screen.

It melted her heart. Sweet Jhoe. She wished him every happy thought his mind could hold.

"What?" Jhoe demanded, beginning to frown.

"Nothing," she said. "I was just thinking. You just gave me one good idea, though; I'll call my great-grandfather."

"Really? Why?"

"Because he's an Original. I bet he'll have some ideas for us."

"I don't see your point."

She shrugged. "They were explorers. They roamed this planet when it was new, and they never knew what they were going to find next. Centuries ago, I guess, but some . . . spark of that time must still be with them."

"Huh," Jhoe said. "Maybe. I guess Jack-Jack Snyder does seem pretty spry for a man of his years."

"You know him?" Luna asked with surprise.

"Huh?"

"Jack-Jack Snyder, that's my great-grandfather. Well, one of them."

"Really? I didn't realize. Actually, other than the president and the director of fleets, he was the first Malhelan I met."

She grinned. "Jumped on you first thing, eh? That sounds like him. Of course, *I* always had to *fight* for his attention. When I was little, he had about ninety great-grandchildren. By now I think it must be twice that many."

"Wow."

"Yeah. Wow. Lots of the births were artificial in the early days, but he really did get around. Six wives, one right after the other. Hey, are we still going out tonight?"

"Um, I guess so." Jhoe looked embarrassed.

Oh, damn, she'd just mentioned marriage and their dinner date in the same breath, hadn't she?

"Darkness. That, uh, wasn't what I meant." She kept her tone light. Really, that *wasn't* what she'd meant. She hadn't even been able to hold things together with Dade, whose voyages carried him no farther than the Centromo. Jhoe's range was considerably farther than that.

What is this then, dear? Some kind of fling?

"Okay." Jhoe's smile was thin, his voice ironic. "Sure. No reason to cancel a date just because . . ."

Just because the sky was falling? Just because Malsato was inexplicably throwing eggs, and they might all soon be dead? She shook her head. "You're right. I guess it does seem sort of odd."

"Yeah, odd."

"Well. Will I see you tonight anyway? For an odd time?"

"Sure." Jhoe paused, looking as if he had more to say. His mouth worked, as if it were thinking about trying to form some additional words. Tender words? But nothing came out, and after a few moments Jhoe rang off instead. Blank screen replaced his image.

"Yeah," Luna said to the blankness, "me too."

"Jack-Jack? It's Luna Shiloh. Korina's daughter, you remember?"

The old man's face lit up. "Luna, my very favorite. Of course I remember. And how is dear Korina? Still reading tea leaves?"

"I don't know," Luna said. "We don't talk much."

"Well neither do *we*, little girl. When was the last time you called here?"

"I don't know. Fifteen years ago? When was the last time *you* tried to call?"

"Ah, you brat. Never tease an old man."

"I'll keep that in mind when I meet one."

He smiled, and there was brief silence between them. Then: "You want to know about the eggs."

She nodded. "You've heard, then."

"Oh yes, I got the news this morning. I gave what's-his-name a call, you know, that president fellow. Thought I'd give him a few pointers. But who listens, hey? He was working on a speech. Now that's one I'd like to hear!"

Luna felt small, talking to Jack-Jack. She remembered sitting in his lap, rubbing against the unshaven bristles of his face. . . . So long ago. Her fingers tried to reach out to the telkom screen, reach out across time and space to stroke her great-grandfather's cheek. It took effort to hold the hand back.

"What were you going to tell him?" she asked.

Jack-Jack shrugged, looking suddenly more forlorn than she thought she'd ever seen him. "I don't know. Be brave, keep the peace, that kind of thing. People don't fold up in a crisis, they . . . sort of come alive. I guess I wanted to tell him that."

"Some people fold up."

"Yeah, some do. Not many."

"I love you, Jack-Jack."

Now he smiled again, and his eyes crinkled up in just the way she remembered. "Well. It's been a long time since anyone's said that. I love you, too. I love just about everyone on this dustball."

"Yeah." She found she couldn't meet those jolly eyes. "Grandfather, what are we going to do?"

"Do? Well, that will depend on what happens, won't it? I'm told the eggs are probably empty."

"I hear that, too," she said, in tone that indicated her precise level of faith in that prediction.

"Oh, perk up. Maybe they want to be friends with us. For all you know, that's why they're coming out."

"And if they don't want to be friends? I mean, they *live* in a black hole. . . . If they want to do us harm, I don't think we can do much about it."

Jack-Jack tipped back his head and actually laughed at her. "Listen to you! Oh, Luna, you're never helpless. Never. When you run out of options, it just means you've stopped thinking. Okay? Don't stop thinking."

She sighed. "You're oversimplifying."

"Never. Have you heard of bullfighting? *La Corrida?* People sticking swords in a cow, waving flags around to confuse it until it bleeds out and collapses. Life is like that, and the one thing age can teach you is to ignore the flags. There's always so much going on in the world, and very little of it actually pertains."

"I guess," she said with a little more hope. "You really should tell this to the president."

"Oh, I will. He'll break down and call me in a few days, and if he doesn't, I'll show up in his office. 'You can't throw me out, I'm the oldest man in the world!' "

"Typical, typical. I'm at work here. I guess I should go."

"You feeling a little better?"

"Yeah," she said. "I guess I am. Thanks, Jack-Jack."

He smirked. "What am I here for? By the way, tell your little Earthman I said hi."

"Darkness, do you know everything?"

"I think so," he said. "Yes."

The telkom screen went dark.

MANAKA: Pawn to king four. You'd like it here, Tomus. This ship offers a bit more room!

KREIDER: Pawn to king three. *Rockhammer*, humph. Have you got drunk with the crew yet?

MANAKA: Drunk? Ech, Dade's bottle swore me off it. Such a headache it gave me! Knight to king's bishop three. And how goes the quark balancing?

KREIDER: Slow, and you know it. Bishop to queen three. The job does not go well with only one person working on it. I've tried to teach Dade, but he . . . well, his own job suits him better than ours does. So, I take it you've heard about this emergence thing?

MANAKA: Hyperbolic orbits, yes. It surprises me that we realize this so late. But so many things come late, I suppose. I wonder what will happen. Pawn to queen four.

KREIDER: Always hogging the center. Tsk. Pawn to queen's bishop four. Do you still believe the time capsule theory? Some of my latest work indicates that if the centrokrist contained more bottom quarks, the gravitic interactions might actually block the transmission of inertia. I mean, if you think backwards, picture inertia as a dynamic quantity acting on a static object. . .

MANAKA: The pink centrokrist contains a lot of bottoms, doesn't it? Pawn to queen's bishop three. Do I hear you correctly? You mean to imply that the ellipsoids have shielded their interiors from gravitational acceleration? Blocked, in effect, the tidal stress?

KREIDER: The pink centrokrist contains *too much*

bottom matter, and we find it all crowded on one side of the vein. If we knew what sort of process had formed these deposits, we'd have an easier time sorting all this out. Oh, pawn to king's bishop four. And yes, you understood my point correctly. If the ellipsoids are hollow, and if they really do shield their interiors from inertial and gravitic interactions, they could contain anything. Anything at all. Even live aliens.

MANAKA: If you want a formation process for the pink centrokrist, consider a high-velocity impact. Such as, for example, pawn takes pawn at your king's bishop four.

KREIDER: One of the ellipsoids smashing into the planetoid? No, that doesn't work. How would the centrokrist get so deeply buried in the rock, without vaporizing the whole thing? Pawn takes pawn at king's bishop four.

MANAKA: You picture a simple event. Let's not make that mistake again, ah? Imagine an ellipsoid smashing into a very large object, shattering it into molten fragments, and melting itself in the process. Can centrokrist form a liquid? Certainly, yes. And could such an event produce the configuration we see? Bishop to king's knight five.

KREIDER: Hmm. I suppose it could, yes. Chondrite would just come apart into dust, but this matrix is stony-iron, so it *would* have cohesion after a violent upset. Based on what I know about the centrokrist, I'll try to work out a collision velocity. Standard asteroidal collision models should apply. Uh . . . knight to king's bishop three.

MANAKA: Queen to king two. Check. Remember that the material may in fact be metamorphic. A really violent impact could certainly disturb its structure a little.

KREIDER: *Obviously* it disturbed it, Yezu. Something drove the bottom quarks right out of it, slammed them up against one side. Like you have just done to me! King to king's bishop two.

MANAKA: Knight to king five. Check. That seems like a big assumptive leap, all of a sudden.

KREIDER: Well, doesn't it make sense? Bishop takes knight. Here, my simulation results have just come through. Good *lord*, this stuff runs right off the toughness scale. I get an impact velocity of nearly half the speed of light!

MANAKA: Certainly? You've made no errors? Ech, that matches the velocity of the emerging objects! We have found something, my friend. We've made an important connection of some kind.

MANAKA: Pawn takes bishop. My apologies, Tomus, I forgot.

KREIDER: Here, look at this! A typical ellipsoid, smashing into a stony-iron planetoid 150 kilometers in diameter. . . . You get tremendous ejections. This could account for all those small centrokrist deposits in the Aurelo and Centromo. But here, look: the object was already liquefied before impact. And hot!

KREIDER: Rock to king one. Apology accepted. What have we found, Yezu? What does this mean?

MANAKA: Queen to queen's bishop four. Check. It could simply mean an even more complex event than you've already assumed. Perhaps an initial collision with a smaller body? At any rate, the exact details don't matter so much. What we've found is that at least one of these ellipsoids came to grief before entering the hypermass. Whatever guides them, it does not do so perfectly. I find that significant.

KREIDER: Hmm. Yes. Perhaps we should contact Mr. Barta with this information. Uh, king to king's knight three.

MANAKA: Bishop takes knight.

KREIDER: Pawn takes bishop.

MANAKA: Damn me for not paying attention! Bishop to king two.

BARTA: The hell, you say! Explain this file!

KREIDER: Oh, hello. We thought you might like to know about the accident our little friends have had. Pawn to queen's knight four.

MANAKA: It troubles me. Queen takes pawn at your queen's bishop four.

BARTA: You play chess at a time like this? Gentlemen, please! Give me the details of your analysis.

KREIDER: You know as much as we, Miguel Barta. And you have real computers, as well, so any further progress will likely come from your efforts rather than our own. Pawn to queen three.

MANAKA: Queen takes pawn at your queen's knight four.

KREIDER: Pawn to rook three.

BARTA: Okay. I've elaborated on your simulation a bit. Let me fix a few things and send the results back to you.

KREIDER: You really needn't bother, Miguel. Trajectories and such don't really lie within our expertise. Just let us know when the show will start.

Chapter Fourteen

The captain had taken her thing-face off, so that Miguel could speak, for the second time, with the human face beneath it.

"Please explain that again," she said calmly.

Miguel took a breath, calmed, backed up. "A billion years ago, they had a crash. At least one crash, at relativistic velocity, with most of the debris ejected clear out of the system. The remainder of it forms the centrokrist deposits our passengers came out here to study."

"And this worries you? Why?"

"*We* avoid accidents like that when we plan our trajectories. Not difficult, right? If the ellipsoids, or whatever controlled them, had planned ahead even slightly, the crash couldn't have taken place."

With a thoughtful look, the captain leaned back into the cushions of her couch. Like Miguel, she seemed not entirely at home here, in this rarely-used briefing room. Like Miguel, she seemed a trifle uncertain, operating now well outside her nominal job description. But definitely, she hid it better. Calm, unhurried.

"What does this, ah, suggest to you, Mr. Barta?"

His fingers gripped the soft fabric of the couch. He fought the urge to leap from his seat and run around waving his hands. "I don't know. I don't. A nebula used to fill this whole region of space, and they flew through it without scoping a completely safe path. At relativistic velocity! Why the hurry? And then, they dove straight into a pair of black holes and stayed there a long, long time. *Why?* Those seem like desperate measures to me."

"Running from some kind of danger? I see." She sat up straighter. "Mr. Barta, you've done an excellent job in the face of extreme difficulty. You make quite a detective. I'm tempted to put your name in for another promotion when we get back home."

"Save it, Captain; I plan to retire when we get back. *If,* I should say."

She made the calming gesture again, like a mother or grandmother might with an anxious child. "Don't let this frighten you. Whatever happened to those ellipsoids happened a long time ago."

"Not so long from their viewpoint."

She huffed. "Look, if anything *lives* inside them, which I very much doubt, we will run through standardized alien contact procedures. You've had the course?"

Of course he'd had the course. The SolCom cadet had never lived who could avoid Unusual Situations 101 and still graduate flight certified. But Unusual Situations had not included reckless ellipsoids caroming up out of black holes.

"Yes, I've had the course. But Captain, we have some evidence that the centrokrist hull may *shield* them—"

"I will *handle* this, Mr. Barta. Do you trust me so little?"

"I . . ." He dropped his gaze. "No. No offense intended."

"And none taken."

Lin Chelsea had proved herself a cool head, and

thoughtful, and responsive to Miguel's needs when they
arose. Probably, as she said, the ellipsoids would do
nothing, would simply emerge and fly away, lifeless and
inert. *Introspectia* could capture them for study, then,
earning Chelsea and her crew the largest science bonus
in the history of interstellar commerce.

And if something else occurred, if the objects proved
somehow non-inert, she would probably react less
wrongly than anyone else he knew.

"Dead or alive," Chelsea said, "we will handle them.
And I'll want you in a calm and professional mood
when we do. Clear?"

"Yes, clear." This time he did rise. "I guess I'd better
. . . start preparing."

The captain also rose, and clapped a hand on
Miguel's shoulder. "Yes. And Miguel?"

"Captain?"

"I've sent a message back to Earth, detailing everything we've found so far. In case something happens to
us, you understand? We can update it just before the
emergence. I think the Malhelans were planning a
broadcast, also. Many of us . . . share some of your
concerns. Please keep that in mind."

"Thank you, ma'am. I . . . understand."

He saluted, then turned for the door. It *whoomped*
open ahead of him, and he turned down the corridor,
and then just before it *whoomped* closed behind him he
caught a glimpse of the captain, still sitting in her
briefing couch, a frown of deep worry carved across her
features.

PART FOUR

EMERGENC (E/Y)

Who sees with equal eye, as God of all,
A hero perish or a sparrow fall,
Atoms or systems into ruin hurled,
And now a bubble burst, and now a world.

—Alexander Pope,
  An Essay on Man, 1734.

Chapter Fifteen

"Scratch the 'inert' theory," said Beth Lahler.

Miguel grunted. Object 30 had just turned on some sort of thruster...

Miguel$_{(1)}$: Hydrogen gas expelled at 0.9998 C
Miguel$_{(2)}$: $\delta M/\delta T \approx 35$ kg/s

... and had begun accelerating. Like mad! Like nothing he'd ...

Miguel$_{(3)}$: $\delta V/\delta T \approx 3310.5$ m/s$^2 \approx 337$ g$_e$

... ever seen or heard of. Insane, crushing acceleration.

"Work with me," he called out to Lahler. "Plot the trajectory. This maneuver serves a purpose of some kind. Find it!"

The image of the thing-captain appeared on the holie before him. "Mr. Barta, I trust you are monitoring this phenomenon?"

Miguel$_{(1)}$: Object 34 has begun to accelerate.
Miguel$_{(2)}$: Object 39 has begun to accelerate.
Miguel$_{(*)}$: Stop. Let me know if any member of the primary group *doesn't* accelerate.

"On it, ma'am," he said to the holie.

"Good."

The thing-captain's image vanished again.

Lahler: Thrust vector, though variant, remains be-
    tween 170 and 180 degrees from hyperbolic de-
    parture asymptote. The maneuver will slow the
    objects down.

"Acknowledged," Miguel said aloud. "So they won't
fire off into empty space. They have business here,
still."

"Business with *us*?"

"Hmm." Miguel scratched his chin. "I doubt it. . . .

Miguel$_{(1)}$: $\gamma = \gamma_1 \gamma_2 = 0.662$ (nondimensional)
Miguel$_{(2)}$: $T_{el} = \int_{Tnow}^{To} \gamma \cdot \delta T = 1209.4$ s

. . . Time dilation is down to sixty percent and dropping
rapidly, but from their point of view we only discovered
them about twenty minutes ago. I don't know if they've
detected us or not, but whatever they plan to do, I
think they planned it long before we came around."

"I hope we don't get in their way!"

He nodded. "Me too."

Miguel$_{(1)}$: Angle between thrust vectors and depar-
    ture asymptotes continues to drop.
Miguel$_{(\cdot)}$: Lahler?
Lahler: Integrating. It looks to me like a circulariza-
    tion burn.
Miguel$_{(\cdot)}$: Time to completion? Radius and velocity
    of final orbit?
Miguel$_{(1)}$: $T_{circ} = 43826.1$ s
Miguel$_{(2)}$: $R_{circ} = 2.7335E+07$ m

Miguel$_{(3)}$: V_{circ} = 6.9869E+06 m/s = .0233 C
Lahler: In that orbit, time dilation will have dropped
to 0.14%. They will have returned to normal
spacetime.

"Acknowledged," Miguel said. Then, "Huh. Still very close to the hypermass. Why don't they come all the way out? They spend extra energy in order to not come all the way out."

"Could it have something to do with the other group?" Lahler asked.

Miguel nodded sharply. "Yeah. Yeah, probably."

Behind and beneath the fourteen emerging ellipsoids, there rose a second group; slower objects, and smaller, still egg-shaped, but longer and thinner than the ones ahead of them. Eight of the smaller objects. Eight. They would emerge into normal spacetime in another day or so, and at hyperbolic velocity.

Unless they maneuvered, too.

"Look at the two groups," he said. "Trace out the trajectories. It looks almost like a dance."

"Yes, kind of," Beth Lahler agreed.

Miguel signaled for the captain. Almost without delay, her thing-face appeared once again on the holie.

"Chelsea."

"Captain." Miguel returned her blank, inhuman gaze. "The outer object group has initiated a circularization burn which we estimate will finish in approximately twelve hours. The resulting orbit lies fairly close to Malsato, well within the gas halo, though out of the major spacetime distortions.

"The, uh, inner object group continues along its original hyperbola."

Some mechanical thing twitched on the thing-captain's face. "I see. I see. You've spent a lot of time inventing threats in your mind, Mr. Barta. Invent one for me now: what do you make of this?"

He shook his head. "Not a direct threat to us, Captain, at least if we stay out of their way. Even if the objects have detected us, they haven't had time to do much about it. Right now, I think they're running through some program of their own."

Offering calm words to the captain. So their roles had reversed, at least temporarily.

But Chelsea said, "Staying out of the way is precisely what I do not intend. We have found active artifacts of an alien intelligence, and that hardly seems like a time to hide ourselves away, yes? What would our superiors say? How would history judge us, if we let this moment just . . . slip us by?"

Miguel's innards went cold. "What exactly *do* you intend?"

"Why, to bring us in closer," Chelsea said, her thing-face still ticking mechanistically, "to beam a prime number signal at them over as much of the spectrum as we can manage. To make contact, Mr. Barta, as detailed in Operations Manual Five, Appendix C."

Make contact? *Down there,* in the maelstrom of white dwarf matter spiraling into the hypermass like water running down a drain? Oh, Lordy, Miguel had not signed on for this. An archaeological mission, a fucking *passenger* mission, that was what his contract had said, and neither that document nor Chelsea's precious OPM5/AC, nor any other piece of Solar Commercial literature known to Miguel, had mentioned anything about flying deliberately into the fires of Hell.

"Feed your trajectory data through to the helm, and keep me apprised of any changes."

Miguel said nothing. Tech Aid Lahler, frozen in the chair beside him, said nothing. The sounds of the ship, the humming of air vents and fluid transfer pipes, seemed awfully loud.

"Courage, crewmates," the captain said gently. "We have to do this. I'll inform the rest of the crew."

Her image winked out.

"Gravity gradient at 0.003 gee per meter and climbing," Miguel reported in a tone that could not disguise his alarm.

Introspectia had eased in slowly toward the black hole, toward the waiting ellipsoids, for the past several hours. But in the past few minutes, the ship's orbital velocity had increased sharply, to over one percent of the speed of light. Relativistic orbital velocity! The idea of it frightened him.

The period of *Introspectia's* orbit had shrunk, too, from the eight weeks of their original Lacigo/Malsato park orbit, to three-hour swoops through the swirling gases around Malsato. Then one hour, then half an hour. At least, as they got in closer to the black hole, the gases cooled, being much farther from their parent in both time and space. Lifeblood chilled down from the star's infernal body temperature. And scattered, strewn. Less dense than the near-vanished atmosphere of Earth's moon, but charged (and still very hot) so that it emitted a diffuse glow.

Dynamic pressures on the hull no greater than in a low planetary orbit, usually. But *Introspectia* shuddered sometimes as it passed through a pocket of higher density. At other times, Miguel fancied he could hear the wind whistling by outside the hull.

Now, they swung round the collapsar once every two and a half minutes, on an orbit only half a million kilometers in circumference. Twice the altitude of a terrestrial communications satellite, and yet moving a thousand times as fast!

Still, the gravity gradient bothered him most of all. At 0.003 gee per meter (no, 0.004!), it had begun to tip the potted palm trees over, to spill things off tables, creating dozens of little messes for the homunculi to clean up. Begun, also, to change the angle of the internal centrifuge gimbals as "down" ceased to fall completely perpendicular to *Introspectia*'s long axis. At the low and high sides of the ship, perceived gravity jumped by ten percent and fell again as the 'fuges rotated away from the invisible line connecting them with the hypermass.

It made him a little queasy.

No, more than queasy. If *Introspectia* lost attitude control, even for a short time, its long axis would swing around to face Malsato, creating a gravity differential of nearly 0.1 gee across the length of the ship. Enough to play hell with the centrifuge gimbals, enough to place serious loads on a structure designed for weightlessness.

"Beth!" he called out, raising his voice against sounds that were mainly imaginary. "This gradient worries me. Can the ship withstand a point one gee gravity differential on its long axis?"

Pause. "Yes it can." Pause. "It can hold a sustained differential of point four gee and limited transients up to about two gee. Estimates, of course."

"Of course," he said. "Let's hope we never find out the truth."

The potted palm fell over again, spilling dirt and leaf fragments on the brocade carpet. A panel slid open in the wall and, chuttering with mixed delight and annoyance, a homunculus leaped out to deal with the mess.

"Just take it away!" Lahler snapped at the little creature. "We don't need that in here anyway!"

"Relax," Miguel said as the homunculus scurried to obey her. "Pay attention."

"Apologies."

"Forgotten. Now hang on a second."

Miguel$_{(\cdot)}$: Gravity gradient at ellipsoid park orbit? Equivalent gravity differential across length of *Introspectia*?

Miguel$_{(1)}$: $\delta g/\delta R \approx 0.13 \ s^{-2}$

$\Delta g \approx 3.9 \ g_e$

"Yeah," he said quietly. "I thought that. Lordy, we can't do this."

"Miguel?"

He signaled the thing-captain.

She appeared.

"Chelsea." Her voice quicker, more anxious than usual. "Just a moment, please."

"Captain, I recommend we stop the descent. Gravity gradient at twenty-seven thousand kilometers will induce serious loads on our centrifuges, and if the ship somehow gets pointed down toward Malsato—"

"Busy right now," Lin thing-Chelsea said. "Just a moment, please."

Then, something changed in her manner. In her posture, perhaps, or in the inhuman jumble of linkware that formed her thing-face. "Yes? Centrifuges? We can shut those off. In fact, we probably should."

Miguel tried again. "Captain, we consider temporary disablement of the attitude control system a class-one failure scenario, yes? Moderate probability, adjust all plans accordingly?"

"Yes, Mr. Barta," the thing-captain said. "Your point?"

"We have no problem as long as we stay above, uh . . .

Miguel$_{(1)}$: 3.4E+07 m

. . . thirty-four thousand kilometers, but the ellipsoids will probably top out at only *twenty*-four thousand. We could survive at that radius if we stayed pointed along our orbit, but in the event of an attitude control failure, our long axis would pitch down toward the hypermass. The resulting tensile forces would pull the ship in two."

A pause. The thing-face somehow managed to look angry. "Why didn't you tell me this before?"

"I've warned you about environmental hazards from the beginning. The details of this particular one have only just become clear. Under pressure here, ma'am, we can't stay on top of everything."

"Nonetheless, I expect you to try!"

"Yes, ma'am."

Chelsea sighed. "My apologies, Mr. Barta. We *have* experienced problems with attitude control. Multiple causes, we believe—we haven't finished looking into it yet. Fortunately, your information has arrived . . . in time."

Miguel cleared his throat. "Captain, can I ask you the exact purpose of this descent? What, precisely, do you hope to accomplish?"

The thing-captain made an angry noise and leaned, suddenly, closer to the screen. "Do you mean to question my judgment, Tech Chief?"

"Huh? Oh, no ma'am. I simply wonder if a landing craft could accomplish the job."

The captain paused, then nodded. "I understand. The . . . objects have not responded to our prime number signals, and we can't tell what that means. The handbook recommends establishing unassisted visual contact, and I concur with it on that point. This means we have to get a lot closer. Would a lander survive the gravity at twenty-four thousand meters?"

Miguel$_{(1)}$: Working
Miguel$_{(2)}$: Working

"A moment please, Captain," he said. "Um . . . Yes. With a little margin, even. It . . . might take a while getting in and out, though. Underpowered."

She nodded again. "I see. I'll have a lander outfitted with science instruments right away. Were you volunteering to go along?"

A spear of ice rammed suddenly through Miguel's guts as he realized just what the captain was asking. Into the heart of the fire, into the teeth of the dragon?

"Um," he said. *No! Absolutely not!* "Sure, okay."

"You seem a little hesitant."

"Well, I've . . . never done this before. Who else would accompany me?"

Certainly not you, Captain Lin Chelsea. Regulation conveniently prohibits you from leaving the ship unless it is docked. But Lord, don't send me down there alone.

Beth Lahler rose from her chair, yanking the link harness from her head and leaning over the holie screen. "I volunteer, Captain."

Miguel turned. "Beth! No, the danger—"

"Stuff it. I don't want you going down there alone."

Barely visible beneath linkware, lips curled upward exposing teeth, and for the second time, Miguel saw the thing-captain smile just like a real human being.

"Ah," she said. "Tech Aid Lahler, isn't it? I find your dedication admirable. Do you feel certain about this?"

"Yes, Captain." Lahler snorted, clearly miffed by the question.

The icicle in Miguel's guts began to move in slow circles, stirring, churning. . . .

The thing-captain nodded politely. "Then I gratefully accept your offer. And yours, Mr. Barta. I shall do my best to find you a pilot."

The thing-face vanished once more from the holie screen.

No hurry about that, Miguel thought at her, loudly.

He turned again to Beth Lahler and frowned at her. "What do you mean by all that? I don't want you down there!"

She glared. "Has my work fallen below your standards, Tech Chief?"

"You know what I mean, Beth. You know exactly what I mean."

"Relax," she said, in the same tone he always used to tell her the same thing.

At that point, he realized she really did mean to go along, and that he couldn't stop her from doing it. Angrily, he turned away and jammed his mind back into the link harness. He would damn well go over the threats again, and again, and *again* before they left!

"Lock yourselves in, people," First Mate Peng called back over his shoulder. A small man, and quick, with narrow and restless eyes, Peng had volunteered to pilot this tiny lander on this risky and quite ill-advised expedition. Miguel had met him for the first time only five minutes before, as the two of them had knocked heads trying to climb through the hatch simultaneously. Beth had then collided with both of them, and nervous laughter and introductions had ensued.

For the moment a mere tenth of a gee pressed

Miguel back into his seat. Not a lot, but then none of it came from thrust or centripetal acceleration. Pure gravity gradient, and too much of it! Against his recommendation, Chelsea had ordered *Introspectia* into an elliptical orbit whose periapsis lay all the way down at thirty-four thousand kilometers. Reluctantly, he had agreed with her about the "safety" of the maneuver— very low probability of catastrophe. If attitude control died and the ship went nose-down, and then main propulsion somehow also died, the ship would suffer tensile oscillations, peaking at a two-gee differential every forty-five seconds as it swung through the lowest point on its orbit.

Even then, it would take hours for the structure to fail. A reasonable risk, in the captain's opinion.

The advantage, of course, lay in that same gravity differential: release the landing vehicle from its moorings near *Introspectia*'s forward end, and it would "fall" thousands of kilometers closer to the hypermass. Firing the motors then at periapsis would circularize them, saving hours of slow and costly descent.

"Acknowledged," Miguel said, reeling his harness straps out and buckling them in a star pattern across his chest. In light of where they were going, it seemed a laughable precaution, but he would wear it, nonetheless.

"Acknowledged," said Beth Lahler beside him. The harness seemed to give her a bit of trouble before she had it latched and snug around her.

Miguel flashed her an urgent look. "You don't have to do this. Please, there's still time to back out."

Lahler made no reply, but seemed to find something fascinating about her harness buckle.

"Beth, come on. *I* don't want to do this, and I especially don't want us both to do it. One of us should stay on the ship."

She looked at him. "Why don't you get out, then? It should frighten me, I know, and it *does* frighten me. But I want to go. I want to meet the aliens."

Peng looked over his shoulder again. His eyes glittered with mischief, with excitement, with a sort of calm, channeled fear that Miguel had rarely seen. "Courage, crewmates. Prepare for rotation. Captain Chelsea?"

"Yes?" the captain's voice rose up from a holie panel somewhere in front of the first mate.

Peng smiled at Beth and Miguel, paused for a long moment. "Let her go, Captain. Anytime you're ready."

"Acknowledged, First Mate. Good luck to you all."

Miguel's stomach quivered, then lurched as *Introspectia,* all three hundred meters of it, disengaged its attitude control thrusters and began to pitch downward. Miguel did not perceive rotation as such, but as they swung down into the gravity gradient he felt himself grow heavier in his seat. And heavier, and heavier still. Too much gradient! Too deep in the grip of the hypermass! Soon, he squashed the seat padding beneath him with the weight of a full gee.

Then his weight declined again, and held, and grew once more as *Introspectia* swung back and forth through the nose-down position. *Gravity gradient produces a stabilizing torque,* he thought. *Greatest force when the alignment is vertical.* Indeed, the oscillations damped out rapidly, and *Introspectia*'s control thrusters kicked back on to finish the job. In moments, his perceived gravity had stopped fluctuating.

"Ready to unmoor," Peng said. "Everybody hold on tight. Blowing the clamps in five . . . four . . . three . . . two . . . here we go!"

Miguel jerked in his harness at the loud banging noise the clamps made as they let go, then jerked again as the lander kicked away from *Introspectia*. And fell! Miguel's stomach fluttered, weightless and empty. The viewports, no longer nestled against the lander's mooring cavity, came alive with light and motion, the bright image of *Introspectia*, its navigation lights ablaze, falling rapidly away from them into a sky washed pale with starlight and white-dwarf haze.

"Wheeee!" said First Mate Peng. "I haven't done anything like this in a *long* time!"

Miguel, dizzy and nauseated and frozen with terror, said nothing. Nor, he noted, did young Lahler, her courage apparently fled.

Introspectia dwindled rapidly, becoming a festively lighted toy, and fell off to the side as it dropped behind the (now lower and, consequently, faster) lander in its orbit. Too quickly, it slipped toward the edge of the lander's broad fore-viewport, and then past the edge and out of view.

"Rotating to burn attitude."

Behind the haze of Lacigo's stolen gasses, the stars, already wheeling with the alarming speed of the lander's orbit, began to spin even faster. Miguel pulled his eyes away, looked down at his fixed, non-wheeling, non-terrifying science monitor. Ah, yes, the sight of it reassured him. No link harness, here, just a holie screen piping numbers and graphs from the various instruments the lander had been fitted with. Peng had, apologetically, referred to the whole thing as a "hasty and awkward assemblage, unfit for such duty as this."

But in truth, it resembled the science equipment Miguel had used for most of his life, in the relativistic-

ally distant days before *Introspectia*. Subjectively, no
more than six months ago!

"Lander," said the voice of Lin Chelsea, "report your
status."

"Doing fine, Lin!" the first mate called out cheerfully.
"Preparing to fire circularization burn."

Already? Lord! Miguel's eyes darted over the science
monitor, pulling data off here and there. Indeed, their
orbital period had plunged to twenty-nine seconds
upon their release, and periapsis had come upon them
once again. He had a hard time remembering how *fast*
their orbit here really was.

"Firing now."

Miguel's weightlessness went away, a comforting acceleration taking its place. A third of a gee? Yes, 0.314;
the instruments confirmed it. He turned his head,
looked over to see how Beth Lahler fared just now.

Not too well, apparently; her face had gone instantly
puffy with the loss of gravity, and the puffs were sag-
ging, now, as the fluid looked for a place to go. Her
tight mouth and slitted eyes, her hands in a deathgrip
on the seat's armrests, bespoke deep terror on an in-
stinctual level. Fear of falling, fear of darkness. Fear of
falling *into* darkness.

I told you not to come, Miguel said to her with his
eyes.

"Engine cutoff," said Peng. The acceleration eased,
vanished. "Next burn in twenty seconds."

"I'll get by," Lahler croaked. Her face, in addition to
its other obvious discomforts, had begun to go a little
green.

"You don't look like it," Miguel said.

She shot him an ugly glare. "Shut up."

Colors shifted, darkened.

Miguel looked up sharply, saw what lay outside the

forward viewport: yellow surrounding orange, fading to a tiny dab of red in the middle, like a bullseye seen out of focus. The Malsato hypermass. So small, so trivial in appearance; no larger than a grapefruit held at arm's length, and not much brighter than a campfire. Even close enough to shake and sicken them with its gravity, it did not look like much.

He saw, of course, not the tiny hypermass itself, only twenty-nine kilometers across, but the light emitted from the dense Lacigo-haze immediately surrounding it. Pure, white light, like that of the dwarf star itself, but whose wavelength had been stretched by the wearying climb out of Malsato's gravity, so that it appeared yellow, or orange, or, nearer the edge of the event horizon, a dark and malevolent red.

Even much closer, though, he knew he couldn't see the actual collapsar. Emitting no light, consuming the light that touched it, and *bending* the rays that brushed close by. The Lord's own telescope lens. The very close rays would bend a full 180 degrees around, swinging back to the direction they came from.

Even at fifty meters altitude, the ellipsoids could never see the object they orbited. What would they see? A nightmare Bosch-Escher world of gravity-lensed double images, false images, images distorted beyond all recognition? A scream of blueshifted light falling in from the outside universe? They would need something like the softlink, something like the obediently fractured mindlets of thing-Barta, to make any sense of it. If the very attempt did not drive them to blindness and madness and worse!

The view outside the lander continued to wheel sickeningly by. The hypermass slipped from view, replaced by cold stars and pale haze.

"Next burn in five seconds," said First Mate Peng. "Three. Two. One. Firing."

The acceleration returned, and Miguel's stomach lurched for the hundredth time. No carnival ride had ever jerked him around so much, spun or disoriented him so completely. Damn, damn, why had he ever agreed to do this?

Something on the science monitor caught Miguel's eye. Something. . .

"Stop the burn!" he shouted.

Instantly, unquestioningly, Peng slammed his fist down on a button. The thrust died. He turned, looked hard at Miguel. "What happened?"

Miguel, his eyes still riveted on the screen, waved a hand at him. "Wait . . . okay, we've passed them. Remember that our periapsis lies right on the ellipsoids' orbit, but we pass through it with a velocity much higher than theirs."

"Do you mean we almost had a collision?" Peng asked, his face a mask.

Miguel shrugged. "Well, we came within a few kilometers of one of them. Considering our relative velocities, I didn't feel comfortable with that."

"I didn't see anything," Peng said. Not skeptically, but rather with regret.

"You will," Miguel assured him. "I don't doubt it."

Malsato swung into view again, washing them in yellow-orange light.

Lahler squirmed in her seat. "Miguel, I can't read these instrument displays. Just numbers and colors and lines! How do you read it? How can you tell where the ellipsoids are?"

"Relax." Miguel reached out to place a reassuring touch on Lahler's shoulder . . . but he groaned and pulled his hand back before doing so. Vertigo! Vertigo! Oh, Lordy!

Gravity gradient pressed his rear into the seat with considerable force, now, almost a gee. Now less . . . now less . . . Now increasing again . . . But the unseen forces pulled considerably harder on his feet and less hard on his upper torso. His head, apparently higher than the lander's center of mass, was paradoxically pulled *upward*. Well, a little forward now, too.

Though weightless, suspended between the forces of Heaven and Hell, his outstretched arm had felt little tugs in every direction, like strings glued to his skin, pulling lightly outward. As if, given time, his arm might swell and burst like a sausage left too long in the cooker. Piled on top of the rotation and the other forces twisting Miguel's guts, the feeling had blown his equilibrium, spun him off into mindless horror for a brief, falling-nightmare moment.

Now, he cleared his throat, tried to look relaxed. "Damn, that feels weird. Keep your hands in close. I think you want to avoid that. In fact, keep your body as small as you can." He tried to smile, felt that it didn't quite work. He left it on anyway—this woman deserved a smile at a time like this!

"Beth, a lot of people have done a lot of good work on equipment like this. Some of them not so quick on the uptake, you know what I mean? Try to relax. This thing in the upper right-hand corner—" he pointed at his own screen rather than hers "—is the tracking display. Radar, lidar, passive optical and gravimetric. At the center of it here is our lander—"

"I'm skipping the periapsis burn!" Peng called out.

"Okay," Miguel said back to him. "Don't skip the next one, though. We need it to avoid contact on the next pass."

"Avoid? This mission it not about avoiding contact."

"Damn it, Peng, you know what I mean. Smashing into them at five kilometers a second won't help!"

"I see the tracking display," Lahler said, pointing at her holie. "But I don't get all this stuff on it, up here."

He nodded, pointed at his own screen. "The radar and lidar beams don't bounce back from the hypermass, except for the fraction that get turned around at the event horizon. I think our sensors can actually look their own selves in the eye, and not understand what they see! Anyway, don't pay attention to anything past about here. A lot of what you see there will be ghost images."

Yes, he felt he could almost grasp it now. An object close by would project two images: one very near its actual position, and the other, coming the long way around the black hole. A distorted ghost over Malsato's shoulder, many light-seconds away and many time-seconds out of date. And an object actually perched in that position behind the hypermass . . . would it produce a clear ghost that hovered nearby? No, certainly, it would produce a scattered image, enormously magnified, perhaps spread out to the point of invisibility.

Well, never mind that. It confused him, and it would confuse Lahler if he tried to explain it, and neither of them could afford confusion right now.

"Just worry about the close images," he said, "in this area here."

"Okay." She nodded once, calmer now with something to focus on.

"I'm firing the periapsis burn!" Peng said.

Oh, damn. Miguel tightened his muscles as the acceleration squeezed at him again. At least thrust acceleration came all in one direction, didn't pull on him in directions he wasn't meant to bend. Still, he didn't like it.

Lahler cried out, as if in pain. Miguel turned quickly (dizzyingly! nauseatingly!) toward her, and saw her face contorted with wonder, not pain. She looked out the forward viewport.

He followed her gaze. Outside, ahead, down below them hung an object the size of a pebble. Sparkly-white, like a centrokrist, but egg-shaped. It moved away from them, shrinking, blending with the haze. The edge of the viewport swung around to cover it before it had disappeared completely.

"Good Lord," Miguel said quietly.

Peng sat riveted. "Oh, my. Oh, my."

The periapsis burn terminated. Gravity gradient tugged and pulled, stronger than ever.

"Lander," said the faint voice of Lin Chelsea. "Rep . . . y . . ."

"I'm sorry," Peng said into the panel, his voice soft. "I didn't catch that."

"Report your status." The captain's voice was clearer now, louder, slightly higher in pitch.

"We, ah . . ." Peng paused, tilted his head over and scratched it. "We made visual contact with an ellipsoid, Captain. Gone now, but we looked right at it. We looked *right at it*—an alien machine. An alien spaceship. About twenty kilometers away?"

He looked back at Miguel questioningly.

"Eighteen point four," Miguel confirmed. His skin tingled. His pulse pounded loud in his ears. *Alien spaceship. We have made visual contact with an alien spaceship.*

For an instant, he was back on Earth, at the Merchant Academy. Parked in a glossy gray desk, with Captain Professor Pence leaning over him. "And what would *you* do, Mr. Barta, upon visual contact with a spaceship of alien manufacture?" Miguel smirked. "Offer them a beer, sir." Laughter. The sound of Pence's crop slapping hard against the desk. . . .

" . . . approximate position of the . . . " Chelsea's voice had dropped in pitch again, and faded. A few seconds of silence, and then, " . . . in line . . . we expected?"

"It has gone now, Captain," Peng said, not seeming to mind that he hadn't heard the question.

A pause. "Proceed with your descent, Mr. Peng, and rendezvous with one of the ellipsoids. Advise us when you have reestablished contact."

I want you to get co-orbital with one of them, Chelsea had instructed them before their departure. *Maybe half a kilometer ahead, and then take over the prime number transmissions from us. Flash your navigation lights at them, too, in synch with the prime signal. We intend to introduce ourselves, no? If anything sentient lives in the object, I want you to make sure it understands this fact.*

Fairly straightforward. Right out of the manual, in fact, in an almost literal sense. In the implementation, however, these orders seemed rather more complex, and certainly a lot less desirable. Nothing seemed easy or familiar down here.

Yellow and orange, the Malsato hypermass rolled in and out of view again, faster than ever.

"Understood, Captain. Crewmates, prepare for periapsis burn."

"Prepared," Miguel said with some annoyance. As if he and Lahler, dizzy and sick and twisted by gravity, had anything left to prepare.

The burn fired. Acceleration vectors danced and

quivered and inflicted discomfort. Patterns shifted on the science displays. The burn ceased.

Peng started banging out a quick sequence on the controls. "Tech Chief Barta, please select an ellipsoid for us to rendezvous with. Please design a final periapsis burn to match our orbit with its own, approximately one kilometer ahead. Please feed this information through to the helm."

"Acknowledged," Miguel said. Stretching his arms out for the controls brought new dizziness and discomfort, forces trying to lever him up out of his seat, and he dealt with these feelings in silence. Trajectory design . . . Lordy, it felt weird to do this again with the old equipment. But not too terribly difficult, no. In moments he had the information Peng had requested, and with a flourish he brought his hand down on the XFER and NAV tabs, transferring the maneuver to the lander's helm system.

"Completed."

Lahler looked over at him, smiled vaguely, then turned back to her science display. Her face dropped back into a frown of concentration as she tried, clearly, to reconstruct what he had done, and the method he had used, and the precise effect it would have when all was said and finished.

"Acknowledged," said Peng. "Rotating to new burn attitude."

The stars and vapors wheeled by as they had done, and the gravity gradient pulled as before. Miguel had computed a small maneuver, less than ten degrees of arc, and he could not perceive it now in the dizzying wash of background sensation.

Malsato's glow came and went.

"Prepare for final periapsis burn."

"Prepared!" Miguel snapped.

"Prepared," Lahler echoed, but with a ring of anticipation rather than Miguel's anger.

Yes, he should take this cue from her and calm the hell down. When had she gotten calm? *How* had she gotten calm? In seconds they would rendezvous with an alien spaceship in the murky depths of a black hole.

"Firing burn."

Higher thrust this time than ever before. Parts of Miguel's body strained against six gee's or more, while other parts remained sickeningly feather-light.

"Here we go, crewmates!" Peng called out over the hum of engines. "Settling into nose-down attitude. Prepare to get *stretched*!"

Rotation, and oscillation. The forces churning Miguel's body doubled, almost. Yuck! Uncomfortable! But really, not as bad as all that. Given time, he could probably get used to it. But how much time? How long would they—

An object, thumb-sized and glittery white, swung into view, wandered for a moment, then settled to a stationary position near the center of the forward viewport. Its long axis, a little over 100 meters long, pointed straight down, aligned with Malsato's gravity gradient. The short axis was about half the length of the long, so that the object looked very much like the egg of a quail or other small bird.

An alien machine. An alien spaceship.

The hum and pull of the engines died away, leaving only the hiss of ventilators and the soft *chunk-chunking* of the attitude control jets. Miguel checked his panel, saw that their new orbit lay right atop that of the ellipsoid.

"Rendezvous achieved," he said, in a voice that had

once more attained some measure of professional calm.

"Acknowledged," said Peng as he worked more controls. "Captain Chelsea? We have rendezvoused with one of the ellipsoids. Preparing to initiate prime number transmissions."

The captain's voice came back staticky and faint: ". . . please repeat . . . ge . . . didn't receive all of that."

"*I said we made it,*" Peng shouted into the holie. "*Shall we start transmitting?*"

"Acknowledged, lander." Her voice clearer now. "Yes, begin prime number transmission."

Peng looked over his shoulder at Miguel. "Mr. Barta, please initiate a wideband prime number transmission, with synchronized strobing of the navigation lights."

Miguel nodded to show that he had had heard, then turned to Beth Lahler. "Tech Aid, would you do the honors?"

Lahler gaped at him for a surprised moment, then looked down at the science displays in front of her, then back at Miguel again. Her expression hardened into a sort of professional scowl. "Of course, sir."

She turned, hunted on her panel for a few seconds, then started working controls. She looked as if she'd never used her hands before, as if they were themselves alien objects of mysterious origin and purpose. But she operated them with reasonable skill, finding and activating the functions she wanted. Soon, the lander was sending its signal to the alien ship.

Beep! BeepBeep! BeepBeepBeep! BeepBeepBeepBeepBeep! BeepBeepBeepBeepBeepBeepBeep!

And also *Flash! FlashFlash! FlashFlashFlash!* Running through all the prime numbers between one and 997, all the integers which could not be divided by any other integers (aside from the number one) and still leave an integer result. No natural phenomenon could produce a signal like that, so conventional wisdom had long maintained that sentient, technological aliens, if they existed, would instantly recognize such a signal as the work of another intelligence.

Miguel had always doubted conventional wisdom, on that point and on many others. How could anyone know what sentient aliens would or would not think? And anyway, the lander itself presented far clearer evidence of intelligent origin. Anyone who mistook it for a natural object could not, in Miguel's opinion, be classified as sentient.

"Object shows no response," said First Mate Peng.

Time rolled by like the starscape outside the viewport, first seconds and then minutes reeling away. The object did not move, did not transmit on any of the frequencies the lander used, nor on any other frequencies in the EM spectrum. Miguel pored over his instruments, looking up only occasionally at the ellipsoid outside to confirm, visually, with his own two eyes, that it continued to ignore them.

"Object shows no response," Peng repeated.

"Acknowledged," said the disembodied Lin Chelsea.

Miguel fiddled with controls, adjusted instrument gains and filters, swapped out one set of pattern recognizers in favor of another. And still, the ellipsoid changed neither its attitude nor its orbit, broadcast no radiation, emitted no particles. In fact, it seemed to *absorb* particle radiation rather well, particularly the neutrinos screaming up out of the depths, fleeing the slow death of matter taking place down there. Centrokrist made a good neutrino catcher, didn't it? He seemed to recall that the Malhelans had discovered it that way.

Something attracted his attention. Neutrino gravimetry readings . . . Wait a minute! He made an adjustment, and another. Yes, the mass of the neutrinos that had passed through the ellipsoid was measurably smaller than the mass of the ones which hadn't. And the ones which passed through the ellipsoid's edges were less massive than the ones which passed through the center.

Oh, hold on just a minute!

"Hollow!" he said out loud. "The hull material steals energy from neutrinos passing through it, but the *hollow* space inside does not! Or not as much, anyway. Lordy, something very strange goes on inside that object. It seems almost as if spacetime curves differently inside of it than out. Which, I suppose, fits with the evidence of inertial shielding based on the fact that they didn't fly apart into fucking *dots* down at the event horizon."

First Mate Peng turned all the way around and gave Miguel a hard look. "What the hell are you talking about?"

Miguel glared up at him for a moment. "Nothing. Thinking out loud. Can we, uh, move a little closer to the object?"

"I would prefer not to. What did you have in mind?"

"Well, if it won't talk to us, at least we can get a good look at it. Possibly even at the insides of it."

"I see. Hmm."

Lin Chelsea spoke up: "Mr. Peng, would you please move the lander to within five hundred meters of the ellipsoid?"

"Yes, ma'am," Peng replied cheerfully.

Engines groaned for a moment. The ellipsoid drifted toward the top of the viewport and began, slowly, to grow. Soon it had expanded to fist size, and the top edge of the viewport bulkhead began to eclipse it. Then it grew to two fists, and then a small melon. Engines, this time on the lander's "top" side, fired once, paused, fired again. The ellipsoid, now comfortably melon-sized, drifted back toward the center of the view and stopped there, hanging motionless before them once more.

"Status of prime number signal?" Miguel asked, glancing over at Beth Lahler, who now looked very disheveled indeed.

"Up to three fifty-three," she said. Her eyes darted back and forth between the science panel and the forward viewport, trying to drink everything in at once.

"Still no response from the object," said Peng.

Miguel turned back to his neutrino gravitometer readings. Important data lay buried there, he sensed, and not very deeply. If he plotted the neutrino mass-deltas as a function of cartesian coordinates . . . Could he form a picture? Yes, certainly! He'd have to set up the mapping algorithm by hand, of course. Damn, where were the mindlets of thing-Barta when he needed them?

"The object draws still closer, Elevated Creature."

Frills expanding, contracting, expanding, contracting . . . Not angry, yet, but tense with the anticipation of it.

"It is not the Enemy."

"It emits patterned radiative pulses. It has moved down into Fleet's own orbit, and approaches the Elevated Vessel. With what intent? With *what intent*?"

Muscles bunch, contract, quiver as they store up energy, and suddenly Elevated Creature is in motion. Even anticipating the attack, even knowing the precise moment at which it must occur, Lesser Being cannot avoid it. Mass slams into mass. Momentum becomes pain.

Out of the deeps at last! Out of the contracted spaces where to look lowside within the Vessel is to look into pits of red slowness, where shouted orders stretch to clicking groans that the incompetent cannot decipher! Where timespace slopes twist the body, forcing rate gradients and spacial distortions upon it, so that time torque may break the bones and rupture the organs of those who move incautiously, of those who move at all.

Talons on spiracles now, squeezing, sharpened points penetrating here and there. Weakness becomes death, if Elevated Creature decrees it!

"It is not the Enemy. Do not be distracted, vermin, by extraneous phenomena."

Lesser Being does not flinch. "And if it proves a second Enemy? Or a new aspect of the first?"

Talons on spiracles, still. Squeezing, almost crushing.

"Then it will no longer be extraneous."

Elevated Creature pauses momentarily, breathing, and then sinks talons in, to the root and beyond. Fluid emerges, coloring every surface. But lo, steadfast bravery spouts also from the wounds! A message to all, from death's deliverer and its recipient both: Lesser Being unravels calmly, never deigning to scream.

Peng shook his head. "No. *Still* no response from the object. Maybe we should pull back and approach a different one."

"Hang on," said Miguel. "I need more time."

On his science holie, reconfigured to display two-dimensional images from the neutrino gravitometer, a fuzzy picture had finally begun to form. Each passing second added thousands of faint, tiny dots to the image, gray on gray but with striking cumulative effect as the exposure time wore on into minutes.

He saw there a hollow ellipsoid, its hull just over one meter thick, with fainter, less intelligible structures inside it. Mysterious shapes, neither formless nor Euclidean. Some smeared more than others, as if they moved slowly or vibrated in place.

He adjusted a gain control, upped the image contrast, plugged in a primitive clarifier module. The picture changed, sharpened. The inner structures vanished, then slowly began to reemerge. Miguel switched clarifiers, and everything changed again.

"Hurry up, will you?" said Peng with obvious annoyance. "What's got so much of your attention?"

"Looking inside the shell," Miguel replied shortly. "Just wait, I'll send you the image when I get it focused a little better."

"Send it to me now."

"Okay." Miguel's tone was skeptical, distracted. The first mate should just let him rivet his attention on the task at hand, let him finish it. Miguel hated to show unfinished work, hated the hasty, half-assed look of it and the resulting implication about his own abilities.

"Oh!" Peng said as the image sprang up on his holie.

But Miguel had not finished. Over the next few minutes, he processed a handful of clear images from his stored neutrino gravimetry data, and found that he could blink back through them on the screen, like a child's cartoon flip-book. And in the cartoon, gray on blurry gray, those humped, elaborate shapes . . . moved. Like living beings, they moved. Thick limbs and other projections emanating from bodies that seemed heavy and sinuous at the same time. They had parts that looked like beaks, parts that looked like claws. Parts that looked like nothing Miguel had ever seen.

"You can see them move!" Peng said. "You can actually see them move!"

"Wow," echoed Lahler.

Miguel ignored them. As he watched, one of the creatures flew from one side of the ellipsoid's interior to the other, colliding with another humped shape in a tangle of limbs and . . . things. Then the cartoon, its five frames over and done with, went back to the beginning and repeated itself. The creature launched itself and collided solidly with one of its fellows. Back to the start again. The creature bunched up and launched itself, savagely, premeditatedly, at one of its fellows, colliding with talons outstretched. Inertially shielded, the centrokrist ellipsoid did not shudder with the impact.

The creature, preparing to jump, gathered itself—

"Mister Barta!"

Miguel looked up from the display. "Huh?"

"I asked you a question!" Peng shouted at him.

Question. "I, uh, didn't completely hear you. Could you please repeat it?"

"Can you *clarify* the lower left portion of the *image*? We're looking at *actual alien beings*, here, and I want a better look at that one that's moving!"

"This display maps a very subtle phenomenon, sir," Miguel said.

"Does that mean you cannot enhance it?"

Miguel huffed. "Peng, I just thought up this imaging process right here on the cusp of the moment. I don't have any experience with this sort of thing. Do you? I'm certainly open to suggestions."

"Think for a minute," Peng said, turning, propping his elbow up on the back of his seat. He looked eerie in the strange light of the hypermass. "Just relax, don't answer right away. I know you're frightened and uncomfortable and you'd really like to get out of here. So would I! It feels like I'm drowning. But this time, this very special time, will not come again. So *think* for me."

Nodding made Miguel dizzy. He closed his eyes, did a breathing exercise for a few seconds. Opened his eyes again. "I can fiddle with it, I guess. If I filter out the noisier—"

"Uh, Miguel," Beth Lahler said beside him, "the second group of objects has—"

Miguel turned a withering stare on her. "A minute, please, Tech Aid." He turned to his panel again. "If I *filter*—"

"Tech Chief Barta," Beth persisted, raising her voice a little. "They just kicked their engines on. Accelerating at three hundred eighty-five gee's."

Miguel froze, then turned back to Lahler. "The second group? How far away?"

Lahler fairly smirked, obviously pleased with her quick mastery of the equipment. "They'll cross this orbit in approximately ten minutes. Moving fast, though. Moving almost straight out of the hole."

"Wonderful," Peng said, jerking an elbow hard against his seat as if to punish it. "There they go, off to deep space, and here we sit, talking to the furniture."

"Not furniture," Miguel said. "Let me finish with the scan."

Suddenly, the image before him went white and featureless. Damn!

"Damn it! Explanation?" he barked at Lahler.

"The object started spewing out neutrinos," she said quickly, her eyes on the holie in front of her. "Wait a minute, all of them did. All the ones in this orbit, I mean, all fourteen of them."

"Oh." Miguel cooled a little. He'd thought at first

that this "primitive" equipment had failed under the gravitational stresses, much as his knees and spine achingly threatened to. And it had occurred to him, too, that Lahler might have fumbled on her controls, somehow erasing his image buffer. But these things had not happened. Instead . . .

"Oh, Lord. Peng, I think the furniture has answered you after all."

Lahler nodded vigorously, an enterprise that must have caused her extreme discomfort. "Yeah, I think so, too. Look at these modulations!"

"Not on my display right now," Miguel reminded her.

She waved her hands. "It's . . . a digital signal of some sort. Very short pulses. This would eat a lot of bandwidth as a radio transmission. It . . . Wow, it wouldn't even *fit* in the radio spectrum, it'd overlap into infrared. Encyclopedias worth of information, here. Libraries worth."

"Record it!" Miguel shouted, not in anger but in gut-trembling fear. Here they'd found exactly what they came down here for: a conversation with alien beings! They mustn't lose any of it!

Miguel's screen went gray-on-gray again.

"The broadcast has ceased," Lahler said. "But I—"

"Damn it! Is it over? Damn it to Hell!"

"No!" Lahler shouted back triumphantly. "I had the recorders on already. I've got it! I've got it all!"

"Oh, my," Peng said quietly. "Oh, my. Can we decode it?"

Miguel gaped at his tech aid, his assistant who only minutes ago could not work the equipment. "Good . . . good job, Beth. That shows remarkable foresight."

Lahler, grinning broadly, blushed. "Purely accidental. Thank my luck."

"*Can we decode it?*" Peng repeated.

Miguel turned to him. "We're in the middle of a black hole, sir."

"Yes. And can we decode the signal?"

Lahler's grin vanished. She looked blue-purple, suddenly, as a wash of color swept across her holie. "The objects have begun emitting a particle stream down toward the hypermass. Correction, toward the second group of objects."

Miguel craned for a look at her screen. "What sort of particles?"

"I don't know. Um . . . antimatter of some sort . . . very massive."

"Antimatter? That would be *dangerous* as a—"

Everything went yellow-white. Everything glowed.

Crying out, Miguel raised an arm to shield his eyes. But the light was dimming already. He lowered the arm, and saw the ellipsoid outside the viewport, radiating like an incandescent light fixture. No, not radiating, *reflecting;* the light came up from below.

"What happened?" shouted First Mate Peng.

Lahler blinked, held her hands out in front of her face, fingers wiggling. Then, apparently satisfied the light had not struck her blind, she looked down at her holie. She blinked again. And began to look alarmed.

"Beth?" Miguel said with more than a little concern.

She turned to look at Miguel, her eyes narrow, a vague almost-fear still clinging to her expression. "One of the emerging ellipsoids has vanished," she said. "And a cloud of plasma has taken its place. The others have changed their thrust vectors, all in different directions. They scatter. They look . . . like startled birds. They look scared."

"That does it," said Peng. He grabbed his controls and hunched over against the gravity gradient. "I'm taking us out of here."

Miguel's skin broke out in shivery goose-pimples. "This is a *war*," he said wonderingly. "They weren't talking to us, they were talking to each other. About a *war*."

The lander's engines whined to life. Thrust acceleration tugged, perpendicular to the gravity gradient. Outside the viewport ahead and above, the ellipsoid grew, and moved up and to the side. Soon, it vanished off the edge of the viewport.

"I'll bet they chased each other in close to the hypermass," Miguel said hurriedly. "They must have been fighting a long time! A *long* time!"

"Ellipsoids are firing antiparticle beams again," said Lahler. "The plasma cloud down below us is dispersing rapidly, but its velocity remains at zero point five six cee. Parts of it will hit us if we don't get out of here."

Peng slammed his fist down on a button and shouted into his holie. "*Introspectia!*"

The holie's reply was little more than a burst of static.

"*Introspectia!*" Spittle flew from purple lips, hooked away in the gravity gradient.

Then, Lin Chelsea's voice came faintly through: " . . . read you, lander."

"Good, come pick us up! Forget the safety crap, we've got to get out of here!"

"Uh, negative . . . " Chelsea's voice sounded agonized, even over the static. "We've got rapid variations in particle flux up here, hammering the conversion fields out of alignment. We have to withdraw to a safe distance. In fact, we are already doing so."

Peng paused for a moment, then slammed his fist down on the panel again. "Damn it! We'll die down here!"

"I . . . My deepest apologies to all of you. But you've

taken triple-dose radiation prophylactics, yes? Believe it
or not, this makes you less vulnerable than *Introspectia*'s engines."

"Correct," Beth Lahler said, almost calmly. "We may
survive the plasma wave, particularly if we get medical
treatment after it passes. The lander, however . . . Well,
we may end up stranded."

"Not if I can help it," Peng snarled, working the controls with stiff, angry movements.

" . . . ive . . . th . . . " said Lin Chelsea.

"Repeat!" Peng screamed at the holie panel.

"I said, please forgive me. I really don't have a choice
in this."

Peng inhaled, paused, let out a heavy sigh. "I realize
that, Captain. Can you explain your plans in greater detail?"

"No plans, First Mate, I haven't thought that far
ahead. Once we clear this gas halo, we'll light up the
main engines and get the hell clear. If we can get a
few light-hours away, we can shut down the whole
conversion field and bring it up again on a higher setting."

"That will take days," Peng said.

"Yes. Again, let me offer my very deepest apologies."

"Oh, save it. Get out while you can."

"That— Oh, I've been informed we can fire the main
engines in another minute. Good-bye, crewmates. I
wish you luck."

Peng did not reply.

"Plasma wave will hit us in just over a minute," said
Lahler.

Miguel squirmed in his seat, suddenly aware of the
solid weight of harness buckles biting into his flesh. He
had heard and understood the entire exchange, and
had felt a kind of disconnected fear as he thought

through its implications. But in truth, his eyes had been mainly on the science holie in front of him, his hands mainly on the instrument and automation controls.

"Mister Barta!" Peng shouted. "What attitude would best protect the lander from the plasma wave? Engines away? Engines toward?"

Miguel thought for a (where was thing-Barta at a time like this?) moment. "Uh, I don't know. I guess it doesn't really matter."

"Why not?"

"Relativistic protons will pass right through us and keep going. Like little bullets, unstoppable, leaving little bullet holes."

Miguel's voice was thick with fear, but still its clarity surprised him; through the panic crowding and clouding into his forebrain, he found it a struggle to speak or think at all. And yet, deep inside a part of him felt calm. As if he'd split a mindlet off after all, one that could observe and react without getting emotionally involved in the situation.

"The electrons will stick," he continued. "I guess we'll build up a charge on the leading edge, disperse it throughout the hull and then discharge it again as the protons fly away. So they'll kind of crawl around the outside of the hull."

Peng scowled. "Do nothing, then? You sound pretty fatalistic all of a sudden."

"Fatalistic?" Miguel almost laughed. "Peng, I sure don't want to get hurt."

Lahler pressed a control on her panel, glanced over at something. She stiffened. "Brace for it! The—"

"Shit!"

"Aaah!"

Lahler's panel exploded in white light, as did

Miguel's, as did Peng's. The viewport showed only the blank, rotating starscape, wholly innocent in appearance, as sparks began to fly and a terrible thundering/crackling/sizzling sound split the air like nearby lightning. Miguel was jerked hard against his harness buckles and he felt his neck snap, felt his shoulders snap, felt his back give way and come apart into separate pieces. Lightning sounds swallowed his scream.

Too fast for pain, too fast for fear, but even so Miguel felt a certain relief when the sounds quieted and everything around him went black.

Chapter Sixteen

From the deputy administrator's floor of the Power Board building, Jhoe had quite a good view of the sleeping city. No, not sleeping, *hiding*. Middle of the day, he reminded himself. Never mind the darkness. In the distance, he could see a tent building that had fallen in the evening quakes. No flashing lights around it, no response teams hustling to clean it up. Hiding, almost all of them.

"It looks so quiet," said a voice behind him. Uriel Zeng's.

"Yes," he said without looking away from the window.

"A million people crammed into those shelters. Ugh, it must be awful."

Indeed, panic and chaos had filled the streets a few hours earlier, only recently dying away to the present state of quiet as the last of the people made their way to the shelters.

"You don't plan to join them," Jhoe said. Not a question, but an observation of fact.

"We can't. Power's more critical now than ever before; if the shelters lose coverage they have only two hours of battery life."

"And then it gets dark inside?"

"No, then the air vents shut off and everyone suffocates."

Jhoe sighed. "Uriel, nobody's welded the doors shut.
People can just walk outside."

"Well, then they wouldn't be sheltered."

"Just like you and I, right now. God, won't you two
see sense? I hear the radiation levels have already gone
two hundred percent above normal, and the aliens
haven't even gotten close yet."

"Doctor," said Uriel, prompting him to turn. Uriel's
so-young face looked tired, drawn. But her expression
showed vigor just the same. "Two hundred percent
above normal is still way below crisis level. Radiation is
all around us, all the time. We've got two black holes
and a white dwarf in this system, spewing out radiation
all the time, not to mention Vano—" she pointed at the
huge, smoldering ball in the sky "—which is *spitting*
distance away. The atmosphere absorbs a lot of crap.
It's much denser and higher than Earth's, you know.
But we absorb the rest of it in our bodies."

"And without radiation pills." He shook his head in
amazement. "That's . . . that's basic molecular medi-
cine. You all must get cancer all the time."

"Not all the time," Uriel protested, her crabby expression slipping back into place.

"You will get it," he said to her. "Standing out here in
the thick of it all, I bet you'll get it really bad. Don't you
even care?"

She shrugged, a little angrily. "I'll get over it, Doctor.
I work around dangerous equipment and chemicals all
the time. This isn't so different. I'm not going to abandon my post."

"You have no sense. You and Luna have no sense."

"It's not just me and Luna. About half the staff are
still on the job. Not all in this building, but around
somewhere, keeping an eye on things."

"Uriel."

Jhoe and Uriel both turned toward the sound of Luna Shiloh's voice.

"Uriel," Luna said, striding forward with long, quick, urgent steps. "The south junction is losing voltage, and I think the transformers are heating up. Can you round up some people and go take a look?"

"Sure," Uriel said, "but could you cut the district load by fifty percent in the meantime? Makes my job a lot easier."

Luna paused. "Can . . . we do that without cutting off any of the shelters?"

"Uh, I think so. I'd have to look at the board to be sure."

"I'll check the board," Luna said. "You get that chopter in the air."

"Okay." Uriel pushed away from the window and trotted off.

Luna smiled, put a cool hand on the back of Jhoe's neck. "You'd better get to one of the shelters soon."

Jhoe glared at her. "But not you."

"Jhoe, I can't. I'll be thinking about you, though."

"Great."

Her gaze moved away from him, toward something outside the window. Her eyes widened.

"I'll be damned. Look at that!"

She pointed, and Jhoe followed her arm and her eyes to see . . . Lacigo. The tiny, starlike white dwarf had . . . grown? And brightened. The ring of sky immediately surrounding it looked distinctly greenish.

"It got bigger," Jhoe said stupidly.

"No," Luna corrected, "it's splitting into separate pieces. Look there. Could those be the alien ships?"

Jhoe looked at her for a moment, saw that she wasn't kidding. "Uh, so far away? It doesn't seem like we could see that."

"Really? Why not? If they're accelerating as fast as they're supposed to, they must be burning awful lot of energy. I think we could maybe see them from here. *Introspectia* was much closer when we first saw it, but it looked like a blobby white star, just like that."

Jhoe looked more closely. Lacigo, never bright enough before to hurt the eyes, hurt him a little now. But, as Luna indicated, it seemed to have split into several distinct pinpoints of light, which did not quite touch one another. In fact, with effort he could see the most central pinpoint as a tiny disc of brightness. And he could see the others as . . . streaks? They seemed to lengthen even as he watched.

Blinking, he looked away. Pink and green spots danced in front of his eyes. "Ow," he observed. "This is probably bad for your eyes."

Luna nodded. "It is bright; it looks like welding torch. I guess we shouldn't look directly at it. Look how blue the sky is getting!"

Jhoe let out a breath through pursed lips, almost but not quite a whistle. "It looks almost like dawn on Earth."

"Like what?"

"Dawn. Um, before the sun comes up. The horizon goes from black to purple to blue, and then the whole sky starts changing color."

"Then you're right," Luna said, "it is like that."

He dared a glance up at Lacigo again, and the streaks had gotten longer and brighter, and had separated themselves more distinctly from the light of the white dwarf. A whole region of sky around them had turned a deep but rapidly brightening blue.

"Quakes," Jhoe said, using the Unuan invective for the first time. "In a few minutes we'll have an ordinary sky-blue sky!"

"How wonderful," Luna said, sounding as though she meant it. "I've always thought Earth must have a beautiful sky. Oh, look at the clouds!"

Above, the haze of Unua's cloud deck had begun to pale, gray-brown giving way to beige and then, in the wisps reaching closest to Lacigo, fading to a color that approximated Earthly white. The sky behind them had gone a pure azure through which the stars, other than Lacigo and its strange new companions, could not be seen at all.

"The clouds, yes, I see them," Jhoe said.

"Is that what it looks like on Earth?"

"Well . . . sort of."

Hostile aliens had changed the color of Unua's sky. That should terrify him, he knew, but somehow he did not feel terrified. No more than he would at the sight of a waterfall, or a snow-capped mountain, blue-white in the moonlight. This just didn't look like something dangerous.

Luna caressed his neck for a moment and then took her hand away. "I have to go back to the coordination center. You'd better get going."

Jhoe's eyes didn't leave the blossoming of the sky. "Do you need anything before I go? I feel like I should help, at least do *something*."

Luna half-smiled at him. "You? The dispassionate observer? I thought you weren't supposed to get involved."

"I could take that as an insult," Jhoe said. "Can I help you or not?"

"Actually, you can," Luna said. "We're pretty short-handed. Can you get down to the supply room and dig out box of glowpegs? We're going to need them for the board."

"I think I can manage that."

"I think so, too. They're in the northeast corner, bottom rack. Yellow boxes about this big." She held her hands a few centimeters apart. "When you're done, you'll go to the shelter? I'd really prefer that you did."

Above, one of the streaks, now well separated from Lacigo and clearly visible, had begun to curl. White on azure, it looked much like the contrail of a high-flying atmospheric transport soaring through the skies of Earth. Familiar and yet . . . not the same thing at all. He knew that it should frighten him. Cancer. Radiation. Death.

"Yeah," he said. "I'll go."

Luna looked up once more at the sky, drinking in the images there, and then in near-synchrony she and Jhoe broke away from the window and stomped off on their separate errands.

The elevator took Jhoe down to the basement, and when its door opened he stepped out into dimness and gray. A large room, rows of shelves and cabinets lurking in the shadows. In general, Malhelan architects threw light around as if their lives depended on it, but this place seemed forgotten, an afterthought, underground and therefore hidden from even the wan glow of the Unuan sky.

Hidden from the radiation as well? No, certainly; the building, designed to be light and flexible, probably offered no more protection than a heavy coat. Suddenly, he felt its weight hulking above him, ready to crash down at any moment. Unpleasant.

He hurried to the northeast corner of the basement, looked for something that could be called a "bottom rack," and then for yellow boxes the size of paired fists. Spying them, he grabbed one in each hand. The shadows seemed to advance on him as he stood up again. He hurried to the elevator.

It had closed.

Awkwardly, he stretched out a finger around the box of glowpegs and pressed the VOKU button. The door did not open, and from the sounds behind it he could tell that the elevator had gone up to another floor. He found the air whooshing in and out of him in quick, shallow breaths. He tried to slow and steady his breathing, but without success. He had to admit, he felt more anxious now than he had in decades. Here in the basement, he found his earlier numbness had fled, leaving his nerves bare to the fact that Unua's ground could not be trusted, that aliens ran unrestrained through its skies, that he had no truly safe place to retreat to.

This is not my planet! he wanted to shout. *This is not my danger to face!*

And yet, he had come to this planet of his own free will, and the danger had followed regardless of his wishes. Luna and Uriel and the others, facing the same peril as he, seemed not nearly so afraid. This *was* their planet, their city, their own little place in the vast universe, and they seemed stubbornly determined to protect it, if only in the smallest of ways.

The elevator door opened suddenly, ringing a bell at him. He jumped, then relaxed a little and stepped inside.

It took him up to the deputy administrator's floor, and his feet took him the rest of the way to the coordination center. Orange and yellow and red lights burned against the black city map on the diagnostic board. A knot of people stood in front of it, arguing heatedly.

Jhoe held the glowpeg boxes out in front of him like wards against evil.

"So shut them down!" Luna was saying. Her arm swept an arc across the board. "Here and here and here. Isolate the problems and deal with them separately."

"Can't do it," one of the men was saying. He stabbed a finger at one of the red glowpegs on the board. "You see that? You see that? I can't get a signal through there with the lines out. It's *defunct*, Luna. Can you say that word?"

"Shut them down manually," another man called out from a workstation in the far corner of the room. "Send Uriel out on it."

"I've already sent Uriel out," Luna said, "to the north side, too far away. Listen, I could call every team we have, but they *can't be everywhere at once*. Those substations need to go down right now!"

"Fine," said the man in front of Luna, his voice and movements tight. "I'll get in my car and *drive* out there. Isolate the whole neighborhood, yes? There's nobody out there anyway. I'll just throw the switch."

Luna blinked with surprise. "Oh, I didn't even think of that. Quakes, I'm really frazzled."

"What's going on?" Jhoe said. He stepped forward, his hands still partly extended. "What's wrong?"

Luna turned toward him, looking as if she'd forgotten about him and was annoyed to find him still in the building. "One of the big transformers finally blew," she said, "about one minute ago. Voltage is going unstable, and it's chewing up three substations on the south side. It's bad. It can bring the whole grid down if we don't isolate it."

"Shall I go?" said the man in front of Luna.

She nodded. "Yes. Take the Fourth and Jewell station, and cut switch number *two*. Elle, you take South Jama. Cut five through eight. I don't care what order you do it in. And—" She looked around, frowning. "I need someone for First and Quincy. Damn it, where did everyone go?"

"I'll do it," said the man in the corner workstation.

Luna turned on him angrily. "No, you will not. If your ass gets out of that chair again I'm going to kick it, hard. Is anyone else *not busy* right now?"

"I'm not," Jhoe said calmly.

"Jhoe!" Luna rolled her eyes at him. "Will you get out of here? I thought you were going to the shelter."

"I know how to throw a switch."

She sighed. "These people have years of training, Jhoe. They have special licenses and special equipment."

"Luna, I know how to throw a switch! Lend me your car, okay? Lars has been teaching me how to drive."

"Lars has been teaching you how to drive," Luna echoed darkly. "Oh, well, that's different, then! We'll just trust the whole city to you, right?"

Gritting his teeth, Jhoe stabbed a finger at the man in the corner workstation. "Can I do what he's doing?"

"No," Luna said.

"Can I do what anyone in this building is doing? Darkness, Luna, you obviously need some help, And *I know how to throw a switch.*"

She paused, appearing frozen, for a moment, with in-decision. "Shit," she said then, and handed Jhoe her keys.

Oh, for a pair of sunglasses! Jhoe thought as he drove along the deserted street. Above and ahead of him, Vano, now approaching its zenith, looked as huge as ever but significantly less imposing; a pale, peach-colored disc against a blue-white background. The sky around it had gone as bright as Earth's own, and Jhoe found himself squinting against it. He was no longer

accustomed to such glare. Alas, he would bet his own
teeth that sunglasses had never sold well on Unua. If
he looked hard enough he might find something like
welding goggles, or perhaps he could simply reprogram
his corneal symbionts to filter and soften the light, but
either of those options would take time, and right now
he didn't have any. Urgent mission! Save the city!

Spaced at intervals along the sides of the street,
stringy, red-brown trees grew two and three and sometimes four meters tall. Choker trees? Yes, the little bun-
dles of dark berries confirmed it. He'd tended to think
of those as rather ugly plants, but actually, in this light
they possessed a certain dignity he had not previously
noticed. By contrast, the buildings he passed appeared
surprisingly shabby—cracked and wrinkled and old,
like mummies dragged out into the sunlight.

He wheeled cautiously around a corner, and the
power substation, object of his quest, came into view.
He pulled up in front of it, working levers and pedals,
bringing the car to a sudden, lurching halt. Its engine
growled at him and died. Jhoe growled back at it as he
removed the enabling key and climbed out.

His body cast a deep shadow against the unnaturally
illuminated pavement. His breath came heavy and
quick. *I must have lost my mind,* he thought. *I shouldn't
have volunteered for this; I should have gone to the shelter.* He imagined the radiation like a fog surrounding
him. Well, more like a rain, he supposed, and a deadly
one.

Still, the rain had come a thousand times harder and
faster during the journey on *Introspectia,* and he hadn't
given it much thought then, merely taking his weekly
radiation pill and leaving it at that. Why should this
seem any different? He hadn't had a pill in several
months, true enough, but he was pretty sure the pro-

phylactic effect was supposed to last awhile, fading slowly as the body flushed and renewed itself. Would his last dose still have enough strength to fight off this weakened threat?

Bah. Luna Shiloh needed his help. The city of Verva needed his help. Soon enough he could indulge the instinct to cower and cringe.

Behind its high fence of white plastic, the power station formed an unpainted tangle of metal wires and shacks and towers, the whole assemblage half again as large as Luna's house. Jhoe strode up to the gate, studied its locking mechanism, inserted the sharp wedge of green metal that was its key. After a few moments' fiddling he popped the gate open and swung it wide. The machinery ahead of him emitted a soft, disturbing whine, as if in anxiety or pain. The sound seemed to reach right through him, wiggling his teeth, wiggling his internal organs. Already, he didn't like this place.

Luna had drawn a crude map for him on a sheet of paper, and he dug it out now and looked at it as he walked, taking the steps and the turns that it indicated. Soon, he found himself at the door of one of the shacks, metal against metal, gray against gray. He took out the green key again and used it, and, squealing on its hinges, the door swung back into shadow.

He stepped into the shack, into the darkness of its interior. Felt for a light switch, didn't find one. He took a step . . . took another . . . His eyes began slowly to adjust, and with some surprise he realized that the lights were on inside, typically and dazzlingly white in the Unuan style, but still as nothing compared with the brightness outside. Just as well the Unuans were mainly in hiding; how would they react to such an astonishing reversal?

Pull switch number five, Luna's note said. He looked

around, spotted a row of hand-sized switches along one wall. Numbers sat above them, painted on the wall in bright yellow. Number five was right in the middle.

"Well," he said out loud, "what now?"

"Throw the switch," he answered himself after a brief pause.

He stepped up to the bank of switches, grasped the handle of number five. Pushed it upward, felt it lock into place. Instantly, something shifted in the character of the background whine. It dropped, becoming softer, less insistent.

"Huh," he said. Had he just saved the city? Had he completed his mission as simply and effortlessly as that? He began to feel a little insulted. Luna had doubted his ability to do *this*? Did she think him so helpless, he who had traveled among the stars?

Shaking his head, he moved away from the switches, walked back to the rectangle of bright sky and ground that was the world outside the shack's doorway.

The car, when he got back to it, hummed to life on his second try, its electric motor engaging, jerking the whole machine into sudden motion. He fought the controls for a moment, then settled down for the drive back to Luna's office. He negotiated one corner, then another, and then sped up for a long, straight section of road.

Above him, shaded slightly on one side and burning with unholy fire on the other, an edge of Vano peeked out from behind the car's opaque roof of painted, padded metal.

Something about the image nagged at Jhoe's mind, disturbed him in some subtle way that he could not quite put his finger on. Vano looked like that, held that position in the sky when—

"Oh, right," he said, suddenly and brightly. "The *quakes*."

At that moment, the ground began to shake violently. The car's control wheel popped out of Jhoe's grasp, and the trees and buildings around him lurched for a few seconds, until a wall of plastered, whitewashed brick seemed to swerve out in front of him and smash the car to a halt. He was thrown forward against his restraints as he heard the sounds of buckling metal, of smashing glass and plastic.

Almost as an afterthought, he screamed.

And then, suddenly, the quake had ended and Jhoe's voice sounded loud in his ears. He let the scream die away. He looked around him, at the odd sculpture Luna's delicate vehicle had become.

"Oh, my God," he said softly.

He sat there for several minutes, feeling another brief tremor come and go, later feeling the slow, mild rocking sensation that signaled the probable end of quake time. Then he sat for several more minutes in relative silence, the only sound the hot breeze blowing through the car's smashed windows.

Eventually, it occurred to him that he should restart the car and continue on his way. His time out here could have no benefit to his health, surely. Feeling a little sick, he engaged the INVERSU gear, then leaned over, grasped and turned the enabling key. The engine groaned, but did not start.

He released the key and then turned it again, with the same result.

"Oh," he said. "Oh, damn." How would he explain this to Luna? The little vehicle had cost her dearly, he knew.

And then, he became aware of a growing, gnawing sensation in the caverns of his stomach. Damn the

money and the vehicle, he was going to have to *walk*
back to the Power Board building! The drive out had
not taken long, but on foot he could be several hours
getting back. Could he find a shelter that was closer?
No, no, he didn't know his way around well enough for
that!

He pulled up on the door handle and pushed out on
the door, which moved a little and then pushed back.
Had he become trapped? With a surge of energy he
heaved his weight against the door, and then it gave
suddenly and fell open with a squeal of metal.

Anxiously, he hopped out onto the street. From the
outside, the car looked even worse, so he turned away
from it and, without further ceremony, started off down
the street at a brisk walk.

His head was throbbing right along with his stomach, he now noticed, and when he reached a hand up
to touch the center of the pain, the pain sharpened tre-
mendously until he pulled his fingers away again. They
came away slightly bloody.

"Oh, wonderful," he said, and wiped the stain off on
his shiny blue Malhelan trousers. And this gesture
caused him to notice the back of his hand, whose color
had shifted somehow from its normal tan to a sort of
pink-brown shade, like meat just beginning to cook.

A sunburn? Or, well, what would you call this, "alien
spaceship burn"? Or could it be something more sinister? Would radiation damage turn the skin red?

The choker trees seemed to glare at him as he hurried down the empty street.

Chapter Seventeen

"Damn the radiation," Tom said to Dade Soames. He had not raised his voice, but with the icy tone he'd conjured he hadn't really needed to. "I will not burrow underground like a mole while the most important discovery in human history unfolds around us! *You* go hide in the mines, but get that damn telescope working first!"

Dade looked angry. "Don't give me orders, Doctor. I am the second in command here, you'll recall, and if I order you down into the mines, you'll damn well do as I say."

"I damn well will not."

A sigh. Fingers running through bristled hair. "What do you need the telescope for? Specifically, I mean?"

"To observe the objects as they cross the Aurelo debris ring!" Tom said, and this time he did raise his voice. "And if I don't get to it in the next few minutes, they'll have got through and I'll miss the whole thing!"

Dade shook a hand, flat, as though it were an edged weapon he might possibly use against Tom if he had to. "That's all? That's *all*? Tomus, Yezu Manaka is in the Aurelo, in much better position than we are to observe the event."

"Think, Dade. Think! At these angles two observations will give us almost full holographic coverage of the passage. One just gives us a flat picture, with no depth. Which would you rather analyze? Anyway, if luck does not favor Yezu in his placement, his observations may never even reach us."

That seemed to wake Dade up a bit. "Yezu is in danger? Is that what you mean?"

"Quite possibly," Tom agreed. "My friend, and yours too, I think. He may find himself in the objects' path as they blast through. I suspect not, I damn well *hope* not, but I'll need a look through the telescope to know for certain."

Dade's face froze for a moment, and then his eyes began to roll and glitter. "Okay. Okay. You and I will both stay. I'll inform the captain and get the telescope fired up. Meet me on the bridge in two minutes."

It took more than a moment for Tom's anger to fade. "Thank you!" he called out as Dade skated away.

Dade raised a hand and waved it in a gesture which said, rather unmistakably, *yeah, yeah.*

Tom stowed his gear again and skated off after the first mate.

Yezu's eyes flicked from instruments to viewport to instruments again as the ellipsoids zoomed silently past. Tiny pinpoints of blinding light, blue-tinged as they approached, then white and then a throbbing red-orange as they swept away again with those great, bright, diffuse smears running out ahead of them. Like backward-flying comets, but *fast;* bright fireworks tearing across the nighttime sky. Light seconds away, and yet they moved with tremendous angular motion, ten or twenty degrees per second. He should know how to compute their velocities and trajectories from that. He should, but he didn't.

Oh well.

He fancied he could feel the radiation firing through him, gamma rays, protons and electrons kicked relativistically from the ellipsoids' rear ends to rip tiny tracks through his flesh, through his organs and bones. Properly, he should have radiation prophylactics coursing through his system, sensing the passage of charged particles and high-energy gamma rays and rushing in to plug the damaged places, to grab the ends of damaged molecules and piece them quickly back together again.

Properly, the *Rockhammer* should be sitting in a cave somewhere, with full 360-degree shielding instead of the 175 or so they got from huddling against the side of this small planetoid.

Properly, Yezu should view these events from some great far vantage point. Back with Tomus, for example, in the distant Centromo.

Oh well.

He fingered a switch, leaned over to speak into the audio plate mounted on the panel. "Rook to king's rook five, Tomus. Can you see this light show? It will have finished, of course, by the time you hear me say this, but you'll have just started seeing it. Isn't the speed of light funny sometimes? Well, anyway, I admit to a certain discomfort with being this close to the action. I worry for my genome. We all worry, all of us here. Still, since I cannot escape this extraordinary view, I shall take advantage of it.

"I must say, I never expected to find myself in a position like this. I gave up everything I had, for much less than this. How perverse and ridiculous, the twistings and turnings of life, and yet how grand.

"Oh dear, I've begun talking like a poet or a philosopher or something. I think that happens when you've gone petric with fear. I . . . let me end this transmission here, with my dignity still intact. I shall speak with you soon."

Another ellipsoid tore by outside the viewport. So fast! And so close this time! Were these the pursuers or the pursued? Attackers or attacked? Did it matter? Earth had not known a war since his early boyhood, so long ago, and his schools had never taught the subject in detail. He couldn't remember the protocols, who was supposed to do what to whom and at what time.

Or did war even have a protocol? He supposed, after all, that it probably did not. How could anyone enforce such a thing? What use the *threat* of retaliation, when actual, physical violence, without referees or regulators, formed the only medium of exchange?

An endless series of killing and destruction, without governance? How terrible for the combatants, and how much worse for defenseless innocents caught nearby! He shuddered. This thought disturbed him even more deeply than the goings-on outside the viewport.

"There they go," said Dade, his face still pressed, ridiculously, against the telescope viewpiece as if he could crane for a closer view.

Tom grunted. He watched the image repeater's holie screen more comfortably and with probably just as good a view as Dade had.

One of the ellipsoids, having punched through the Aurelo, burning a path for itself by running tail-first with engines on, had flipped around again and made a hard sprint for the distant Soleco hypermass. Now, hours later, it approached its target with no signs of slowing. Half a light-hour behind it, another ellipsoid followed, accelerating even harder. It had gotten a late start, but made up for it with raw speed, shrinking the distance slowly, steadily. It seemed to Tom that it would not catch up, not before the leader had reached Soleco.

The leader already has *reached Soleco,* he reminded himself. The events he witnessed now had already occurred, hours ago.

"Is that one chasing the other one?" Dade asked. "Does it mean to approach and attack it?"

"Presumably so," Tom said, even though he suspected Dade had meant the question rhetorically. "But unless its weapons have terrific range, I don't think it will make it."

"I don't think so either. Hey, does that front one look different to you? Little bit skinnier? Maybe slightly different color?"

Tom grunted. "Yes, I had thought about that. I really find it hard to tell at this range, though."

Indeed, ahead of their plumes of relativistic flame the ellipsoids appeared as little more than dots, and he had to squint hard at them to see any detail. Not that they had much detail to be seen.

"How fast do you think they're accelerating?"

"I don't know," Tom said. "I would think you more qualified to answer that than I."

"Oh," Dade said. "Yeah, I guess so. Hang on a minute."

He pulled away from the viewpiece and swiveled, almost weightless on his feet, to face a computer station. He took up a stylus and began sketching and tapping.

Tom watched the ellipsoids on the telescope's image repeater. The pursuer had a much longer and brighter plume behind it, and yes, it did appear somewhat fatter than the vessel it pursued, and somewhat redder. Could that simply be a function of doppler shift? Oh, of course; it moved away from him more quickly. The light reflected and radiated from it would have its wavelength stretched by that greater velocity.

"Several hundred gee," Dade said. He paused, put the back end of the stylus in his mouth for a moment, then took it out and resumed feeding sketches and figures to *Wedge*'s computer. "Uh . . . about four hundred gee for the leader, and almost five hundred for the pursuer. Their velocity is up around sixty-five percent of lightspeed. I'd have better numbers if I knew the ranges more precisely."

"Ah, well, later when we've got *Rockhammer*'s data we should find it easier to piece this all together. Speaking of which, let's look back at Lacigo again."

"Okay." He twitched his hand, spun the stylus in his fingers. "You know, these guys are *really stupid*. Here they are, inertially shielded and practically massless. . . . For them, that huge acceleration is just about free, and they're pissing it away like it means nothing. Darkness, you give *me* one of those ships, and in three weeks I'd own the cosmos."

Shaking his head, Dade put the stylus back in its niche and pressed a pair of buttons, then went back to the telescope controls again. The image on Tom's repeater screen swung rapidly, taking the two ellipsoids from view. Within a few seconds, the not-quite-blinding glare of Lacigo filled the screen. The dwarf star, with its tiny, vampiric companion, looked like a glowing hand with fingers outstretched.

Only one ellipsoid could still be seen close by, a tiny pinpoint at the head of a curling comet's tail, a tail that formed a thirty-degree arc measuring probably several light-minutes in length. As he watched, the shape of the tail distorted as the particles which comprised it continued their relativistic scattering, moving in straight lines while their point of origin hooked away.

"Where have they all gone?" Tom asked, rhetorically.

"I don't know," Dade answered. "It looks like they're well away from Yezu, though. I'm switching to the spotter scope."

Tom's image remained unchanged.

"Ah. Ah. Look at this!"

Dade pulled his face back, worked the massive dials controlling the telescope's orientation, pressed his face back in the viewer again, and pulled back to work the dials once more.

The repeater image jumped, and jumped, and jumped again. And when it had finished moving, Tom saw the tangle of contrails Dade had intended him to. Good . . . good Lord, what was going on out there?

"You see that?" Dade asked, his face down in the viewpiece again.

"Oh yeah."

"What mess. What do you guess they're up to?"

Tom, not replying, studied the image and thought for several seconds. He saw five trails: two farther ahead, twisted and contorted like carelessly tossed yarn. The other three, considerably less wiggly, seemed to close, purposefully, menacingly, on the pair two or three light-minutes ahead of them.

"The ones out ahead, the ones who flee . . . I think they've attempted to conceal their true position. The pursuers see an image several minutes out of date, and can't detect course changes until well after they occur. Oh, but . . . let me think. The pursuers close in from the sides, yes? You agree, you see that as well?"

Dade grunted noncommittally.

"If the pursuers avoid a stern chase and select a path so that they can move more slowly than the pursued, they take advantage of a smaller time dilation. They can think faster!"

"No, hang on," Dade waved his arms around as if erasing Tom's suggestion from the air between them. "Time dilation isn't a big factor at those velocities. I think they're trying to catch up, but they just haven't managed it yet."

"Hmm. Maybe, yes."

Light blossomed on the repeater screen. Brightness, pouring from the telescope viewpiece, illuminated the side of Dade's face. Tom winced, blinked . . . and stared. One of the ellipsoids under pursuit had disappeared. Had, well, exploded into a ball of glowing gas. The trail behind it went arrow-straight for a moment, and then stopped. The comet's head, diffuse and expanding, had separated from the tail.

"I guess they didn't conceal their location well enough," Dade said.

Tom pointed. "Look at the other one. Its course changes have become more violent. Does it accelerate faster, as well? It looks that way to me."

"Uh, yeah, I think so. He didn't like losing his friend like that."

Tom thought that comment a little overly anthropomorphic, but didn't say so out loud. The object *did* look, well, *unnerved*.

Tom and Dade watched the chase in silence for a few minutes.

The sharper course changes seemed to have done the fugitive some good; it had pulled farther away from its enemies and had even begun, in a tentative sort of way, to loop back around behind them. Tom doubted it could complete this maneuver, but he found he admired the attempt.

"I don't think anything more is going to happen in the next few minutes," Dade said. "Look, they're not on his tail anymore, but it will take him forever to get around onto theirs."

Tom nodded. "I agree. He seems a spirited little fellow though, doesn't he?"

Dade snorted. "Let's take another look at Soleco, you think?"

"Oh, yes. That fellow should be right up to the hypermass by now."

Dade worked the controls for a while, until he'd conjured the proper image. That fellow had, in fact, gotten right up to the hypermass. Its pinpoint glare pushed at the edge of the lens, the distorting mirror, the puckering absence that was Soleco. Behind, the vehicle's plume remained unbent, a result of sustained linear acceleration. But time dilation had caught hold of the craft already; its color had shifted strongly toward the red, so that it looked like a very bright, very twinkly star with a wineglass held up in front of it. Its apparent velocity had dropped by over twenty percent.

The harder it runs, the slower it goes.

Tom knew what that felt like, to be sure. Relativity and hard work and boredom and anxiety—these things had formed the very texture of his recent life. Along with sleep deprivation! He had last closed his eyes twenty hours before, and then only briefly. Still, he suspected the ellipsoids' pilots were having a much longer day.

The pursuing ellipsoid had also turned redder, and while its velocity continued to increase, its rate of visible acceleration was down considerably. Only minutes, now, behind its quarry. The distance between them shrank.

"Ouch," Dade said, pulling back a little from the viewpiece.

Tom squinted as well—the pinpoint glare of the fugitive ellipsoid had grown *really* red, without diminishing in brightness, until Tom found his eyes unable to focus on it. Unable to localize it against the starry background. Unable, soon, to see it at all. Soleco had swallowed it up in layers of dark, gravitational amber.

Tom shook his head in wonder, and in horror. They did this willingly. They dove straight into the hypermass, willingly, without even the slightest effort to scoot around it at the last moment.

"Darkness," Dade Soames muttered quietly. "Bloody, quaking, stinking, festering darkness. And damnation."

Driving as hard as ever, the pursuer slowed as it approached the edge of Soleco's distortion. Twinkling like a garnet under fluorescent light, it reddened. Deepened. Lost focus, vanished. Back once more into the deeps. Brave fellows, or stupid, to continue the chase with such a destination ahead of them.

Darkness, and damnation.

"Yes," Tom agreed. "Quite."

Chapter Eighteen

Miguel awoke to numbness and the sensation of smothering. Something moved against his chest, moved against his face. Covering his mouth, covering and penetrating his nose, a *thing*, a solid, squirming *thing*!

"Don't try to move," said a soft, androgynous voice Miguel did not recognize.

"Mmf!" he said, and tried to sit up.

"Don't try to move," the voice repeated more firmly. "Your nerves have not finished reintegration. Please be patient."

"Miguel," said a more familiar voice. "The first aid kit can't help you if you don't sit still."

He couldn't focus his eyes. Before him, twin images danced, blurry beyond recognition. It seemed very dark, as well, though something told him that was not his vision playing tricks. Not many lights on here. Here . . . in the lander? The floor beneath him hummed, and he could hear and feel warm air hissing from a ventilating unit somewhere not far from his left ear.

He forced his mouth open, spoke around the strange rubber thing that pressed against it. "Beth? Beth, what's happened? Why can't I move?"

"You've broken your back in four places. Now hush, the kit is almost finished."

With effort, he worked his eye muscles until the

twin blurs above him merged into a single, very fuzzy, image. A human form, long-haired and pleasantly curved, sat in a chair at what might be one of the lander's makeshift science stations. And sitting atop Miguel's chest, a squat, white object with stubby protuberances (legs?) that made footprints of aching pressure against his flesh, pressure he had felt before but had not identified.

The object was white, and it had little black arms, little gray tentacles. And limbs that seemed stranger still, and more sinister. Knives and needles? Shiny things, certainly. Shiny things that moved and whirred and rotated in unsettling ways.

Beyond this strange machine, and beyond the vague form of Beth Lahler, he could see other sources of movement. Small lights seemed to crawl up and down the walls, and small shadows with them. Actually, now that he thought about it he could hear the clitter-clatter of tiny metal legs against the panels and bulkheads of the lander. As if an army of insects had arrived to cut it all apart and carry it away.

Of course, they must actually have the opposite intention. Like thing-Barta, *Introspectia* and its children could, on demand, split pieces of themselves off as separate machinelets, and then gobble them up again when they'd finished their tasks. A technologically sensible development, yeah, but creepy enough to keep surprising him, to keep him from ever quite getting used to it.

He thought of insects, with their exoskeletal bodies and their bulging, faceted eyes. Sensible, you had to admit, sometimes even elegant in their physical design. But no matter how fastidiously they cleaned themselves, how scrupulously harmless they kept their activities, even the prettiest of them was still a *bug*—a nasty, unclean thing you didn't want crawling around near you. Particularly not on your face.

He relaxed his eye muscles again and let the view slip back to doubled blurs. He did not want to see the giant bug, no matter how wonderful and helpful, doing its work on top of his body.

"Peng took a bad blow to the head," Beth said, her blur shifting slightly. "I can't figure out what he hit. I mean, his harness doesn't have much give to it, and there just aren't any sharp, solid corners within reach of his head. And nothing big came loose and flew around, either. Anyway, he's got some kind of concussion or something. The kit had to induce a deep coma to keep his blood pressure down."

"Ungh," Miguel replied.

The double smear of Beth leaned over toward him. "You may have noticed the gravity gradient's gone down a bit. I've got a couple of the thrusters working again, and we've sort of limped our way up out of the hole. I think the lander's had it, though. I can't fix it much better than I already have. Even in drydock, I bet they'd just part it out and build a new one."

"Ungh."

"You know, I think this is the longest I've ever had your attention. You always . . . I don't know, turn away when I try to speak to you. I wish I knew why you did that."

He tried to sit up again, winced when the first aid kit trundled higher up his chest to force him down again.

"Don't move. Relax," it said. "If you continue to move, I will administer a disabling current to your motor nerves."

"Get this thing off me!"

"Just like that," Beth said. "You always change the

subject that exact same way. The first aid kit doesn't bother you, *I* do. Why is that?"

Miguel sighed. "Good Lord. Listen, I like you just fine. I just . . ."

"Just what?"

He worked his face muscles, pushing aside the mask that the first aid kit was trying to hold over his mouth and nose. "Damn. Damn. Get this thing off me."

"Don't try to move."

Beth's blur moved again, took up a stiffer posture. "Just answer my question."

"I don't want to get in trouble, all right? As soon as we get back to Earth, I hit the bricks a free man. I don't want a bunch of fines and hearings and stuff slowing me down."

His vision was definitely clearing, now. He could see her frown. "I don't think I follow you."

"Fraternization," he said. "Against policy, right? As I'm sure you're aware."

Beth snorted, beginning to look angry. "You take a lot for granted, mister. I was just talking about *talking*. I do know the regulations, and frankly, I know when to keep my legs crossed. Lord, you've got some nerve!"

Miguel tried to raise his hands, remembered that he could not. But he did feel a tingling in them now. An unpleasant sensation, actually, like sharp objects jabbing him repeatedly, harder and harder.

"I can feel my hands again!" he said.

"Hmph," Beth replied.

Oh, it had become one of *those* things, had it? Like a game of "wimp-out," where the first to swerve from collision course must then admit defeat? It was his turn to snort. "You have me at a disadvantage, Tech Aid. If I've . . . misinterpreted your overtures, let me apologize."

His tone indicated exactly what he thought of that possibility. And hearing that, Beth turned away slightly and did not reply. Had he overstepped himself? Lordy, it felt good to have this out in the open at last, but how much of it, really, existed only in his own head? In these days of long life, popular wisdom maintained that humanity had risen above the absurd tyranny of its hormones. As with the bit about prime numbers, Miguel had his doubts. He had scars enough, both physical and emotional, as evidence to the contrary.

"Maybe I should shut up," he said, more quietly. "For whatever trifling value, Beth . . . Uh . . . Lord. If I did want to get in trouble, you would . . . I would . . . "

"Yes, you should shut up," Beth said. She'd swiveled back toward him again, and now she rose from her chair, did a giddy dance for a moment as her personal gravity shifted. She stooped over, letting her hands and knees drop to the floor. Her face moved right over Miguel's, her breath warm against his skin. Her lips brushed his forehead, and then she pulled away again.

She looked down at him, and though her face was comically sideways, her expression held no trivial emotion. She brushed her hair back, tucked it behind an ear. "After the plasma wave hit, you and Peng both looked dead. My harness had jammed or something, and for a little while I couldn't get up out of my seat. I kept . . . screaming your name, waiting for you to wake up. But you didn't wake up. When the first aid kit pronounced you alive and recoverable, I . . . was very relieved. I didn't think about Peng until later."

The jabbing sensation had spread to Miguel's lower body. He twitched. "Hey, I can feel my legs."

Beth said nothing.

"Oh, I guess I changed the subject again, didn't I? Wait, I can feel my feet!"

"Stop moving," said the first aid kit. Its neutral, androgynous tone had taken on a distinct ring of irritation. "This will stop you from moving."

Miguel did not lose the tingling sensation in his limbs, but a sickly quivering suddenly slammed down on top of it and then vanished just as suddenly. He found, once more, that he could not move.

Fuck! Get it off me! he tried to say, but got no more than a gurgling sound.

"What happened?" Beth snapped, sounding frightened.

"Don't be alarmed," said the monster on Miguel's chest, its calmness of voice now restored. "The patient faces greatest danger of self-injury during the final stages of the reintegration process. I have immobilized him as a precaution."

"Fu . . . uuck," Miguel managed to say.

"The patient will regain mobility in a few minutes, at which time he may resume limited physical activity. Thank you for your patience."

"Get off me . . . you piece . . . of junk."

"I have not finished administering treatment." The first aid kit's voice had taken on a long-suffering quality that, despite its fleshless, genderless tone, sounded remarkably human. An appendage twitched, rotating a hypodermic needle back into its tool caddy and putting a glittering scalpel out in its place. Miguel felt a jolt of alarm for a moment, but the twitching and rotation continued, the scalpel vanishing and a gray, rounded instrument clicking into position instead. The arm moved, then, touching the rounded thing to Miguel's exposed chest.

Exposed? Oh, Lordy, was he wearing any clothing at all? He tried to look down at himself. Bare chest, yes. He couldn't see farther than that, though, with the damn first aid kit in the way. Plus, his eyes wouldn't bulge out far enough. Ow, even the attempt brought a biting pain behind his forehead.

"What troubles you?" Beth asked, seeing his exertions, his facial contortions. "Aside from the obvious, I mean."

Miguel's face burned. "How much clothing . . . have I got on?"

She grinned down at him. "Afraid I might sneak a peek at your equipment and lose control, Tech Chief?"

"Beth," he pleaded. She seemed to enjoy his discomfort a little too well!

"You've got your trousers on, don't worry."

"Ah. Good." Relief washed over him like a cooling breeze. "The embarrassment of this situation . . . you have no idea. Remind me . . . not to break my back in the future."

Her face grew serious at that remark, and she glanced over in the direction of First Mate Peng's seat, at the fore of the lander. "It could have been worse. Really, you should have seen yourself an hour ago."

Miguel could think of nothing to say to that, and so they remained silent for a while. The tingling in his arms and legs intensified gradually, and then began to fade away again after a minute or so had gone by.

Experimentally, he wiggled his fingers. They wiggled, sure enough. He tried his toes, and then his ankles and knees and wrists, his hips and his elbows and shoulders. Everything responded. Small movements, yes, and a little weakly and sluggishly executed, but still a great improvement over his earlier paralysis.

"I can move," he said, to Beth Lahler and the first aid kit both.

The kit trundled another few centimeters up his

chest, stuck an instrument in front of his left eye and fired a blinding purple light into it.

"Ow!"

"Pupil dilation normal," it said. "Neuro-electrical field status approaching normal. Reconstructive agents have begun self-disassembly. Do you feel an itching or burning sensation in your back and neck?"

"No."

"Excellent. I will now permit you to resume limited physical activity. Please move cautiously for the next several hours."

For his first trick, Miguel tried to knock the first aid kit off his chest with a lateral sweep of his arm. Unfortunately, his muscles proved somewhat difficult to control, and the kit, with its low center of gravity, proved difficult to tip. As if hurried by his motions, though, the kit tucked away several instrumented arms and stepped quickly onto the floor.

"It has pleased me to serve you," it said, with what sounded like a sincere tone. "Please call out if you experience any further discomfort."

Miguel attempted an obscene gesture, failed.

With surprising speed, the kit scuttled across the floor and, turning on its side with a little hopping motion, slapped into a wall-niche obviously shaped and sized to accept it. It tucked its limbs in still further, and a panel door slid down over it and merged seamlessly with the gray bulkhead. In that brief, flickering moment, Miguel had gotten his only clear look at the machine that had saved his life. It did, vaguely, resemble a box with handles, like something he might actually recognize as a first aid kit from his own time and place. If such a box had mated with live crabs, the offspring might look like that: smooth, antiseptic-white carapace arching over an array of specialized limbs. It had had a bright red cross painted across its back.

Miguel tried to get up. His limbs didn't feel much like helping him, though, despite what felt like a quarter-gee or less in the gravity department.

"Here," Beth said, offering him a hand. She pulled him into a sort of sitting position, and he curled his legs, crossing them slightly so he had something stable to balance on. His head pounded. The lander swam and shivered around him.

Sighing, he put a hand over his eyes. Buzzing, blackness at the edges of his vision. The taste of metal. As slowly as he had sat up, it was still too much for him in this weakened state. Slowly, his bearings returned.

"Okay?" Beth asked as he took the hand away from his face again.

"Yeah, I guess." He put his hands flat on the floor to steady himself. They felt stronger, more clearly under his control. "Where, uh . . . how far out of the hole have we got?"

"Not too," she said, grimacing and shaking her head. "I can lift you into your chair if you want to see out the viewport."

He thought about that, nodded. "Yeah, well, hold on to me, at least. I'm going to try and get myself up."

Pushing with his hands, he levered himself up a bit and slid his legs underneath him until he knelt on the hard floor. Then, with greater effort, he straightened, bent a knee up and put one foot down flat against the floor. He swayed a bit, until Beth's steadying hands tightened on his shoulders. Oh, her touch tingled, it threatened to stun him more thoroughly than the first aid kit had.

He pushed up and got his other foot under him. Like a child attempting a first walk, he stood splay-legged, arms waving around for balance. His head swam as its local gravity dropped to zero, and even a little ways beyond. Swaying, he caught the edge of his seat, gripped it tightly. His strength picked that moment to fail.

"Falling," he said, with as much calm and dignity as he could muster.

"Nope." Beth had shifted her grasp to his armpits, and she lifted with them, simultaneously raising him to his feet and pulling his body tight against hers. Her curves pressed against him, warm and soft and immediate. Something stirred and stiffened inside his trousers.

"We're going to turn," Beth warned. Her tone held no trace of embarrassment, nor of passion. Only a sort of brusque cheerfulness, the voice of one stranger to another on a crowded skytrain.

"Okay," he said. Together, they swiveled until he felt the chair against the backs of his legs. "Does that . . . can I sit?"

"Wait a second." She did something with her foot. Behind him, the chair shifted slightly. "Okay."

Gently, she began to lower him into the seat.

The floor, no, the entire *lander* jerked upward and to one side. The lights went out. Miguel fell into the padding, and Beth tumbled in on top of him. Both cried out, and instinctively he wrapped his arms around her.

"What happened?" He shouted. "*What happened?*"

Beth struggled against him. "We've had a deuterium leak since the plasma wave hit. Damn, I didn't think it would run out so fast. Let me get to the panel."

Miguel's grip remained tight. "We've run out of fuel? We've stranded ourselves?"

"Miguel, let me go. Let me get to the panel."

"Why? What can you do?"

"Let me go!"

Her breasts felt hot against his bare chest. Her hair

had tumbled across his face. White light spilled in through the viewport, casting shadows across her. She had never looked so beautiful.

Regretfully, Miguel unlaced his fingers and loosened his grip on her. She flopped against him for a thrilling moment, then rose a bit. But rather than rising fully, she paused, and then settled back down into his lap again.

"The panel lights have gone blank," she said, with an oh-yes-of-course sort of tone. "The batteries shorted, and the generators have no fuel. Right. We *are* stranded, Miguel. We can't do anything. We can't even call for help."

He should answer her intelligently. He should let her up, and get up himself, and they should find a way to fix the lander and get out of here. But Lordy, he just couldn't help himself.

He kissed her. She had no reaction to that, so he kissed her again, and again, and then his hands were roaming across those beautiful curves he'd admired for so long.

"Miguel!" she cried out, struggling in his arms.

His heart sank. Hormones had betrayed him after all, seizing him in this moment of weakness. What troubled realms had they just cast him into?

"Miguel," Beth said, turning her face toward his, brushing long hair out from between them. "The first aid kit said, 'limited physical activity.' Let *me* do it."

Suddenly, her mouth moved against his skin, and her hands roamed across *his* curves, quickly finding the bulge in his pants and the means to free it from bondage. Her breath shuddered, her voice moaned with unfettered desire.

Astonished, Miguel could not think what to do. Could not think . . . Did not need to. His muscles still felt weak, but his blood burned, it boiled inside him. And Beth's muscles were doing just fine. He sat back into the chair's thick padding and let his hormones take over.

"Doctor Manaka?"

A hand shook Yezu, firmly. He opened his eyes. Techman Chase stood beside his bunk. Or hovered, actually, in this planetoid's abominably weak gravity.

"Yes? What?"

"Doctor, your spectral analyses are complete. You asked me to wake you when the data was ready."

"Oh." He rolled away, covering his eyes against the light. "I've changed my mind. No, wait. I haven't."

"You sure?"

Rising, Yezu gave a weary nod. "Yes, thank you. I'm afraid my stronger guilt defeats my strong intent. I've monopolized your computer long enough."

Chase snorted. "You certainly have. If there were any gravity around here, Captain would be pacing holes in the floor. As it is, he's bouncing around, making everybody crazy. He loves to keep a few trajectories in his pocket, just in case we need to move in a hurry, but this time we just haven't had the chance to compute any."

"Go any direction," Yezu said, tiredly swinging his feet out, then grabbing the edge of the trunk to steady himself when, nearly weightless, they continued to swing past the "down" position. "I bet you a pound of centrokrist you'll never come to grief."

Chase shook his head. "Bet me all you like. Captain won't believe it unless it comes out of the computer."

"Ech. I find that odd, considering the quality of your computers."

"Now, now," Chase said. "Be nice. We've been very accommodating to your needs, I think."

"Of course. Of course you have."

Malhelan computing revolved around the quaint and practically useless notions of central processing and random-access digital memory. One had to feed the computers endless streams of didactic, excruciatingly explicit instructions to get them to do anything at all, and even then the slightest error sufficed to bring them, messily, to a halt. The systems employed a number of elaborate schemes for trapping and correcting errors, but these didn't help much. Dressing up a stone ax, as he sometimes said to Chase and the others, did not make it steel.

"There's still some food in the galley, if you'd like to eat while you work."

Yezu waved his hand dismissively. "Not hungry, thank you."

Chase nodded, more from impatience, Yezu thought, than out of any real sense of politeness. He turned and, bracing a foot against one of the bunks, shot through the hatch and away down the length of *Rockhammer*'s central corridor.

Yezu slid from his bunk, drifted for a moment before finding stability in the near weightlessness. His stomach churned. He wondered when he would get out of this rotten place, when circumstances would again let him find his work and his comfort in the same vicinity. Not soon, he supposed.

Minutes later, he found himself at the computing station he thought of as "his," the one with the window and the telkom and the almost-sensible layout of controls and displays. In point of fact, the crew shared this little niche in the same way that they shared the galley and the showers and the gruesome "sanito" facilities.

But Yezu hogged the station whenever he could, and complained when he could not, and for the most part, the crew humored him in this. His projects had frequently kept the computer at a deathly crawl anyway, so they'd found little need for the workstation.

"Queen to king's knight four," Yezu said into the telkom plate, holding down the RECORD/TRANSMIT button. "Good morning, Tomus, or have you had your morning already? Good evening, then, or maybe I should just say 'good.' Unfortunately, I have precious little 'good' to speak of myself. The living conditions have really begun to wear me down. Oh!"

He took his finger off the button. What in heaven's name . . . ? Outside "his" window, he could see a peculiar smudge of white, about the size and shape of his thumb, with a much brighter speck at its center. He depressed the button again.

"Well, one of our friends has come back for a visit. From the look of things, I'd say his course is on a line with *Rockhammer*'s current position. Moving which way? I cannot tell. Hold on while I inform the bridge."

He pressed some other buttons. The INTERKOM light came on. No picture appeared on the screen before him, though, no doubt because he hadn't tripped the right controls. Well, to blazes with it.

"Bridge. First Officer speaking."

"Navel of the world. Manaka speaking," Yezu said, following the informal protocol of Rockhammerian humor. Had he been farther forward, he'd have said "nipple" or "cake-hole." Farther aft, he'd have named a less pleasant anatomical feature.

"Go ahead."

"Have you spotted the, uh, bogey outside my station?"

The first officer cleared his throat as if preparing

to deliver a criticism. "Repeat and confirm, Manaka. Bogey at two-seventy by ought? Range presently indeterminate?"

"Yes." He sighed. He tired of the Malhelans' professional banter, their steadfast refusal to speak normally when discussing matters pertaining to *Rockhammer*'s maintenance and operation. Still, refusing to go along with the joke would get him nowhere. "Bogey at two-seventy by zero zero. Range indeterminate. I confirm."

"Acknowledged. Bogey is on our scopes. Radar soundings indeterminate at this time."

Yes, of course. The ellipsoids did not reflect radio waves in the same way they did visible light, so that *Rockhammer*'s old-style radar equipment gave decidedly questionable readings at times. This left them with little means, other than patience and sharp eyes, to determine the objects' ranges and velocities.

"If it helps," Yezu said, "the ellipsoid has brightened and shifted colors. It appears distinctly bluish in hue."

"Acknowledged. We confirm your observation."

He sighed. So early in the day, conversations like this one did not amuse him.

"Manaka out." He switched communication modes, went back to his Centromo transmission. "Tomus, these Malhelans can wear me farther down in an hour than convention lectures could in a four-day weekend. Really, *Wedge* has a completely different personality. Count yourself luckier than I. Now, where were we? Have I moved yet? Yes, I have."

The computing station had grown brighter, and bluer. He looked up into a dazzling blaze of sapphire light outside his window. It filled the entire view, swelling and brightening rapidly.

"My God," he said, "Talina. Be happy, my love, wherever you are. Tomus, I believe that thing is going to hit us."

He stared silently for a few moments. Such a *pretty* shade of blue, such a *pretty*—

His universe ended.

Chapter Nineteen

Tom ran to the viewport as light blossomed outside it, blossomed through to *Wedge*'s interior despite the instant polarization of the glass. He had to close his eyes, turn his head aside, and even then the glare burned like hot sunlight. And then it faded, and he opened his eyes, and he saw a small star burning a little ways off from the Lacigo/Malsato pair. Right where the Aurelo cut around it. Right where the Malhelan ship *Rockhammer* had been parked.

Presently, the star dimmed to a cloud of murky gray vapor. Not large; he could easily cover it up with two fingers.

"Yezu?" he said quietly, uselessly. He skated backward, bounced lightly into the com station once again. Activated the telkom. Transmitted.

"*Yezu?*"

Distant, of course. He wouldn't hear a reply for hours. He wouldn't. Hear. A reply. He depressed the transmit button again.

"Come on, speak to me. I don't find this funny."

Indeed, tears had begun to form and sting in his eyes. What an abysmally bad joke, not funny in the least.

Dade Soames appeared, looking stricken.

"What an abysmal joke," Tom said to him.

"Tomus, were you watching that? Did you . . . Darkness, I . . . "

Tom attempted a smile. "That sewer rat, he hates to lose. I'd have beaten him in another three moves."

Dade nodded, his facial expression peculiar, concerned. He reached a hand out toward Tom, paused, retracted it.

"I suppose I'll miss the whiny sound of his voice," Tom remarked. Indeed, the universe already seemed a larger place, colder and emptier without Yezu Manaka to fill it. Tom choked, gagged on the bolus of this damnable thought. And the tears came forth.

Jafre stepped away from his window, back toward his desk and the telkom there, the telkom to which he had been almost surgically attached for the past fifty hours. All traces of that hellish light outside had faded.

Damnation! Lacigo and Malsato were on the other side of the sky right now, the whole planet of Unua standing between them and himself. And still the explosion was visible! How far out would conflagration like that be fatal? Could anyone in or near the Aurelo be left alive? He doubted it.

How many people dead up there, five hundred? Nine hundred?

He boiled, suddenly, with feeling akin to rage. How *dare* they? How *dare* these aliens shoot up his star system, murder his citizens? It was *personally* outrageous, *personally* unacceptable.

"Yes," he said to Gerane on the other side of the telkom. Gerane, in the city of Brava, five thousand kilometers away. "I saw it."

"Streets have been filling up again," Gerane said with clear agitation. "Everyone wanted to get out and see the blue sky, and then nobody wanted to get back in the shelters again. Even after Lacigo set. All night long, wandering around, looking up at the stars. Like some quaking festival!"

"The explosion was not far below the horizon for you people," Jafre said. "Correct?"

"Yes. Darkness, we're lucky it wasn't right overhead. That's all I need, half a million people staggering around blind."

Jafre nodded at the telkom image. "Yeah. Yeah. Now listen to me: I don't want you running around with your head chopped off and your dick hard. Do you hear me? I find any panic over there and I'll see to it you dig tunnels out on Dua for the rest of your miserable life. Clear?"

"Crystal," Gerane said. He did not look happy.

"Round up the civilians and get them back in the shelters. *Do not* let them out this time. I will not be held responsible for any further loss of life. Do you understand me? Have I made myself perfectly clear?"

"Yes. Perfectly." The words crisp, distinctly angry now. And that was fine. Anger would harden Gerane, firm his resolve, and an explicit enemy, even if it was Jafre himself, would lend him the crucial sense of focus he would need in coming hours.

Jafre cut the connection without further ado, and punched in the code for Port *Chrysanthemum,* director's office.

A man's face appeared on the screen. Wendall, that new secretary of Asia's. He looked as harried as everyone else Jafre had been speaking with lately.

"Get me Asia," Jafre said. "Now."

Wendall didn't nod, didn't speak, didn't appear to move at all. But his image vanished, and Asia Gill's took its place.

"Madame Director," Jafre said formally.

Asia glared. "Drop the shit, Jafre, I'm very busy right now. Did you see that explosion?"

"Everyone saw it, Asia. How is the station?"

"The station has been better. Lacigo was dead center above us when it went off, and we've lost a bunch of instrumentation. If you think that event was visually bright, you should have seen its emissions down in radio frequencies. Played hell with the electronics. It'll be a few minutes before we recover."

"I think," Jafre said, "that one of the eggies hit a rock in the Aurelo. Moving *fast*, I mean. Releasing a *lot* of energy."

Asia nodded. "I think that, too."

"If they can screw up like that, my light, they can hit Unua as well. Drive their fist right through the heart of Malhela. There'd be nothing left of us, nothing but handful of ships, plus the mines and prisons out on Dua. How many women and children are there off the Unuan surface right now? One hundred? With ninety of them right there on your station?"

She waved her hands at him, shutting him up. "I've been thinking the same thing. If Unua gets it, *Chrysanthemum* gets it as well, and suddenly there's no colony here at all. I'm going to move the station."

"Can you do that?"

"The original engines are still intact," Asia said, "and I keep small amount of antimatter in containment. My staff has always complained about the cost and the risk, but I thought it would be stupid to lose that capability."

"Bravo, my dear. Bravo. Get out as quickly as you can. Have you had any contact with that bitch Lin Chelsea?"

"Yes. She's back in the inner system again, looking for some kind of shuttlecraft. Apparently she lost some people down near Malsato or something. I'm not sure of the details."

Jafre seethed. "Damn her. Damn her. You tell her to get her ass back *here*. We need protection, and she's the closest thing we've got."

"You tell her. She won't listen either way."

"She might. I doubt her employers would be very happy if we transmitted a formal complaint."

"You would do that?" Asia looked astonished. "In the middle of all this, an interstellar broadcast? Damn the cost, damn the consequences? Just to get her in trouble?"

"Yes. Absolutely. I need leverage on that woman. I *need* her, but she won't ever do what I tell her to do."

Now Asia's eyes narrowed, her lips drawing together. "I smell hidden agenda, mister. What are you up to?"

He flashed her a look of annoyance, a warning beacon in the night. "Don't start with me, Asia. You've got a station to move, and I've got a bitch starship captain to speak with."

He cut the connection. Quaking hell, but he wanted to rest. But like a machine, like a thing never permitted a moment's leisure, he was on the keys again, placing the next call. Not to Chelsea, not yet. He had first to look after the city of Fiera, and the mining stations at the poles and at the oceans.

So many people scurrying around the planet, and he'd be damned if he'd let any more get themselves killed while he was on duty.

Chelsea stared wearily at the holie screen in front of her. Crap and crap and more crap, why couldn't she just send a personality fax and have done? Jafre Shem demanded such a ridiculous share of her waking time, wanting constantly to be briefed, and comforted, and obeyed.

And now he'd stooped to petty threats in order to have his way. She felt sorely tempted to ignore him altogether, to let him vent his rage to the empty ether on whatever schedule pleased him most. But perhaps the man had some valid concerns, after all.

Yes, his planet faced a terrible danger. Yes, the technology at her disposal far outstripped anything Jafre had access to at home. But still, weaponless, and outfitted with only a rudimentary array of science instruments, *Introspectia* couldn't actually *do* anything to help the Malhelans, aside from jaunting around, recording and analyzing the events as they unfolded.

Indeed, she felt a terrible impotence about the entire situation, and a constant fear that this feeling would leak through to sully the confidence of her crew. How much more helpless must Jafre feel, cringing on the surface of his little planet, unable even to move out of the way should danger approach? His reaction to the stress manifested in unpleasant ways, but even so she should try to maintain a little empathy.

She was, after all, a sort of ambassador. And given the magnitude and importance of the circumstances, she felt the eyes of history looking back at her, watching every word, every decision with the cool, smug detachment that came from *knowing* how things would work out in the end. Oh, how critically they would dissect her!

Best face forward, then. Make it look good.

She cleared her throat.

"Mr. President. Although your threats have scant meaning for me, the fact that you resort to them shows me how deeply your convictions run. I believe I understand your position. Once we've completed the retrieval of our crewmates, *Introspectia* will proceed with all possible haste to the vicinity of Unua. We will then do what we can to assist you. I hope you find this satisfactory."

And fuck you, history, she wanted to add, but did not.

Asia gripped the arms of her seat as Port *Chrysanthemum* trembled. Like a quake that never quite ended, the shaking rose and fell in intensity, produced sounds that were louder at some times and softer at others.

"Structural failure in the docking port," someone called in through her office door. "The rivets are popping!"

"Fine," she called back, though she knew full well that it was not fine at all. After four centuries of slow modification, Port *Chrysanthemum* had almost as much in common with the city of Verva as it did with the spaceship it once had been. The rumbling antimatter engines could produce no more than a twentieth of a gee along the spin axis, hardly significant by propulsive standards. And yet, this twentieth of a gee fell perpendicular to the centripetal "down" so much of the port had been designed for, like stiff wind through old and fragile trees. Things were breaking all over.

She could only hope that nothing important broke loose, that the hull did not burst, that the superstructure did not lose axial integrity and collapse the whole ship like an empty gourd.

On the holie, Verva looked small and distant. Funny; for so long the planet had hung there, rotating slowly but seeming otherwise not to move. Then, as the acceleration began to pile up into serious delta-velocity, Verva had suddenly begun to shrink. Now, she felt she could almost watch the changes with her eyes. Well, maybe not quite.

They had broken away from Unua orbit, though, and leaped out onto ellipse that circled giant Vano, ellipse that stretched and widened each moment as the engines continued to fire. At this rate they would reach cold, airless Dua in thirty-five hours. And then . . . well, she didn't want to think that far ahead.

It occurred to her, suddenly, that she had fulfilled her childhood dream, earning the title of starship captain. On the very tub she'd administered for the past eighty years! Her destination might be somewhat closer than the stars, but that couldn't be helped. And anyway, she'd long ago left childhood behind.

"Asia, the reactor is still running much too hot."

She sighed. "I see. Did you open the coolant valves all the way?"

The young woman, Lisa Jan, nodded. "Yes, we did. But there isn't enough coolant to fill the entire system. We've got these big air pockets circling through the pipes, and everytime they cross the reactor the temperature jumps another half a degree."

Asia fought back anger. So her starship was misbegotten and klugey. No one had ever expected it to move at all!

"Okay," she said. "Okay. Siphon water out of the waste recycling systems—*clean* water, mind you—and add it slowly to the coolant."

"I don't know how we'd cross-couple those systems," Jan protested.

"Find a way!"

"Yes, ma'am." Jan turned, stomped off to her duties.

And so it went for awhile. The image of Unua was distinctly smaller now, and the edge of Vano had begun to creep into view. In a few hours, Unua would be a dot on the brown dwarf's smoldering face.

Later, it seemed to her that the shuddering of Starship *Chrysanthemum* had begun to intensify. She paused, looking around her office-cum-bridge, watching the walls vibrate around her. Yes, it had definitely gotten stronger!

Fumbling at the telkom which was her viewport holie, she punched controls, paged Lisa Jan. There was a pause, and then:

"Yes? Lisa Jan here. Yes?" There was no picture.

"What the hell is going on?" Asia demanded.

"We added water to the coolant loop," Jan said quickly. "But it burst! One of the lines burst! Reactor temperature is *really* climbing now."

Asia pounded a fist on her desk. "Darkness, woman, I told you to add it *slowly*! The cooling oil is over five hundred degrees; it'll turn water to instant steam! What the hell is wrong with you?"

"We did add it slowly, Asia." Lisa Jan sounded offended. "Ten cc's a second. That pipe must have been about to split anyway. Oh no, the reactor walls are melting! Darkness! Shut it down! Shut it down!"

This last was directed, not at Asia, but at someone behind and away from the telkom Jan was using.

Asia leaned forward. "Have we lost containment?"

No answer. The other end was a chaos of shouts, machine noises, distant alarms.

"HAVE WE LOST CONTAINMENT!"

A new voice, unfamiliar. "The reactor is ruined, we're shutting it down. Antimatter containment is intact."

She breathed a sigh of relief. "Okay. Okay. Who is this? What do you mean when you say 'ruined'?"

The shuddering of Starship *Chrysanthemum* rose to a new peak and then suddenly ceased.

The silence came as a shock, like a physical blow that left Asia weakened and empty.

"Uh," said the voice on the other side of the telkom.

"Hello? Yeah, little melted pieces of it are floating out the back."

"I see. How long before it can be repaired?"

The voice barked out a sort of laugh. "Is this Asia Gill?"

"Yes."

"Uh, Madam Director, the reactor core looks like grilled cheese on toast. Nobody's going to be fixing it anytime soon."

Asia felt tickly sensations in the pit of her stomach. "But . . . we're out in the middle of nowhere. How are we supposed to get out of here?"

The voice on the other end declined to respond.

"Jafre, I think the battle is coming closer, and we're just hanging here dead. Can you send *Introspectia* out here to rescue us? Can you send *anybody* out here to rescue us?"

Thanks to the light-lag, Jafre's image took several seconds to respond. "I'll see what I can do. I think *Introspectia* is still hanging around at Malsato. There's one ship in orbit right now, but they seem to be low on fuel or something. They were very upset when they learned Port *Chrysanthemum* had been moved."

"We have no shielding out here. I've got most everyone holed up between the water tanks, but I'm not sure how much good that'll do. Please, come get us as soon as you can."

After the usual pause, Jafre grimaced. "Nobody's coming to grief if I can help it, Asia, but you've got hundreds of people up there. Even if I can get hold of this ship, it can't take everyone. What's it going to do, push the whole station?"

"*Introspectia* could do that. I'm sure of it."

Jafre's face was serious. "There's no way *Introspectia*

is going to reach you before the eggies do. I don't think *anyone* can reach you before then."

"Darkness!" She pounded her desk. "Damnation! These 'eggies' are a threat to public safety. I'm ordering them destroyed."

Pause. "I was thinking the same thing. But how? Pull alongside them with mining lasers? They're made of centrokrist; how are we supposed to hurt them?"

"Damn it, we'll just *drop* stuff in their path. They can't always steer so good, we've seen that."

Pause. "Asia, my light. The eggies have ignored us up to now. Is it a good idea to stir them up?"

"Sit up here and ask me that," she fumed. "How many people are dead already? Those exhaust plumes are half million kilometers long and maybe ten thousand wide, and in a few hours we could have dozens of them swinging around Vano like planet-sized welding torches. They could hit you, they could hit me, they could hit the stations on Dua. . . . " She paused, glaring at him with all her fury unveiled. "They have no right to do this. We've worked hard in this system, it's *ours*. They have no right to be here."

Pause. *Long* pause. "That strikes a chord," Jafre finally said. "Indeed, who do these . . . *people* think they are? I'll talk to Chelsea; you talk to our own ships. If we can hurt the eggies, or at least frighten them away from the inhabited areas, we should start immediately."

"Agreed," she said in her best official tone.

The telkom went blank.

Chapter Twenty

Miguel sat up suddenly. What was that noise? Like a giant hammer had pounded a metal plate, once, firmly. He looked around.

The light had gone. The white glow of Malsato's halo had vanished from the viewport, replaced with blank blackness. Not even starry blackness, but a total void. A few lights winked here and there inside the lander, driven by capacitors that had not yet failed, and these reflected from the viewport as if from a shiny black mirror.

He tried to scratch his mouth in puzzlement, and then knew a stronger puzzlement when he felt the mask there. But yes, he remembered, the first aid kit had made them put on gas filter masks when the air circulator's main capacitor cut out and the backup switched in.

"Don't worry," it had said. "Between the masks and the remaining capacitor power, you can easily survive another six days." That news had not exactly comforted them.

SlamClang! That noise again, real, not something he'd dreamed or imagined!

He shook Beth awake.

"Mnuh?" she said through the filter mask.

"Wake up," he said quietly. "Something going on here. I don't know what."

She sat up, the emergency blanket spilling down around her. "What? What? Who is that?"

"Shh!"

"Oh." Quieter. "Oh, Miguel. You startled me. What happened to the light?"

"I don't know."

SlamClang!

Beth was staring at the blank viewport. "Wait a minute," she said. "I see *rivets* out there. That's the inside of the docking blister! Miguel, *Introspectia*'s come and picked us up!"

Hurriedly, she took up an edge of the blanket again and pulled it against her, covering her breasts in the dimness.

Just in time.

With a new, different banging noise, the inner and outer doors of the airlock unlatched themselves, one sliding upward, the other down. Yellow light spilled in around silhouetted figures.

"Confirmed, they are alive," one of the figures said, in a masculine voice that rang with amusement. "They're, um, also naked."

Miguel sat stupidly in the wash of light, not moving, feeling his skin turn hot with embarrassment.

"Acknowledged," said another voice, also amused. "I'll inform the bridge."

"First Mate Peng has received serious injuries," Beth said coldly to the men as they entered. "Stop gawking and take him down to the infirmary."

Dade stuck his head into the science niche and grinned humorlessly at Tom. "Secure your equipment," he said.

Tom looked up from the spectrograph to which he'd devoted his attentions since Yezu . . . since . . . "Huh?" he inquired.

"Secure your equipment. We've been ordered to move out and intercept the eggies. We've been ordered to destroy them."

Tom blinked. "What?"

"Please secure your equipment, Doctor. A cluster of ellipsoids will pass near here in just over an hour, headed for the inhabited planets. Captain Vitter intends to put us in their way."

"I . . . see," Tom said.

Dade nodded somberly. "Yeah. Tomus, I . . . yeah." He turned and left.

Chelsea gaped at the holie screen. *You want me to* what, *you puffed-up little fool?*

But the message continued. "I realize you won't take orders from me. I realize you'll object to the very *idea* of this. But listen to me, Captain. I've got five million people who are maybe about to get fried. Please, I'm asking you, please intercept the aliens. Turn your engines on them, melt them down! You are the only one who can help us right now."

Turn your engines on them. Melt them down.

Good Lord, did he really expect this of her? To fire on an alien intelligence, to attempt the destruction of something so obviously valuable and important, something with which she hadn't established even the most fleeting of contact? That would be insane, criminal. The eyes of history would never forgive her, nor would she ever forgive herself.

She configured the holie for a reply, configured herself, her inhuman softlinked face and her all-too-human voice.

"No," she said simply, and turned the holie off.

She would rendezvous with the aliens, yes, but peacefully. She would *make* them listen to her, *make* them understand her.

Through the link, she signaled for data from the tracking systems. State vectors of all known ellipsoids? Identify slow movers. Identify those with low accelerations. There. Yes, and there, and *there* was well. Ah hah. She rerouted the data through to Navigator Jones.

"Lay in an intercept course at maximum acceleration," she said aloud to him. "That cluster right there." She indicated, linkwise, which cluster she meant. After looping around through the empty quarters of Malhela system, this group would soon pass by the Centromo debris field on its way toward the brown dwarf and its planets. Assuming nothing changed too remarkably in their behavior, of course.

Their acceleration seemed surprisingly low, only about fifteen gee's, and they did not obviously pursue or flee from any of the other ellipsoids. A stately patrol, then, perhaps open to communication. If she dared to reactivate the conversion fields with thrusters on full, she could bring *Introspectia* in on a tangent to their course, and hang within visual range for several minutes before dropping behind.

She transmitted the gist of this thought to Navigator Jones, as well.

"Yes, ma'am," Jones replied. "Course laid in."

Everything became a little heavier. And a little heavier still.

"Activate conversion fields."

"Activated."

"Full power."

"Full power."

One gee. Two gee's. Three. Three point two. Three point two three.

"Maximum acceleration, Captain."

Chelsea nodded politely. "Thank you, Jones, I can read the instruments. I can feel it, too."

"Yes, ma'am."

Useless, redundant, without a task to perform, Tom sat and listened to the chatter on *Wedge*'s interkom circuits.

"Approaching intercept point."

"Acknowledged."

"Engaging secondary reaction control."

"Starboard thruster 2AS not responding."

"Acknowledged. Switching autopilot configuration."

"Affirmative. Lock."

It went on like that, without pausing or changing in character. The operation of *Wedge* seemed inordinately complex to Tom, a few small capabilities divided into myriad subsystems and sub-subsystems, each requiring at least one operator while the ship traveled. During mining operations, he understood, many of the crewmates switched stations, or reconfigured the stations they had, to perform a largely different set of tasks. But still the ship required all of them, or nearly all of them, to function properly. And of course, they could all use a pick and shovel when necessary, and on occasion this did occur.

Strange. He felt sure that a ship like *Introspectia* could get by with only one or two crewmates, that the presence of dozens owed more to tradition than to necessity. Well, during emergencies he supposed it would help to have a lot of extra hands. And, probably, the passengers required more direct and careful attention than the starship itself.

Wedge, it seemed, had no extra hands standing by for emergencies, and of course it had no effective means of dealing with passengers, as he and Yezu had come to know well.

Ah, Yezu.

At least you had a window, my friend. At least you could see the thing that ended your life. Damn, how Tom wished for the same luxury! Instead, he lay here in his bunk, out of everyone's way like a self-acknowledged piece of animated uselessness. . . . Bah. Death would come for him unannounced.

Tom did not believe in an afterlife, did not believe he'd wake up, blinking and confused, in a cloudy heaven somewhere. His life would simply end, so swiftly that he would never even know he had died. Like a stage drama with the last scene cut out, the lights suddenly and meaninglessly extinguished, cutting the actors off in mid-sentence. Worse than that, even, for once his curtain had dropped, he wouldn't ever realize he'd lived at all.

Such futility. Such damned futility. For this he had crossed the ocean of stars.

"Anomalous readings on the radar," an interkom voice warned.

"Acknowledged."

"Telescope lock achieved. Tracking targets."

Tom felt his heart beating faster. The moment of truth inched closer.

"Visual contact!"

"Visual contact confirmed."

"Plotting trajectory solutions."

"Acknowledged."

What did Yezu know, in those final fleeting moments? Did everything fall into place for him, his life flashing before his eyes, snapping into focus, becoming a whole, clear entity for the first and final time? Had he simply stared, his mind a blank?

"I get multiple solutions."

"Have you eliminated imaginary roots?"

"Affirmative. I'm still getting multiple solutions."

"Update observations."

"Telescope tracking update."

"Solution lock. Solution lock. Intercept coordinates to follow."

"Acknowledged."

"Coordinates received."

"Dump the hold! Dump the hold!"

Wedge shivered for a moment, and Tom heard the sound of the cargo hatches blasting open, dumping their load of Centromo gravel.

"Dumped."

"Initiate escape trajectory."

"Acknowledged."

"Here they come!"

"AAAAAAAAH!"

Tom sat up sharply, banging his head against the supports of the bunk above his own. They were screaming on the bridge! Somebody was *screaming* on the *bridge*!

"Target course change."

"Course change confirmed. Negative collision."

"There they go!"

"They're going to *burn* us! They're going to *burn* us!"

"Shut the hell up."

"Hey, hey, what is that? There's something behind them."

"That's *Introspectia*! Darkness, look out!"

Silence. More silence. The bulkhead beside Tom reached out and punched him once. Twice. Not painfully, not hard. Silence followed. An odd thought occurred to him: might he escape Yezu's fate and survive these events after all?

"Burners on secondary," said a calm voice on the interkom. "Looks like we made it."

"Secondary burners, acknowledged."

Miguel, having got back to his station and entered the link only a few minutes before, had not really felt prepared to deal with another emergency. But here one came, nonetheless.

"Captain!" he shouted, after activating the comlink. "Discrete gravitational sources ahead. Change course! Right now!"

The captain's thing-face appeared on the holie. "I see it, Mr. Barta. Course change initiated. Analysis?"

Miguel "watched" as the gravitational sources . . .

Miguel$_{(1)}$: One object massing approximately two hundred tons.

Miguel$_{(2)}$: Several million objects massing ten grams and under.

. . . flashed by, barely a kilometer away at their closest approach. He "looked" harder at them.

Oh, Lord. He recognized the lines and contours of the larger object: a Malhelan interplanetary mining ship. What the hell had they been trying to do?

"Captain," he said, "that was a Malhelan ship, dumping *rocks* in our path."

"In the aliens' path," the thing-captain corrected. "The Malhelan government has ordered its ships to attack."

"*What?*"

The captain's thing-face seemed to glare at him.

"The details don't matter right now. Continue your prime-number broadcast."

Beth Lahler growled beside him. "Captain, they don't respond to prime numbers, at least not over radio. Can't we try something else? We have no equipment to produce a modulated neutrino pulse like we've seen from them, but can we do something new with the radio? Pictures, maybe sounds?"

The captain appeared to think about that for a moment. Then: "Yeah. Send anything you like. And keep an eye out for the Malhelans."

Chelsea's image vanished.

Miguel put a hand over his eyes. Too much to concentrate on. Too much even for thing-Barta, who seemed to have a lot of trouble working through the snarl of thoughts and feelings clogging Miguel's natural brain.

He had slept with a tech aid. On the brink of retirement, in the midst of the greatest discovery in the history of space travel . . . He had given in to his hormones, throwing away his pension, canceling all of his hard-won science bonuses. And Beth Lahler's, as well.

He stole a look at her.

As before, she sat stiffly, eyes forward. Not looking at him, not speaking to him unless he hit her with a direct, work-oriented question. *You have ruined me,* her posture said.

Ugh, that thought did not do her credit. Maybe she couldn't face him because *she* felt responsible. Maybe, in her mind, she had ruined *him*! But no, really, he could blame nobody except the hormones. Obsolete software, running ineluctably through the minds and bodies of people with rather loftier concerns.

She had certainly pleased him, though. The feel of her, sliding against him, moaning, rolling in the light of a dying star. . . .

No! He slapped himself mentally. *Stop it!*

"More Malhelans ahead," Beth said coldly. "We'll need a more dramatic course change. I don't think we can keep following these aliens. In fact, if we want to keep out of trouble we'll have to slow way down, and we'll have to do it without burning up those Malhelan ships."

"Beth . . ."

No response. Miguel sighed. Must he lose even the thing for which he had lost everything else? Apparently so.

"Understood," he said. "Feed your data through to the helm. I'll inform the captain."

Beth jerked, sat up straighter. "Miguel, another ellipsoid is coming in. A big one, moving fast!"

He shoved his mind back into the instrument array, and confirmed her observations. "Oh, Lord. We've *got* to pull away from this mess."

He communicated his concerns, and Beth's, to the bridge.

Introspectia changed course. The ellipsoids changed course as well, ducking around the Malhelan obstacle.

The big ellipsoid flickered past, moving at over ninety percent of the speed of light. One of the smaller objects exploded.

Miguel$_{(1)}$: Neutrino density function has suffered distortion along—

Miguel$_{(2)}$: Gamma flux—

Miguel$_{(*)}$: Shut the fuck up. Unless you can figure out how to fix my life, I really don't want to hear it.

The other ellipsoids continued their course change, though the huge interloper had gone as quickly as it had come. They moved, swinging faster, and faster still, through a great, high-gee arc across the starscape. Away from Vano, now, and the inhabited worlds which circled it. Moving back toward the emptier quarter of Malhela system, in the general direction of the Soleco hypermass.

I wish we *could accelerate like that,* Miguel thought, fleetingly.

Introspectia, slower and less nimble than its quarry, continued for a long while on its previous course.

Chapter Twenty-one

Something seemed to have shifted in the battle. Some great milestone had passed, or a pivotal event had come and gone, unnoticed by human observers. The ellipsoids still fluttered around the system like restless insects, and every now and again a group of pursuers would pounce on a group of pursuees, and something would blow up. But a sort of energy loss had occurred, in the spiritual rather than the physical sense; the ellipsoids seemed less intent on hard acceleration and strangely looping trajectories, more concerned with staying apart, keeping large distances between themselves and their enemies.

Captain Chelsea had taken the opportunity to invite Miguel and Beth to her briefing room, outside which they now stood.

Miraculously, Miguel's heart had stopped its hammering. His brow felt cool and dry, his stomach churning only slightly. With the time of reckoning now at hand, his anxieties seemed to float away like so much dandelion fluff. No more waiting, no more choices, no more chance. He drew a deep breath, a calm breath, and let it slowly out.

"Do you want to knock, or should I?" he asked.

Beth said nothing, did not look at him. Nodding to

himself, he stepped forward and knocked on the captain's door.

After a pause, the door *whoomped* open, Lin Chelsea standing behind it, a white-haired angel of justice, clothed in Solar Commercial dress-grays. No smile on her face, no anger.

"Come in," she said, and stepped aside. "Sit down on the couch."

Miguel did as instructed, and Beth followed, sitting down next to him. Not crowding close against him, but not cringing away, either. Her posture and expression announced a firmly neutral formality, the sort of bearing a person might bring to a court proceeding. Which, Miguel supposed, fit this circumstance rather well.

The door slammed closed as Chelsea moved away from it. She sat across from them, placing her elbows on the armrests of her chair, fingers coming together to form a steeple beneath her chin.

For several seconds, she remained silent. Then, tiredly: "You two could have behaved a little more discreetly, don't you think?"

The question seemed rhetorical to Miguel, so he made no reply. Beside him, Beth also said nothing.

The captain rocked her steepled fingers back and forth, touching middle fingers to her face, then swinging them away until her index fingers came up against the bottom of her chin. Then reversing, rocking the steeple back and down once again. Like a sort of machine, one which converted reciprocating motion into waves of grim displeasure, radiating them out toward Beth and Miguel.

"You've both demonstrated considerable bravery," she said, "performing crucial services for the corporation, and for the citizens of Malhela. For the whole human race, really. It doesn't please me to punish you, not at all. But I find my hands firmly tied by the circumstances."

Again, Miguel remained silent. Again, Beth Lahler did the same.

Chelsea's scowl deepened. "Won't you say *something*?"

More silence.

"Okay, fine," the captain said. "Make this as difficult as you like. Miguel Barta, you are formally charged with Conduct Unbecoming an Officer. Upon our return to Earth I will turn you over to Admin with the recommendation that you shall forfeit ten days' pay. Do you understand this charge? Do you understand the proposed sentence?"

Ten days' pay? The words made no sense for a moment, as they bore little resemblance to the ones he had expected to hear. Fraternization charges usually meant truly excruciating fines, along with punitive duties, refusal of discharge. . .

"Ma'am?" He asked.

"Do you *understand* what I have told you?"

"Yes, but—"

She waved him to silence, and turned her disapproving eyes on Beth. "Elizabeth Lahler. You have disappointed me with your ingratitude, and with your lack of judgment. I charge you, also, with Conduct Unbecoming an Officer. Upon our return to Earth I will turn you over to Admin with the recommendation that you shall forfeit ten days' pay. Do you understand this charge? Do you understand the proposed sentence?"

Beth appeared flustered, suddenly. "Ma'am," she said, "I'm only an aid. Second class."

"Excuse me?" the captain barked. "I distinctly recall promoting you to tech officer five days ago. Shall I check the duty logs to confirm it?"

Beth blinked, silent and confused.

"My dear," Chelsea said, more gently now, "the stress of recent events has obviously unsettled you. If you *think* about it for a moment, I feel certain you'll remember."

Suddenly, Beth's face broke out in a smile, and in that same moment it occurred to Miguel just how much Chelsea had done to spare them the company's wrath. Altering her records! Causing Beth Lahler to have been an officer at the time of the . . . illicit liaison.

So, *Introspectia*'s captain had committed Falsification With Intent to Defraud. Good Lord. An offense like that made fraternization look like straight company policy. Good bloody Lord.

"Don't you smile at me, Tech Officer!" Chelsea snapped. Her expression registered not a trace of amusement. "Go on, get out of here. Both of you, get out! And find someplace a little less public the next time you decide to screw!"

Hastily, Miguel and Beth got up and made for the exit. It opened for them, slammed closed behind them.

Once they were a safe distance away, Miguel put his hand on Beth's back. Warmly, affectionately.

She squirmed out from under his touch, stepping back against the corridor wall and raising an accusing finger. "Don't you touch me, Miguel Barta."

Astounded, Miguel just looked at her. Had he misjudged things once again? Did Beth really, actually hate him now? Oh dear.

"Don't you touch me," she repeated, shaking her finger at him. "Not in public. One misconduct charge is quite enough, thank you."

Oh. He let out the breath he didn't know he'd been holding. "My apologies," he said, with a fair attempt at sincerity. "Maybe you'd do me the honor of accompanying me to my quarters?"

Beth scowled. "You take a lot for granted, mister. It takes more than a—"

Warning klaxons went off. Red and yellow lights began to flash.

"ALL BRIDGE, ENGINEERING, AND SCIENCE PERSONNEL REPORT TO DUTY STATIONS." The voice of First Mate Peng echoed down the corridors. "REPEAT, ALL BRIDGE, ENGINEERING, AND SCIENCE PERSONNEL TO DUTY STATIONS."

The captain's door flew open, and the captain herself paused for a moment, flashing Miguel and Beth a look of almost parental distrust before turning and hurrying down the corridor's other way.

"There they go," Miguel said, with no small measure of bitterness. "Look at that, it looks like they're just going to head right back in again."

Through the ship's sensor networks he watched the ellipsoids in a dozen different ways. He saw their electromagnetic emissions and reflections, the whole spectrum from thermal radio right on up through low gamma. He felt their prickly, constantly shifting neutrino flux, and their gravitational signatures. With three spectrometers operating on completely different principles, he sniffed and tasted the objects, and he sensed minute, physical vibrations from them in a way not entirely dissimilar to the human sense of hearing.

Their gyrations continued, but each loop and turn seemed now to carry the ellipsoids closer, ever closer to the time-prison of Soleco. Was the encounter really ending, then? Damn! The most important event in human history, and yet even in the thick of it all Miguel had been an observer, perhaps a minor nuisance, really nothing more than a beetle at the aliens' picnic. Well, okay, maybe "picnic" was the wrong word. He'd braved a lot of dangerous conditions, and he'd certainly be glad if he didn't have to brave any more.

Or would he?

Roughly half the ellipsoids began to chatter, wildly, in a staccato language of neutrino pulses, and to dive even more swiftly toward the sensory null of the Soleco hypermass. *Let's go, boys!* Virtually massless in their centrokrist shells, shielded from inertia and from gravity, they expelled their exhaust of relativistic plasma and roared, with little apparent effort, at hundreds of gee's acceleration.

The other ellipsoids, more slowly it seemed, began to accelerate, and to start up their own neutrino pulse dialogue. The volumes of data they exchanged, very nearly a hundred terrabits in the first second, seemed ludicrous to Miguel. They didn't have anything to *do* other than swoop around and shoot at each other. What could they need to discuss in such volume?

None of it made any sense to him, of course, but he thought he heard a different sort of quality in the voices of the pursuing aliens than he had in the fugitives'. A little harder, perhaps a little colder. Not like the others' complex screams of rage and defiance. Or perhaps he simply read too much into signals which had not, after all, been meant for him.

"Analysis," he said to Beth.

"On what?" she snapped back.

"On the signals. Do they sound different to you? Between the two groups, I mean?"

"Yes."

He gritted his teeth. Did she have to behave this way right now? "In what *way* do they *differ?*"

In lieu of a verbal reply, Beth jammed a load of processed data at his mind. With some difficulty, he accepted and assimilated the bundle.

Average spacing between the neutrino pulses differed by ten to twenty picoseconds between the two groups. Neutrino mass varied by an average of 5.32E-12 kilograms. A thousand such measurements filled his mind, along with occasional annotation and commentary and . . . *and Beth Lahler was deeply, burningly in love with him.* Her feelings throbbed orgasmically in his mind, sought out his pleasure centers and entered them, so that he felt bruised with the magnitude of her desire.

"Ulgh," he said.

Beneath the medusa-sproutings of the link harness, Beth shook her head. "No, damn! I didn't mean to let that through!"

Miguel slumped in his chair, lay almost motionless. Incapacitated, numb with an overdose of love, which was without question the most powerful drug that had ever existed.

"Damn it! Damn it!" Beth said. "There goes the last trace of my dignity."

"Oh well," Miguel said, still sprawled in his chair as limply as if his spine had shattered once again.

Miguel recovered within a minute or two, in time to watch the fugitive ellipsoids descend into Soleco, watch redshift and time dilation and Lorentz contraction take hold of them, blurring and fading and distorting them until, at this great range, he could no longer perceive them at all. Into the hypermass, into the future, forsaking the universe of the present. Another thousand years in the amber? Another billion?

Less than an hour later, their pursuers began to trickle in behind them.

The pursuers have the advantage, he thought as he watched them, thinking about what things *they* might think about as they followed their enemies down into the hypergravitational pit. *You plot the enemies' trajectories, find their velocities and their periapses and integrate forward through the time dilation. Find out when they will emerge, a thousand or a million or a billion years hence, and adjust your own trajectory so that you come out slightly earlier. They might escape you even then, but if you played things right, you could herd them right back into the hole again. You could keep them from ever escaping.*

In fact, you must *keep them from escaping; if they ever got round to the other side of the time hill, they might be waiting for you when* you *emerged! Ready to kill, ready to destroy. You cannot win this game unless you play it forever.*

The thought sent shivers up and down his spine. A war that never ended. Like a *picture* of a war, like a fossil of it. A live battle with live participants, yes, but frozen in amber. Trotted out for show every once in a while, and then trotted right back into stasis again.

Sympathy washed over him. Whatever had set these groups off, whatever word or thing or event had triggered their mutual rage, it must by now have vanished as surely as the nebula from which Malhela system had coalesced so long ago.

He didn't feel quite so surprised, now, that the aliens had ignored *Introspectia* and all its attempts to communicate. On the timescale in which they had forced themselves to live, external events must seem fleeting and meaningless indeed.

But he remembered the images he'd captured, down in the Malsato gravity well. *The creature hunched up and launched itself, savagely, premeditatedly, at one of its fellows, colliding with talons outstretched. Malevolence implicit in the act.* The sympathy left him as suddenly as it had come.

He noticed Beth looking at him, curiously, worriedly. Did these troubling thoughts show on his face, even through all the messy linkware? He transmitted the gist of the thoughts to Beth.

Silence and stillness for a moment, and then he watched her shudder under the burden of what he had given her. So awful. So terribly, terribly awful.

"Better them than us," he said to her, as the last of the pursuers slipped into the arms of the hypermass and redshifted away to nothingness.

GILL: Damn you, *Introspectia*, will you get out here
    and help us now?
CHELSEA: My deepest apologies, Madame Direc-
    tor. We'll be there in five hours. Really, I promise.

Chapter Twenty-two

"Hello, sweet thing," Jhoe said, putting a hand on Luna Shiloh's shoulder. "Have you looked outside?"

His hand, like the rest of his body, had layers of pale, dead skin flaking off it in messy, thumb-sized curls. Fortunately, he seemed to have suffered no other ill effects from his exposure.

"What?" Luna croaked, turning blearily to face him. Her face looked puffy and red, her eyes slitted, her hair an unruly tangle.

Jhoe frowned, looking around him at the coordination center. It stank in here, stank of sweat and farts and partially eaten sandwiches, of improper ventilation, of days of uninterrupted human occupation. Two other workers shambled about, seemingly as dazed as Luna herself.

"Damn," he said. "You people haven't left this room, have you?"

"What?" Luna said again. She blinked at him, then looked over at the diagnostic board and blinked at that for awhile.

Oh, dear. Finding things well in hand after his brief but city-saving mission, Jhoe had evacuated himself to the nearest shelter. To his surprise, he'd found it not too terribly crowded, not too terribly uncomfortable. His bunk space, considerably smaller than the interior of Luna's car, had shrunk his world a bit, but someone had gone through and furnished the bunks with soft pillows and mattresses and blankets, furnished the individual rooms with plants and rugs and great heaps of paper books. Jhoe had actually spent his time quite pleasantly, snacking and reading and sleeping, speaking sometimes with his neighbors or listening to the songs that they sang together and quietly memorizing the lyrics.

He had worried about Luna, of course, but he felt it appropriate to leave her in peace to do her job. And of course, she had promised him she would look after herself and her people, and Jhoe had seen no reason to doubt this.

Here and now, in the coordination center, which looked as if a tribe of primitives had moved into it, he realized his error. Technical people left to their own devices, permitted in their time of danger to ignore such logistical irrelevancies as sleep and hygiene . . . He saw his retreat now in a somewhat gloomier light, less prudent than selfish and cowardly. Clearly, they could have used his help around here.

"Come to the window with me," he said, taking Luna by the elbow and leading her toward the room's exit.

"Jhoe," she said, as if recognizing him only now. "What's going on?"

"I think it's over," he said to her. They stepped through the arched doorway that marked the coordination center's exit.

"Ove—" she started to say, and then stopped when she saw the windows.

Night had returned to Unua once again.

Outside, the sky had the deep, yellow-purple look

that Jhoe associated with summer evenings, when the sun had set but its light not entirely faded.

Neither Lacigo nor the brown dwarf sun occupied the heavens right now, but a kind of star, bright and small and sparkly-pink, glared fitfully near the horizon.

"That's Soleco," Jhoe said, pointing at the star. "You can't see it anymore, but the ships were all diving in there. Dozens of light trails, all scrunching in together and disappearing. It's been going on for hours."

"Why is it red?" Luna asked, seeming more alert now than she had before.

"That has to do with relativity," Jhoe replied. Not that he knew anything about it, of course, but he remembered the example of Black Hole Bahb.

"Oh," Luna said, and sagged against him.

He put his arm around her and felt good for a second, a lover reunited with the subject of his desire. But Luna's slump continued, and he had to move his arm beneath her and lift to keep her from falling. Her body felt a lot warmer than Jhoe thought it should.

"I'm sorry," she said, vaguely. "I feel so . . . tired and I just . . ."

Jhoe placed a finger against her hot, cracked lips, hushing her. "You're sick! Oh, Luna, I *warned* you . . . Well, never mind about that. Your shift is *over* now; I'm going to take you home. No, that's not right. You probably have cancers blooming all through your body. I'm taking you to the *hospital*."

"You can't take me there," Luna protested. "My . . ."

"You'll be just fine," Jhoe said. "If the Unuan doctors can't help you, I feel sure the *Introspectia* ones will. I bet they'll be busy cleaning this mess up. A lot of radiation cases, I would think."

"You can't take me to the hospital," Luna repeated,

more insistently this time. "You smashed up my car, re-member?"

"Oh," he said. "Oh, so I did."

The last of the alien ships vanished into Soleco, leaving the sky completely dark, and Jhoe began, very inappropriately, to laugh.

PART FIVE

HEREDAJO

*Toward the very centre whither
Gravity was most inclined,
There you have made your bed . . .*

—Pedro Calderon De La Barca,
  Life is a Dream, c. 1651 A.D.

Chapter Twenty-three

"You're awfully quiet," Uriel said to him over the thrumming of the chopter blades. "That's not a good note to end your visit on."

Jhoe shrugged, then realized Uriel couldn't see that, so he grunted. Not loudly enough, though, to be heard above the chopter noise. "Yeah, I guess," he finally said.

He was leaving, forever, but the good-bye with Luna had not gone well. He'd shared her home for nearly a standard year, and after Lars had gotten him that ferry-driving job and he finally had some money . . . Well, Luna hadn't let him pay for her ruined car, so instead he'd spent the money on himself, accumulating quite a surprising amount of junk. Some of it, the things he'd grown attached to and felt he couldn't part with, he'd stuffed in a trunk which would ride with him back to Earth. Other things he had given away, and a few he had left behind, so that the inside of the house had a sort of motheaten look to it. As if burglars had broken in and stolen a carload of random, valueless things.

And Luna, limping and wincing with her latest cancer scars, had railed at him, railed at the notion that Jhoe could bear to leave *her*, as if she held no more importance to him than the beryl drinking mug he had ill-advisedly bought with his first paycheck, or the rubber sandals and hat he'd bought with his third. "You might like Earth," he'd said many times. "I think you would."

But this suggestion had not mollified her. "I have responsibility here, Jhoe!" she'd screamed at him. "I'm important, I'm *somebody*. On Earth, even *you* are nobody."

And that had stung him terribly, and so he'd stomped out without another word.

"I love you, Luna," he whispered now, inaudibly. He imagined the whirling chopter blades cutting the sounds up, strewing and scattering them across the sandy hills.

And that thought merely underscored his failure. He had met the Unuan people, lived and worked and loved among them, and yet he knew nothing of them. Their insides, their secret hearts remained as opaque to him as on the first day he'd stepped off the lander. *What will I tell the people of Earth? I've come from Unua, where the sky is dark and folk are a wee bit strange?* Would the people of Earth even care?

"For someone who's going home you don't seem too happy," Uriel observed. She seemed mellower than usual today. Older, quieter.

"How very true," he agreed. "And how nice of you to notice. I feel . . . I think you and I could have been friends."

"I think we have been," Uriel said. "I think we are."

He watched the city lights down below, fading up to the dark horizon and the darker sky above it.

Uriel flew smoothly, delicately, as if afraid to jostle him, as if afraid he might shatter. "I guess you'll miss this place," she said. "At least every now and then."

"Yes."

"But once you leave it you can never come back.

Even if you tried, even if you climbed right back on some ship the moment you got to Earth, the Unua you've seen here would be centuries gone. You'd just be stepping into the amber again, letting the universe pass you by, even more than it already has."

"Uriel, have you got a point to this, or do you just want to make me unhappy?"

Uriel turned for a moment, flashing him an exaggeratedly innocent look. "*I* didn't make you unhappy, Doctor. Not listening to your heart is what makes you unhappy."

"My heart is a muscle," he said. "I've listened to it before, and it . . . it just makes you crazy. It just makes you lose your mind."

"Aha," she said, nodding. "And if you listen to your mind instead? What does that make you lose?"

He thought about that for awhile as the yellow-orange city lights rolled by underneath them. He found he couldn't argue with her logic. He found he couldn't argue with anything she'd said.

He turned to her, almost angrily. "How did you get so wise, little girl?"

She snorted. "Old people think they have some kind of monopoly on wisdom. It isn't true, though. Personally, I think we're born with it." She paused, then spoke, gently: "Doctor Freetz, do you want to stay on Unua? Do you want me to turn the chopter around?"

"Yes," he said, and found, with some surprise, that tears had begun trickling down his cheeks.

"Happy day!" she beamed. "I guess there's space on *Introspectia,* then. Can I have your ticket?"

"*What?*"

"Oh, I won't stay on Earth for long. Just look around some, then hop on colony ship and head for the frontier. Someplace new, someplace that really needs me. What do you say?"

He gaped at her, aghast. "Did you say all that just to swindle your way into the starship?"

"I don't know." She shrugged lightly. "Maybe. If what I said is true, what do you care?"

A spasm of anger came and went. Jhoe found, once again, that her logic precluded any sensible argument.

"All right," he said, giving in. "All right. Your people skills have certainly improved. Just take me back, okay?"

"As you wish, Doctor." Her grin looked wide enough to split her head in two.

"At last, Captain Chelsea," Jafre said into the telkom screen, "I have the chance to speak with you in real time."

Chelsea nodded. "Yes, I gather you have waited a long time for this."

"Much longer than you think," he said. *Bitch,* he added mentally, but found there was no real force behind the thought. "It was I who called you to Malhela in the first place. I've been waiting to speak with you for over eighty years."

She raised an eyebrow. "Really? Well, you have my attention now. What can I do for you?"

"Take me to Earth," he said, simply and unceremoniously.

Lin Chelsea blinked at him. "Did I hear you correctly? You want to leave Malhela?"

"I *despise* Malhela. The dark, the scarcity of resources, the scarcity of *people.* . . . One more decade here will kill me, I swear. I was meant for more than this. Please, Captain, take me away."

"But you have responsibility here," Lin Chelsea protested. "You have position, you have authority! That must mean something."

"Better to rule in darkness, eh? Forsaking Paradise forever? I think Milton was overly romantic and underly clever, and he sure as damnation never had to live on Unua. I'll ... take my chances in the light, thank you."

The captain's expression was skeptical. "Jafre Shem, or should I say 'Mister President'? I have a hard time with this concept. Surely you can't just walk away?"

"Why not?" He attempted a shrug, attempted a casual smile. Neither one felt particularly successful, so he put on a serious expression instead. "Captain, as you so frequently point out, I have no authority over you. I can only ask you, I *do* ask you: will you rescue me from this awful place?"

Chelsea seemed to lose her stiffness somehow, as if a tight belt or harness around her had suddenly been released. She sighed theatrically. "I have no objection, I suppose, though I warn you I will not be held responsible if you later regret your decision."

Jafre sat silently for a moment, savoring his victory. Strangely, he did not feel exhilarated, nor even particularly victorious. Was he just slinking away, after all? Could his long years of scheming really have led up to something so small and so fundamentally petty?

"Thank you," he said to the captain, in quiet voice that felt drained of power, drained of everything. "I'll resign my office in the morning."

"Will your wife accompany you on the journey?"

Jafre sat up in his chair. The question had taken him by surprise. Asia! He *knew* he'd been leaving something out in his planning, but ... Asia? "Oh, darkness. I guess that's *two* things I'll have to resign from."

* * *

Miguel stepped up into the Malhelan lander, then turned, offered Beth his hand. She accepted this with good grace and let him help her inside.

"Well, so much for shore leave," he mumbled at her.

She nodded. "Yeah. I enjoyed it very much, though. Thank you."

"My own pleasure, uh, darling."

He had found, to his amusement and minor dismay, that that was the pet name she wanted him to call her by. She called him "Ace" in return, though, and he liked that. He liked much about her company. Indeed, their week on Unua had passed in a sort of haze of mutual affection, and he felt sure that in later years he would recall little of it besides the sound of her laughter, the feel of her hair in his hands on a hot, dark night . . . or a hot, dark day, for that matter. It made little difference, here.

Together they stowed their bags in the indicated compartment, and moved back to find their seats among the other passengers.

"Hey!" A young woman called out, looking at them and smiling. "Hey, Solar Commercial uniforms! I'm going to be riding on your ship!"

Beth led Miguel to the row of seats in front of the young woman and sat him down in the window seat, taking the aisle for herself.

"Hello," she said, sticking her hand back in a friendly way.

"Um, hello," the young woman returned pleasantly. She looked at Beth's hand uncertainly, then clasped it in both her own. "My name is Uriel Zeng."

"Beth Lahler. And—" she aimed an elbow at Miguel. "—my . . . my boss, Miguel Barta. Chief Technical Officer aboard the Solar Commercial Starship *Intro-*

spectia. It pleases us to meet you. Now, what's this you're saying?"

Uriel grinned, obviously pleased with herself and with her circumstances. "I'm riding back to Earth on your ship. As passenger, I mean. Taking the place of Doctor Jhoe Freetz."

"Huh," Beth said. "I don't believe I know him. Miguel?"

"Uh, I think Tomus Kreider knows him."

"Ah."

Uriel turned, raised a finger to point. "See that guy back there? That's the president of Unua."

"Ex-president," the man called up. He sounded tired. He *looked* tired, and a little bit shrunken, like an inflatable dummy with a good bit of the air removed. "I'm going to Earth as well."

The man seemed at war with himself for a moment, as if agonizing between two difficult decisions. But then he offered a wan smile, and rose from his seat, and moved three rows forward to sit down across from Uriel. He crossed his arms, held them out toward Beth.

"Jafre Shem, refugee. Salutes."

Politely, Beth took the ex-president's hands and shook them. "It pleases me to meet you," she said. She cast a wide glance that took in Jafre and Uriel both. "You must feel very brave, going away like this. Miguel and I were born on Earth, and even we don't know what we'll find there when we return."

Jafre smiled a little more sincerely. "Eagle among the turkeys, that's me. I've got to get away from here, find some place where I can stretch my wings."

"Earth has quite a lot of turkeys, too," Miguel said, perhaps a little unkindly. He instantly regretted his tone, but then, nobody else seemed to have noticed. Or else, in the spirit of the day, they'd let it pass.

"I feel the same way," Uriel said, her eyes glittering. "I may not stay on Earth. I may move on as soon as I get there. But you're right." She turned to Jafre. "Stretch my wings, yeah, that's exactly the way I feel."

She made light fists of her hands, and then crossed them, and then offered them to the ex-president of Unua.

Miguel had the sudden sense that he was observing an event of some significance. A kind of tension crackled in the air, as if lightning might soon strike here. Human lightning.

Jafre stared down at Uriel Zeng's hands for a second or so, and then, though he did not look like a man who often felt happy, an expression of genuine delight broke out across his face. "Salutes, my dear," he said, taking Uriel's hands in his and shaking them, warmly. "I don't believe we've met."

The gangway had crowded up with people of varying heights, varying speeds and directions of movement, and with voices of widely varying loudness.

"So that's it, then," Asia said, bitterly. She had been crying earlier, but her eyes were dry now, and her voice fairly steady. "Eighty years, over like that."

"I guess so," Jafre said. "Such ruts we get into, it's nice to break out. But you make it sound so small, so petty. Can't you be happy for me?"

"Not likely." Her tone fierce, indignant.

And from the other direction:

". . . really won't see anything in the raw centrokrist that resembles an ordinary atom, but Tomus and I have worked out most of the *sub*atomic structure, and it seems likely that, given time, we can duplicate it in—"

And:

". . . with the collision in the Aurelo we should be

finding new veins for the next hundred years. Screw the tin and niobium and all that other crap, we can reoutfit for some *real* prospecting again. You know, helping science and making a little money at the same—"

And:

"Such *busy* little children we've managed to produce. It makes me proud, let me tell you—"

A sort of collision took place, a dozen bodies attempting to occupy a space not big enough for half that many. Everyone stopped.

And then, suddenly, in one of those rare gestaltic moments, everyone in the small crowd looked up and recognized someone else they knew.

"Tomus!"

"Captain."

"Tech Officer. Tech Chief."

"Jack-Jack!"

"Oh, darkness. Don't tell me *he's* coming—"

"Children, look at you all!"

Everyone paused again, and then Jack-Jack seized the initiative and, with his eyes on Jafre Shem, began speaking in an elevated voice: "My boy, I'm not here to board the ship, but rather to bid farewell to these children of Earth, who stood by us so bravely in our moment of peril." He whirled on Tomus Kreider and Miguel Barta, trapped them with a gaze and a grin. "And what wonders have they found? What final news have they got for us? Come on, don't be stingy."

"Uh," Miguel said, looking around him, surveying the faces, marking those known and un-. He did not recall ever having met this man, this "Jack-Jack," but he sensed an importance about him that compelled an answer.

"Well, sir, we may have cracked some of the final secrets of centrokrist's internal structure. Reproducing it, even in small quantities, seems far beyond us right now, but ... Well, according to my calculations, the next emergence will take place in seven hundred eighty-four standard years. By then, quite possibly, we can return to Malhela in centrokrist ships of our own. Shielded from inertia, shielded from gravity ... I wonder if they could ignore us so readily."

"We'll use it better than they have, I daresay," Tomus Kreider broke in. "Centrokrist strikes me as a technology of exploration, meant for looking outward, not in. Truly, I wish Yezu had lived to see this day."

Beside him, Lin Chelsea spoke up, in a peculiar tone that did not sound like her at all. *"Their armor have we stolen, their secrets do we keep. Corrupt as ancient gods in frozen amber do they sleep, unaware that their age has already passed."*

"How lovely!" Jack-Jack exclaimed. "How very charming a quote. *Where* did you find that?"

"I made it up," the captain said, sounding embarrassed. "I don't usually ... Well I couldn't sleep last night, and it just sort of ..."

"A poetess, then." Jack-Jack winked at Miguel, and at Beth. "I'll bet you never suspected such talents of your captain. Guard her well."

"Old man," said Jafre Shem, his tone at once spiteful and amused, "why don't you go find someplace to sit down, and leave the rest of us alone? You'll be dust and gone before the eggies come out of their hole again."

"And so I will," Jack-Jack agreed, turning and beaming down at Jafre, several paces below him on the ramp. "The old will always dry up and blow away, and the young will always inherit. But *wisely,* my boy, if they've taken note of their elders' mistakes. And now, I think I *will* sit down. The excitement, you know. It wears an old man out. Good day to you all."

Jack-Jack squirmed through the crowd, past Jafre Shem to the bottom of the ramp, and strode off down the corridor. To the watching eyes behind, he did not appear particularly tired.

Chapter Twenty-four

Unmooring and pulling away from Port *Chrysanthemum*, *Introspectia* soon found itself surrounded by smaller ships, a Malhelan color guard of miners and prospectors and cargo ferries, along with smaller vehicles—landers and repair boats and such.

Tom and Beth and Miguel stood together by one of the viewports in the observation lounge, watching some of the little ships roll and tumble in salute, watching others stand by with greater dignity, like soldiers at attention.

"How beautiful they seem," Tom said quietly, and Miguel did not know if he meant the ships, or the Malhelan people within them.

"Yes," he said, and beside him Beth grunted her agreement as well.

The floor began to hum beneath their feet. Port *Chrysanthemum* appeared to move outside the viewport, and it moved more and more quickly, and within seconds it had vanished from sight. Farther back, the dark, red-brown ball of Unua had begun to drop back as well.

The Malhelan ships kept up, at first. But *Introspectia* was gaining speed, still, and would continue that way for days, until it had reached the very edge of light-speed. The color guard eroded slowly, its member ships dropping away one by one, but following bravely while they could.

ABOUT THE AUTHOR

An aerospace engineer for the Martin Marietta Corporation, Wil McCarthy has published short fiction in several major anthologies, and also a number of magazines whose names begin with the letter "A." He lives near Denver with his wife, Cathy. This is his second novel.

ROC

FANTASTICS

☐ **THE ARCHITECTURE OF DESIRE by Mary Gentle.** Return to a medieval world of Scholar Soldiers and magic in this magnificent sequel to *Rats and Gargoyles.* "Miraculous!—*Washington Post Book World*
(453530—$4.99)

☐ **DR. DIMENSION: MASTERS OF SPACETIME by John DeChancie and David Bischoff.** Can a questionable robot actually help Dr. Dimension and his sidekick, Troy, escape the trash planet? (453549—$4.99)

☐ **SHADOWS FALL by Simon R. Green.** A town of amazing magicks, where the real and the imagined live side by side, where the Faerie of legend know the automatons of the future. (453638—$5.99)

☐ **THE SEVEN TOWERS: WIZARD AT MECQ by Rick Shelley.** A battle is brought to the heart of the Wizard Silvas' own domain—where he might find himself facing a foe beyond even his magical abilities to defeat.
(453611—$4.99)

*Prices slightly higher in Canada

ENCHANTING REALMS

☐ **SCORPIANNE by Emily Devenport.** Lucy finds herself with a new identity on a new world at the brink of rebellion. Even here, she cannot escape the nightmare memories of the assassin who strikes without being seen, the one who has sworn Lucy's death, the stalker she knows only by the name Scorpianne.

(453182—$4.99)

☐ **THE EYE OF THE HUNTER by Dennis L. McKiernan.** From the best-selling author of *The Iron Tower* trilogy and *The Silver Call* duology—a new epic of Mithgar. The comet known as the Eye of the Hunter is riding through Mithgar's skies again, bringing with it destruction and the much dreaded master, Baron Stoke.

(452682—$5.99)

☐ **A SWORD FOR A DRAGON by Christopher Rowley.** The most loyal bunch of dragon warriors and human attendants ever to march on campaign had just been re-formed when Bazil Broketail and his human boy, Relkin, returned from a search for Bazil's beloved green dragoness. But when the Goddess of Death marks them both as her chosen victims for capture and sacrifice, they must face unexpected danger.

(452356—$5.99)

☐ **THE ARCHITECTURE OF DESIRE by Mary Gentle.** Discover a time and a place ruled by the Hermetic magic of the Renaissance, by secret, almost forgotten Masonic rites, a land divided between the royalists loyal to Queen Carola and the soldiers who follow the Protector-General Olivia in this magnificent sequel to *Rats and Gargoyles.*

(453530—$4.99)

Prices slightly higher in Canada.
